SOVEREIGN

A DARK BRATVA FORCED MARRIAGE ROMANCE

WICKED VOWS
BOOK 1

JANE HENRY

Playlist

Scan QR Code to listen to the playlist for
'Sovereign: A Dark Bratva Forced Marriage
Romance" on Spotify ©

A huge thank you to Noa Shalev for putting together this stunning playlist that captures Mikhail and Aria's story so perfectly!

~Jane Henry

Follow Noa here:
https://www.instagram.com/solariaroyalblue/

SYNOPSIS

Powerful and merciless. Cunning and cruel.

A monster wrapped in luxury and wealth.

Mikhail Romanov is my opposite in every way...

And my new husband.

In exchange for his protection...

He'll demand everything from me.

My obedience.

My submission.

My body.

But marriage is only the beginning.

I'll have his baby, too.

I thought I was clever. A penniless hacker hiding from the world.

That no one would discover who I am and what I've done.

I was so wrong.

The Solution: Marry the man more powerful than my enemies.

While endless wealth and power don't melt his icy glare...

The fiery tension between us threatens to combust every second we're near.

Every command.

Every touch.

If I leave, I have nowhere to go.

I'm being hunted by his enemies.

But if I stay? I'm wedded to a monster who plans to keep me forever.

CHAPTER ONE

Aria

"TODAY, YOU ARE GOING *DOWN.*" I shove my glasses up the bridge of my nose for the umpteenth time with a little smile, blinking at the screen in front of me. Although it's cramped in this small, makeshift home office which consists of a tiny desk I rescued curbside nestled in a corner of the room to give me the best access to my computer screens, here's where I do my magic. While I don't really mind teaching coding at the little community college outside of Coney Island, I don't like the red tape and long hours. I long to get back to my little haven, where my fingers fly over the keys and I truly come alive.

Today, in the most boring white conference room under harsh, fluorescent lights, tepid coffee in hand, I longed to get home to unwrap what I discovered last night: *the* mother-lode of all encrypted goldmines. Way too complex for me to delve into before school, but now, when the night is young and the moon rises, I get to play.

Professor by Day, Hacking Goddess by Night.

At least that's what I like to think.

I glance at the time and stretch. I can out-code anyone in the world, bar none. One day, I'll no longer be known as Aria Cunningham, the nobody, barely scraping by at the local community college. I'll actually make a *difference* in this world.

I blink and stare at the screen.

Wait.

My heart beats faster. Is that...

No.

My mouth dry, I click the little icon indicating my download is complete. I scroll down, my hand covering my mouth as I'm seized with two conflicting emotions.

Elation — *I did it!* I successfully hacked into the most notorious database of criminal activity I've ever seen in my life.

And gripping, terrifying fear.

No one has ever done this before. And unearthing something this massive comes at a cost.

I stare, my mouth agape.

Names. Dates. Locations. Pictures.

Evidence.

Politicians and celebrities, CEOs and religious leaders, military icons and monarchs. I stare in both horror and glee as I realize...it *worked.*

I scroll past pages and pages of information that should be encrypted but reads clear as day now. Oh my *God*. This is worse than I thought. If this got out to the press...if anyone knew what these people have done. *No.*

And worse? If the owners of this information ever realize I've hacked into their database...

"Good thing you covered your tracks," I whisper to myself.

A blinding yellow light flashes. I stare for a second too long.

I leap to my feet. I smack the button on the surveillance camera that overlooks all entryways to my apartment. My blood runs cold at the sight of six armed men at the back door. I might be in an old, mostly unoccupied house that was nearly condemned, but there are still *three* access points, not including windows, and I don't take risks.

Shit.

Oh God.

My heart beats so fast I feel nauseous, bile rising in my throat as I quickly assess my options even as my mind whirs. *How?? How did they discover where I am so quickly?*

I'm so damn careful, sweeping *every* digital footprint as thoroughly as possible. I leave no trace behind and cover every possible angle. I don't have time to unravel this.

I kick my keys into the trash bin and grab my laptop. I have seconds as I scramble to my hideout in the tiny attic. The trap door glides into place at the same time my front door opens.

I slide into position, my heart beating so rapidly I feel like I'm going to be sick.

I listen. It's just as I imagined. I told myself I would never actually *need* a hideout. And yet here I am.

My mind races.

The type of information I discovered was under high profile lock and key. The people responsible for this set up an immediate alert in the event of a security breach and absolutely had the funds and resources for high security measures.

Oh God.

Footsteps sound on the floor below. How long will they look for me? How thoroughly will they search? With a pounding heart, I wait in the corner of the attic, well hidden. If whoever's here had the foresight to bring a search dog, I'll be fucked, but I'm mostly invisible to the human eye.

Glass shatters amid loud, commanding voices. Though I can't make out clear words, I know they're trying to get me out of hiding. I swipe at the tears that fall and clutch my laptop to me at the sounds of my meager possessions being destroyed.

I listen for words but can only hear muffled voices. From my perch in the attic, I crawl on my belly to look through the tiny, triangular-shaped window that overlooks the driveway. Three unmarked luxury SUVs.

Shit.

I hold my breath and pray the camouflaged trap door remains hidden.

The footsteps come closer. Someone bangs a heavy hand on

the closet walls and ceiling. I slap my hand to my mouth to stifle a scream. The voices come nearer.

I hold my breath until I'm dizzy.

I wait until it sounds like every single one of my belongings has been obliterated and the cold, angry voices retreat. I stare out the small window and watch the SUVs reverse onto the street and leave.

I can't go back to any place that's familiar or home.

I have to run.

CHAPTER TWO

Aria

I CLUTCH my laptop to my chest as I stand outside the towering door. The imposing estate alone almost makes me want to flee, but I didn't get where I am by running when I'm scared.

My finger hovers over the doorbell, my hand quaking. I will myself to push it. No turning back now. Loud chimes sound inside the elegant house.

What am I doing? Why am I here? I wish I didn't feel so out of place. I wish I had another option.

My heart's racing when the door opens and Tatiana, my old college roommate and former best friend, stands in front of me.

She blinks. She's barely aged the past few years and looks as beautiful as ever with her pale skin the color of cream, and her ice-blue eyes, a mass of thick dark curls framing her face. "Oh my God. *Aria?*"

"Tatiana," I say with a forced smile as I look over my shoulder. "Please. I need to come in."

The quick snap of her gaze tells me she understands. With a nod, she steps back and slams the door behind me.

"Come with me."

I follow her to a small room that looks like a study, complete with a sideboard and gleaming mahogany desk.

"Sit." She points to a chair. While I never bothered with small talk, Tatiana never bothered with formalities. Without another word, she takes a glass from the shelf, opens a decanter with amber liquid, and pours. "Drink?"

I normally don't drink. It's too expensive and I like to stay in control of myself. But this is good stuff and God, has it ever been a week. I drink what she gives me until ice hits my teeth.

Tatiana gives me a half-smile. "How've you been?"

I swallow. "Been better. You?"

With a sigh, she nods. "Same. I knew you'd eventually come to claim your dues. So let's hear it."

Claim your dues. So that's what we're calling it now. Ah, well. She isn't wrong.

"I need to know that we're safe here. I cannot be overheard."

"We're alone."

My mind whirrs and clicks. I can't help it.

There were two cars in the driveway, four pairs of shoes in the entryway when I entered, and two sets of keys on hooks by the door. Either she likes duplicates, or she's lying.

I know her well, and I think it's the latter.

I give her a look with a pierced eyebrow. "Really?"

"It's recent," she says, clearing her throat, and looking away before she drags her eyes back to me. "I kicked him out. That's all you need to know, Aria. Spill."

At one point Tatiana and I were best friends. Eventually, as our college days passed, we had less and less in common. No one really liked me — I was too honest, too direct. I didn't play well with others. My clothes were never the right style, I didn't know how to drink, how to fit in, and my grades surpassed everyone else's. But we both know I'm the only reason Tatiana graduated from Suffolk Law.

She stares at me. "You've finally done it, haven't you?"

I wince and nod.

A slow grin spreads across her face. "I knew you'd do it someday. You're fucking amazing."

She would know. Whereas others might ask for help with homework or essays, I was the one people came to when they needed hacking skills. She was the one that came to me, tearfully begging me to hack into the school grading system when she was at risk for failing. I did, with the promise that one day she'd pay back the favor.

"Tell me everything you can."

"It's huge," I tell her in a whisper. "The more I tell you, the more danger you're in. You're in danger just being with me right now."

Her brow furrows, and her lips press together. She nods.

"Listen, Tatiana...The stuff that I found...if it ever got out to the press...it would destroy institutions across the world. You remember the Epstein scandal? Think bigger. Multiply it by a hundred, drag in every major institution you could think of, and you'll be getting closer."

"Holy *shit*."

I nod, my belly churning.

"World," she repeats, her eyes wide. I watch her swallow before she clarifies. "Not just the country?"

"*World*."

"My God," she mutters. "So if you're found..."

"I'm fucked." One of the people implicated could have me killed with a simple command, hiding all evidence laughably easily given the lack of contacts and influence I have. I lick my lips and nod. "Even the good guys can't help me this time." Because even the "good guys" are on that list.

"Are you in danger right this very minute? Do you have a place to stay?"

"Yes, I am and no, I don't."

I pull out my phone and tap the article I saved. Wordlessly, I hand it to her.

Mysterious Campus Attack Unleashes Panic as Authorities Hunt for Missing Professor

In a chilling turn of events, the tranquil campus of West End Community College is reeling after a brutal attack last night, sending shock and horror through the community. The assault, which authorities suspect was aimed at locating a missing professor entrenched in a high-profile investigation, has left students and faculty in a state of fear and confusion.

At approximately midnight students and campus security reported masked assailants arriving on campus. Some believe the assailants suspected Professor Aria Cunningham was hiding on site.

The attackers managed to evade capture, disappearing into the night as swiftly as they had arrived.

West End Community College has been placed on high alert, with classes suspended indefinitely, and students urged to stay safe. Officials are urging anyone with information on the whereabouts of Aria Cunningham or the attackers to come forward immediately.

Finally, she blows out a breath and nods. "My God. *Officials.* And you're telling me you found information on said officials that would destroy them."

I blow out a breath in relief. "That's exactly what I'm telling you."

She nods and smiles wanly. "I knew when you came to me it wouldn't be to set you up on a blind date or to borrow some gas money. How much do you need?"

I exhale. "I need more than money."

She stares at me as reality dawns. "You need protection," she says in a whisper. "Someone outside the law."

"Exactly," I whisper back.

She rises to her feet and paces the room.

"Holy shit, Aria. *Girl...*" Her voice trails off as she thinks over the implications of what I've told her. "This is too big for me. You'll need someone who can give you protection and money. You need someone with power. I have money, but money will only go so far." She mindlessly tugs at the delicate gold necklace she wears. "You could — no, no, that's too much. Hmm. That won't work," she says, as she mentally sifts through ideas. "Could send you to — no. Not this time of year, it's too busy and they'll be looking for those records anyway." She blows out a breath. "You can't show me what you found?"

I shake my head. "I don't want to involve you. The more you know, the more dangerous it is."

And honestly? I don't know her. Not really. What if she decides she wants to turn me in herself? Suddenly, the thought of coming here in the first place was the worst thought I ever had.

My heart is beating so fast I'm dizzy. I can't wait any longer. I can't stay in one place.

I stand up.

"You know, I'm good. I think that I—"

"Aria! I've got it!" She reaches for my arm and grips it tightly, her eyes so wide she's scaring me. "There is someone who can help. I mean...he's...vicious. He's scary as fuck. But if you go to him, okay, *them*...and offer your skills...it just might work. I mean, you've got information that law enforcement doesn't want you to have. Your only choice is to go to someone who's *above* the law. Who doesn't care about niceties or following the rules. Who hates the Feds and would likely love fucking them over."

I eye her skeptically. She's right, but..."Okay?"

"The Romanovs," she says in a whisper.

The hair on the back of my neck stands up. "They rule The Cove and they despise local authority," she continues. "They're the only ones *above* local authority."

I lick my lips. "How?"

"Organized crime. You know? *Bratva.*"

Bratva. I do know. When you do what I do, sifting through the vast network of connections and people and places...you know exactly where the most powerful people live.

The Romanovs own The Cove, the large, sprawling "Little Russia" smack dab between Coney Island and Manhattan. That's all I know.

But I have no safe place to go. I could form another identity, uproot everything, and flee the country. I know enough that I could fabricate a new ID and start from scratch.

But I'd have nothing. No one.

"I've lost everything, Tatiana. I'm willing to pay the price of anything at this point."

She stares at me unblinking. "Anything?"

I swallow. "Anything." My small apartment is gone. My identity has been leaked. I don't have a job anymore and had no money to begin with. For the first time in my life, I'm thankful I have no loved ones I could lose.

"The Romanovs are in charge of everything in The Cove. I can tell you right now that whatever you ask of them, it will come at a price. A price you may not be willing to pay. "

My mind goes over every possible price. Debt collection. Forced involvement in crime. Unpaid labor, human trafficking...sexual favors.

What would they demand of me?

"I have what they may find to be a...marketable skill," I say, my voice trembling.

She blows out a breath, and relief floods me when she smiles. "Of course you do. What do you know about The Cove?"

I shake my head. "Honestly, not much." I want to hear what she has to say.

Tatiana's family is Russian, so she's a lot more familiar with it than I am.

"So it's this neighborhood known for having a lot of Russian influence. The shopkeepers speak Russian. There are restaurants, grocery stores, cultural centers. An Orthodox Church. There's like a beach, and a boardwalk. It's really popular in the summer, because people sunbathe and swim, and take walks. In the winter it's less crowded because of the drop in tourists. But that's when the Romanovs come. That's when they set up shop, or whatever the fuck they do. I don't know. They own everything. Literally everything.

The restaurants, hotels, venues. But they also have apartment buildings and single-family homes, you know, residences. They own those, too."

"Wow. Okay."

I can do this. What do I have to lose? I've already lost almost everything. Almost.

She bites her lip thoughtfully. "This just might work."

CHAPTER THREE

Mikhail

"MY CONDOLENCES, MIKHAIL."

I stand a full foot taller than the old man in front of me, but despite Fyodor Volkov's smaller stature, no one ever mistook him for being weak.

Volkov reaches to pour me a shot of vodka, but I shake my head.

"So soon you forsake tradition, son?"

"Call me son again and I'll remind you who I am."

Volkov's bodyguards come to attention at the challenge in the air, but I don't fucking care. "Don't try me," I tell them. "This conversation is between your *pakhan* and *me*. If any of you dare to defile my father's memory, you'll wish you were buried with him."

Other than staff, a few of my guards and Volkov's men are the only ones present for this impromptu meeting in one of my restaurants. I chose this one for the security of its location – the beachfront at my back and only one access point. The secluded room is located deep within the walls of the building.

Though from the outside it appears to be an ordinary restaurant serving Russian cuisine, it's only a front. The atmosphere is thick with the rich aroma of Russian foods, the walls decorated with paintings of Russian landscapes and art, all underscored by the threat of unspoken violence. If these walls could talk...

A muscle twitches beneath the old man's eye, but before he can respond, I lean in closer. "Some men respect the elderly, cousin. Don't make the mistake of assuming I'm one of them."

"If you think—"

"I don't *think*," I snap.

One of his men starts. I know for a fact the last man that interrupted Fyodor Volkov lost his tongue. My fingers itch for his guards to come at me, but they don't.

Volkov holds a hand up, a silent gesture to hold them at bay. I'm done with the formalities.

"I know why you're here, old man. I'd like to remind you that by law we're in our days of mourning. If any of your number breaks that law, retribution will be swift and merciless. The only reason I've given you permission to be in my presence before now was out of respect for my father." I reach forward and adjust Volkov's lapel. "Is. That. *Clear?*"

We have ten days left and he knows it.

Muscles twitch in the old man's jaw, his watery eyes narrowed. He pulls away from my grip on his collar with effort. Though his men outnumber mine, the sheer strength of my cavalcade would overpower them, at least in this moment. My father trained us to be dynamite in human form, veritable panthers.

Volkov would be wise to hire more muscle.

"Ten days left," he says, before playing his final card. "But you know our traditions."

I need no reminder.

I wear the knowledge of my duty like a noose around my neck, tightening with each day that passes. The dissolution of my first arranged marriage agreement on the heels of my father's death was no accident. Volkov is notorious for hitting hard when a man is down, for striking the Achilles heel with no mercy.

My first fiancée went missing, and while we hunted for her, Aleks discovered their financial stability was fabricated. The second arrangement ended as swiftly as the first when my second fiancée was found dead. The third was much harder to secure after my history of arrangements, but we were finally able to. Money talks. And then my third fiancée was found dead this morning.

I nod my head to my cousin's men. "You've outstayed your welcome. You have three minutes to leave before I consider your presence trespassing on our territory and treat you accordingly." My guards practically vibrate with excitement, rabid dogs who smell blood in the air.

I take out my phone to send a red alert.

Krasnaya trevoga

Unlike Volkov's men, greater in number but languid under the leadership of their aging *pakhan,* my brothers obey on command. All are eager to show obedience and homage to their new *pakhan.*

Volkov stares around the room with those narrowed eyes of his for a few beats before he eyes me carefully and gets to his feet. Without another word to me, he gestures for his guards to escort him out. I've already dismissed him as I turn to my phone and send another text.

I tap the computer screen in front of me and wait, drumming my fingers on the mahogany table.

"Another drink, sir?"

I nod without looking at the waiter, scrolling through my notes in front of me. "A bottle of *Stolichnaya Elit* and a platter of appetizers. And send all staff out unless I signal you directly."

In my peripheral vision, I see him nod. "Right away, sir."

Quietly, he evacuates all staff from the room. I pay my employees well to be discreet and obedient, so they know the routine.

Aleksandr is the first to arrive. I wave a hand to greet him at the door, wordlessly point to the seat beside me, and turn back to the computer.

"Heard the news. Bad fucking luck."

I grunt in reply. "Luck has nothing to do with it. Sit."

Aleksandr takes a seat, leaning back and opening up his cell phone. While the rest of the world uses their phones to scroll social media and take selfies, Aleks runs an empire.

He scowls at his phone, his fingers dancing over the screen.

Aleks is younger than I am and in impeccable physical condition. Like all of us, he battles demons, but Aleks schools them under the weight of a barbell. The combination of brilliant techie and sheer brutal strength is useful in our line of work.

He looks nothing like me, which sometimes comes in useful. All of the Romanov men were adopted, a part of our father's intricate plan to build an empire.

It worked, for the most part.

Aleksandr sits brooding, as his fingers fly over his phone screen. He mutters to himself and stifles a groan. Today's news fucked up our plans. But the Romanovs always find a way to prevail.

I tap my computer monitor and pull up the video feed. Viktor is the first that shows on screen, followed swiftly by Kolya, Lev, Nikko, and the rest.

"We have a situation." I quickly bring them up to speed.

"This morning, I got a call. Irina Smirnova was found dead, strangled in her sleep. Of course they have no fucking leads, but we know who was responsible."

Nikko scowls at the camera, his arms crossed over his chest. He's glistening with sweat and I can see the walls of his home gym behind him. Nicknamed "The Steel Serpent," Nikko's our head assassin. "Volkov."

Kolya finally breaks the silence. "Being engaged to you's a fucking death sentence."

Kolya, our group mastermind, served with my father in the army. Though younger than my father, he's older than I am. I respect his brilliant strategic mind.

Our laughter quickly dies because it's true.

He shakes his head at the camera, running his fingers through his short hair streaked with silver. "We don't have much time to arrange another marriage, Mikhail." Kolya's voice is grim. "If we hit that deadline and you're still unmarried, we know the consequences."

The destruction of our assets, the possibility of attack from our enemies, the potential threat they could use leverage against the few people that mean anything to us. Even my tribe of panthers isn't enough.

We're on the cusp of war if I don't have a wife, a war we're not equipped to win.

Kolya continues. "No one in our circles will agree to another arrangement, Mikhail. We'll have to find someone else."

I nod, stroking my chin as I think. The waiter brings our food and pours vodka into shot glasses.

"You have our support and protection, brother," Nikko says, his sober, earnest eyes meeting mine on screen.

I nod. "Thank you."

"We'll find you a wife," Aleks says. "Secretly, of course. We have a network of contacts and resources that can help."

The rest agree.

My phone buzzes with a text. I feel my eyebrows rise with surprise.

The timing couldn't be better.

CHAPTER FOUR

Aria

IT'S LAUGHABLY easy to find the online scheduling software the Romanov assistant uses.

So maybe I planted a little bug. Practically child's play. And when she opens up her computer to the calendar for the day, previously color coded and organized perfectly, she'll see a blank slate.

I feel a little guilty causing someone else anxiety, but I'm desperate. And she must know who she works for.

I can't spend another second wondering when they'll find me. At this point, I'm not even sure who "they" are because the system of corruption runs so deep and wide. I imagine everywhere I turn, everywhere I look, masked or hooded men and women are ready to take me. After the newspaper article...I'm confident it's not just my imagination.

I walk into the lobby of the Romanov business center like I

own the place. Like I belong. Anyone can pretend for a little while, right?

When I reach for the door, it whispers open of its own accord. The entrance exudes opulence and sophistication, topped off with a very clear theme of exclusivity. The spacious, welcoming area boasts sleek leather chairs and minimalist decor, speckled marble floors of black and gray, adorned with a splash of contemporary artwork in bold red and black. It's compelling but a bit unnerving.

A brushed metal desk stands in front of me, featuring an arrangement of fresh flowers. It's so cold in here, the flowers are a nice touch.

I walk forward with my head held high, my gaze taking everything in and cataloging it. The chic seating area to the left, the plush armchairs and sofa to the right. High ceilings with recessed lighting, and discreetly hidden in a darkened alcove is a state-of-the-art security panel that looks complicated enough to launch a spaceship.

I borrowed one of Tatiana's dresses for today. She's thinner than I am, so it's a little risqué, clinging to my curvier body. I declined the heels because I know myself well enough to know that I would keel over and mortify myself if I tried to walk in them. So instead I opted for a pair of sensible but elegant flats.

"May I help you?"

The receptionist is a young, gorgeous woman, *of course*, with porcelain skin and delicate features, luscious blonde waves cascading down her back.

I mentally grimace. *Sorry I fucked up your computer.*

I don't miss the fact that there are six armed guards nearby.

"Yes," I say, keeping my tone even, almost bored. "I'm here for my eleven o'clock meeting with Mr. Romanov."

She eyes me curiously, her head tipped to the side. "Are you sure about that?" I wonder idly if those lashes are falsies, they're so pretty.

"Of course," I insist, my tone hardening. "Is there a problem?"

I'll make it up to you, I promise. A few keystrokes and her bank account will be mysteriously fatter.

Doing what I do means I blur the lines of morality sometimes. Other times, I have to erase them completely. Still, I'm shaking and want to run. I breathe deeply and will my nerves to remain calm.

"Let me see," she murmurs to herself. When she stares at the screen, unblinking, I know exactly what she's seeing — nothing. Her calendar wiped clean and an obnoxious error code.

Pink splotches of color stain her cheeks. My belly dips with guilt. "Just a minute, please."

She stands and walks to another room and knocks politely on its door. I take a deep breath and will myself not to glance at the guards all looking directly at me.

Here we go. Enter, the Romanovs.

When the door opens, the gentleman on the other side looks exactly the way Tatiana described these guys — huge, gorgeous, muscular, with perfectly symmetrical features and stunningly rugged looks.

This is *a* Romanov...just not the one I'm looking for. This one looks younger with his scar across his eyebrow. He has a chiseled jawline etched in neatly trimmed stubble, striking blue eyes, and a close-cropped haircut. A black dress shirt stretches across taut muscles and is tucked into charcoal gray dress pants. He wears no tie, an effortless nod toward business casual. He's ruggedly handsome and dangerous as fuck.

"Yes?" He eyes me suspiciously while she fills him in.

"I'm so sorry to bother you, sir," she says in a low voice. "I can't access our database of appointments and records. It's gone completely blank. This woman says that she's here to see Mr. Romanov, but I have no record to compare or..." she gives me a quick glance and then looks back to him, "... memory of booking the appointment."

The man scowls at me. I shiver and promise her she can buy herself whatever it is her little heart desires tonight. *Just help a girl out, please,* I silently beg.

"Who are you?" he bites out without any semblance of professionalism. I'm reminded of a pit bull.

Fortunately for me, constructing a false identity was also very easy. "Linda Rogue. Mr. Romanov brought me in here as a cybersecurity consultant."

His eyebrows raise. "*I'm* the cybersecurity consultant."

Shit shit shit.

I took a gamble and I lost. Time to pivot.

"So nice to meet you," I say warmly. "My hope is to show Mr. Romanov the latest digital defenses that we have against cybersecurity issues. I'm not here to take your job, of course, but to offer my expertise and services to strengthen your empire. Our goal is to make your security impenetrable." I give him a delicate smile and hope tossing the word "empire" in there stroked his ego just enough.

The way his ice blue eyes narrow on me makes my belly dip. Maybe this was a bad idea.

"Interesting. What did you say your name was?"

"Linda Rogue."

I just have to get into Mikhail Romanov's office. By the time I get in there, they might've already realized this is a front, but I'll have my audience.

"What time is your appointment?"

I glance at my watch and frown. "Five minutes ago?" I say, hoping that they'll believe it. "I'm sorry, but I can't wait much longer. I'm happy to schedule another appointment, though unfortunately I'm booking six months out." I pull out my phone and pretend to open up the calendar app.

I feel the heat of his glare across the room. "Fine. Take her in. I'll get our database back up."

My heart thumps. I swallow. I can almost audibly hear the clicking of an imaginary clock on how much time I have before I'm discovered.

I may have done my research before I came in here. I may know that the man I'm about to face is Mikhail Romanov, eldest of the Bratva brotherhood here in The Cove, and the man that works with him here is either Aleksandr or Lev. Likely Aleksandr, because he's closer in age to Mikhail.

The Romanovs are widely known in these parts for ruthless extortion outside The Cove, but here, they run things at a quieter pace. Most suspect their businesses are a front for extortion and money laundering, but a perusal of the Dark Web reveals contractual assassinations and elite levels of espionage. They maintain respect from those outside their family by exacting revenge on those that betray them and making no effort at hiding the discipline they require within their own family.

The local papers are notably quiet about their presence here, but the Dark Web tells another story – violent turf wars, brutal public punishments for crimes against them, high-profile assassinations to eliminate anyone who stands in their way.

I've made a terrible mistake.

Their assistant's heels click on the marble floor as she walks away from me. "Miss Rogue? This way, please."

I have to do this.

When she opens the door to his office, I have to force myself not to gape. If I didn't already know Mikhail Romanov was a former military officer and billionaire with a cutthroat reputation, his office would tell me. It screams power, efficiency, and ruthless determination.

Dominated by dark yet simple mahogany furniture, the space is immaculate. The largest leather chair I've ever seen sits behind an imposing executive-style desk positioned to command immediate attention.

I nearly salivate at the state-of-the-art computer setup — multiple screens, a custom keyboard you can't find in any shop, complete with an ergonomic wireless mouse. Not a cable's in sight, hidden from view, a wireless charging pad to the right.

"Please, make yourself at home. He'll be right with you. May I get you a cup of coffee? Water?"

"I — water would be great, thank you." I'd kill for a hot cup of coffee, but I don't need to add to my jitters. A shot of whiskey would be heaven.

I take the bottle of water gratefully and give her a smile. With shaking hands, I twist the top off and take a swig.

Heavy footsteps sound behind me. I nearly choke on my water.

"Mr. Romanov! The woman I called about is here, sir. Your brother is looking into the scheduling software now."

Your brother. Of course.

I sit nervously on my seat, my fingers wrapped around my water bottle. I did my research before I came here. I know who he is, and what he looks like. His background.

Mikhail Romanov was a soldier who suffered PTSD after witnessing undisclosed "war crimes." He was born in Russia and is skilled in combat. He's ten years my senior and the eldest in his family.

But one thing you realize about reading details online? Nothing is what it seems.

For example, you can read a person's height is 6'2", but when a man who's *actually* 6'2" tall and 250 pounds of solid muscle enters the room? It's a completely different experience. You can read "covered in tattoos, Russian heritage, pierced ears, scarred upper cheek," but you don't know how terrifying that looks when you see those details in person. And even the Dark Web was eerily absent of any pictures.

And nothing I read said...*dangerously sexy.*

Mikhail Romanov enters — no, *prowls* — into the room with a scowl I feel in my very bones.

It takes everything in me not to run.

CHAPTER FIVE

Aria

I'M unprepared for the way he towers over both of us. For the piercing coldness of his gaze. For the heat that emanates from him as if he's stepped straight out of the fiery depths of hell.

But worst of all? I'm unprepared for the way my body responds to his utter *perfection*.

Deep-set dark brown eyes beneath heavy brows. Golden, tanned skin, and dark brown hair tinged with flecks of gold. A square, clean-shaven jawline. All his features make him arrestingly masculine and undeniably attractive. He carries his large frame effortlessly, corded muscle and strength barely hidden under a crisp white shirt.

I tear my eyes away to prevent myself from gawking and realize my thoughts have come to a stuttering halt. I swallow and regain my composure just in the nick of time.

"Why the hell are you in my office?" Oh, God. That voice. Deep and dark and cold as ice, like a plunge into the unknown depths of a sea in winter.

Don't run. Don't run.

"We had a meeting, sir," I bluff. "Cybersecurity."

"I did not make an appointment with anyone about cyberse-curity. We have a cybersecurity expert. And I wouldn't have made an appointment with someone like *you*."

Great. Add male chauvinist asshole to that list. Or is the direct insult aiming at another one of my traits? The *prick*.

I bite my tongue to keep from snapping at him. It won't behoove me now at all. I have to play nice.

"You're excused, Chantelle," he says seconds before he clicks the door shut behind him.

Fuck.

"Cut the bullshit and stop lying to me about why you're here, and I might let you live."

Wow, so we went straight there, didn't we.

This is my last chance for protection. I take a deep breath, my voice shaking with a mixture of fear and determination.

"Mr. Romanov," I begin. "I am here for another purpose. I needed to speak to you and came here out of desperation."

Still scowling, he rounds the desk. I'm faintly aware of the scent of pine and leather. I watch him pull out the chair and fold himself into it with surprising grace.

"You have thirty seconds."

Before...what?

God.

I speak faster, telling him my purpose in a rush of words. "I've uncovered a ring of powerful and influential people who've committed unspeakable atrocities. They've infiltrated even the highest levels of authority. I need the help of someone who operates outside the reach of the law." I lick my lips and swallow. "Someone like you, sir."

Mikhail Romanov regards me with a cold, calculating gaze as the fingers of one hand come to rest on the desk. I notice the blunt tip of each finger and tattoos on his knuckles. The havoc he could wreak with hands like those...

"Why should I help you?" he snaps.

I lean in and hold his gaze with every ounce of bravery I can muster. "*No one* can out-code me. I will work for you and all I ask in return is that you grant me safety and sanctuary."

Mikhail leans back in his chair, his stony expression hardening.

"What makes you think I need you?"

I can't help it. Tears spring to my eyes. I blink them away, but he doesn't miss them. "I'm out of options. Please, Mr. Romanov, help me. I promise you won't regret it."

"A woman like you is smart enough to know that I don't give a fuck about your cybersecurity bullshit." He gives a derisive look toward my ample chest as if implying he has a lot more use for my body than my brain.

The nerve.

I snap my teeth together. I didn't really expect a meeting with Mikhail Romanov to exactly go swimmingly, but I wasn't quite prepared for this level of dickheadedness. I wish I could slap his beautiful face or at least tell him off, but that's way too risky.

I clench my teeth together. "A friend of mine suggested I come here. I've uncovered information that puts every major institution in America at risk. Your enemies, sir."

He narrows his eyes to slits. "You have no fucking idea who my enemies are." My pulse spikes. I will myself not to shrink back. "So you were fucking around in places you never should have been." His voice takes on a tone of mockery. "The big bad guys found out, and now they want to punish you." He shrugs. "Fair. If you'd hacked into *my* organization the punishment would be swift and severe."

Oh no.

He sneers. "Though I have to admit, I'd thoroughly relish punishing a woman like you."

It takes every effort of self-control to school my features. I feel too hot and too cold and for some reason, a little dizzy.

I swallow. And still, I press on. I can't give up. "I know what I'm asking you is a tall order, but I also know that you're the only person that can actually do this." I'm starting to feel desperate. "Please. I'm crashing on my friend's couch, in hiding. And I *promise* you if you hire me, you'll be happy you did."

He shakes his head. I try not to cry.

"I told you. I have no use for your skills. It's not my fault you trespassed where you don't belong." He dismisses me with a wave of his hand. "Get the hell out of my office." He turns back to his paperwork and doesn't look up when he speaks again. "Oh, and before you leave? A word of advice."

My cheeks flame with embarrassment as he continues. "Never, ever wear your hair like that in front of a man like me, and especially not when you're being tracked. No pony-tails. No buns."

My hand flies to the thick bun at the nape of my neck. I thought I looked sophisticated.

"My – hair?" I ask haltingly.

He leans on his forearm and gestures for me to step closer with a crooked finger. Against everything in me that tells me not to, I lean in.

"It's too easy for someone to reach out"— he gestures to the air in front of him — "and grab it." He makes a fist so suddenly, I jump back, my heartbeat threatening to choke me. "And once you were caught in their grip..." He shrugs. "They could do anything they wanted to do to you."

One last lingering gaze skates over my neck to my chest and all the way down the length of my body.

"Now go." He turns away. "If you're still in here in ten seconds, I'll give you a personal escort out of my office. And just so we're clear." He snaps his gaze back to mine. "If you ever fuck around with me again, you'll deal with me person-ally. I promise you, you don't want that to happen."

I open my mouth to try another angle, but his steely gaze forbids it.

I do the only sensible thing.

I walk out the door with my head held high and shoulders squared.

I outed myself to Mikhail Romanov. I practically flat-out begged. He knows who I am and what I'm capable of.

I offered what I had to give.

He didn't bite.

When my feet hit the ground outside his door, I finally run.

CHAPTER SIX

Mikhail

"FOLLOW HER."

I don't wait for a response. They know exactly who I'm talking about. Hell, they followed her in here. It's cute that she thinks she orchestrated this.

Even though I knew she was coming, I wasn't prepared for how beautiful she was. Nerdy, yeah, but in the sexiest way I could imagine. The brightest eyes hiding behind scratched lenses, thick, dark hair pulled into a bun at the nape of her neck. I imagine pulling on her mane of hair. I imagine pain flashing across her face before she moans when I wrap my fingers around her hair and pull. I want to see her fight me when I take control.

I wasn't giving her a warning when I told her about her hair. I wanted her to imagine me gripping it. I wanted her to imagine what I'd do to her when she was at my mercy.

A knock sounds at the door.

"Who is it?" I snap. I'm not in a social mood. When am I ever in a social mood?

"Aleks."

I grunt in reply, and Aleksandr opens the door.

He nearly slams the door shut behind him, but he's too in control of himself to give way to temper. Unlike the rest of us.

He stalks in and glares at me. "You know her?"

"Of course I don't fucking know her." By the end of the day, I will. By the end of the day, I'll know everything about her.

"But you knew she was coming."

I nod. "I did."

Scowling, he doesn't ask me how I knew. The less we say out loud, the better. I tell my brothers what they need to know, no more, no less. We have informants and allies, and the key to survival is knowing when and how to use them.

"Someone hacked into our data system. Give me ten minutes and I'll prove it was her."

I raise an eyebrow at him and he nearly flinches.

He fucked up and he knows that I know. He also knows what that means.

I shake my head. "You don't need to. I know it was."

She'll pay for that. But so will he.

Aleksandr's eyes grow dark as he glares at me. "And you let her walk?"

I lean forward. "You're hardly in a position to question my decisions, don't you think?"

Aleks is suitably humbled. He swallows and hangs his head. "No, sir." As the oldest, my parents held me responsible for my siblings from a young age. They learned to respect me and defer to my authority, so the transition to me being *pakhan* was almost seamless.

"No. She only thinks she walked. Do you really think, brother, that I let someone hack into our systems, manipulate their way into my office, and leave unscathed?" I shake my head with a sigh. "Sometimes, I don't think you know me at all." A glint of a smile ghosts his lips, but he knows he fucked up. I lean forward, my voice deceptively calm. "But tell me, Aleks. How did she hack into our system to begin with? Think before you answer."

He flinches as if struck and nods.

"Give me ten minutes, Mikhail," he says, unusually subdued and chastened.

"You have five." I tap my phone and send a message.

> Krasnaya trevoga

We need a meeting, now. What if she's working with others? If she could access our scheduling with ease, what else does she have access to?

But I have another purpose for our meeting.

Aleksandr sits brooding, as his fingers fly over his phone screen. He mutters to himself and stifles a groan.

I tap my computer monitor and pull up the video feed to see my brothers as they join the virtual meeting, one by one.

"We have a situation."

Nikko scowls from the screen. "Do we have an explanation?"

I lean back in my chair and raise an eyebrow at Aleksandr.

He flinches. "I'm looking into it now. I'll have a report by the end of the day." Turning to me, his icy blue eyes fairly gleam. "But I'll tell you this, Mikhail. It takes great skill — *unparalleled* skill — to bypass what I've put in place. Genius. Brilliance." He shakes his head, half in awe of the expertise she casually demonstrated without even knowing she did.

Brilliance.

My personal kryptonite. Why have I always been attracted to brilliant women?

I want her.

One of my brothers stares at me, his gaze cold and calculating. "You could use this to your advantage, brother."

"I could."

"He doesn't have time to seduce her," another of them says. They carry on a conversation while I think this through. While they don't say it aloud out of respect, we're all painfully aware of my lack of a wife and how crucial marriage is for me.

"Seduce her?" Aleks half grunts. "If he had ten years, he wouldn't have enough time to seduce her. First, she's not the type to fall very easily. I'm telling you, this woman's intelligence is off the charts. I had a firewall and system in place the fucking FBI couldn't break. Trust me when I tell you they've tried."

"And let's be honest," Nikko says. "Mikhail is good at many things but with all due respect, brother, seduction is not one of them."

I shrug and don't deny it. It's a skill I've never needed.

I want to stare into those eyes again. I want to grip her hair in my hands. I imagine myself cupping her ass and making her moan. I imagine the look of fear in her eyes when I overpower her.

I imagine the way she screams when she can't get away. I imagine the way her face looks when her head is thrown back when she fucking comes.

She's mine.

Kolya shakes his head at the camera, running his fingers through his short hair streaked with silver. "We don't have much time to arrange another marriage, Mikhail."

"We fucking don't." I blow out a breath. "Fortunately, *she* needs protection and money."

He gives me a curious look but doesn't ask questions. As he strokes the stubble on his chin, I can practically see the wheels turning in his mind.

"Excellent," Kolya finally says. "So the little hacker walked right into your lair and practically bared her neck to you."

Little hacker.

"She did. And don't forget she committed a crime worthy of punishment." I give a short nod.

"How many days, brother?" someone asks. I don't bother to see who it is.

"Three."

If I don't get married, I forfeit the alliances and connections a marital statement makes. Marriage can be a powerful force, yes. In some cases if we marry an influential family, we gain access to resources and support, but in this case, it symbolizes unity and loyalty within our group. Marriage means that we immediately strengthen the sheer number of our group.

This time, Volkov won't be able to make a move. He would never suspect I'd marry a penniless fugitive.

The destruction of our assets, the possibility of attack from our enemies, the potential threat they could leverage against the few people that mean anything to us. Even my tribe of panthers isn't enough.

We're on the cusp of war if I don't have a wife, a war we're not equipped to win.

"I'm having her followed, only to see where she goes and what she does. I know where she's sleeping tonight. Her temporary refuge."

Aleks smiles. "Perfect."

My phone rings. My mother's ringtone.

I hold up my hand to indicate silence. My brothers practically hold their collective breaths.

I put the call on speaker.

"Yes."

But it isn't my mother on the other line.

"Mikhail. How are you?"

Volkov.

Aleks narrows his eyes.

I clench my fist. "Fantastic." He waits for me to reciprocate the bullshit formality, but I don't.

"Fine, fine. I was just sitting here with your mother. We were having a nice dinner."

I grit my teeth and force myself to stay calm. Bashing this phone against the wall is a childish move that won't solve anything.

My mother. Of course. She doesn't know who Volkov truly is, and there's a part of her that still trusts him. He's family, after all, but she doesn't know what he's capable of. How he only values family inasmuch as he can use them.

I keep my tone light. "Mama. How are you?"

"I'm well, Mikhail. I miss you. Come for dinner, soon?"

I look at Aleks as my mother continues talking. On the conference screen, Nikko makes a fist, Lev scowls at the camera, and Kolya's body tightens.

We all know why Volkov is there. It's a silent but very real threat. If I don't get married, he attacks. And yes, we lose money and assets but he's not above kidnapping or hurting my mother. He won't give a fuck about retribution.

I have to get married.

"We were just looking at the calendar," Volkov says. "I've suggested a little trip back to Mother Russia. You know we have family there. Your mother says she misses it, Mikhail. Your father never allowed her to go back to Russia."

Of course he didn't. Enemies, history, former lovers. Russia was ripe with memories of my father's past. My mother, though...

"It's hard to believe it's been thirty-seven days since your father's death," he says. "I offer my condolences." He speaks in Russian to my mother, and I clench my hands into fists.

"Leave her alone."

"Leave her alone? What are you talking about? We're just here for a little visit. I wondered if there was an invitation somewhere along the line that I've missed?"

I make a fist. "If you hurt her, old man..."

"Mikhail," my mother says gently. "You're too distrusting, son. We're just having dinner. Come see me this weekend, will you?"

I close my eyes briefly. I can see her now. The matriarch of our family, strong yet graceful, sitting upright with her impeccable posture. People call her a timeless beauty, but it's her indomitable strength they truly admire. Her decisions are made with a blend of intuition, wisdom, and strategic foresight.

Now, though. Now that my father's gone, I value her input, but final decisions rest with me.

"Of course we'll have dinner," I tell her. "Though I'm arranging for you to come to me. I have a surprise for you."

I can practically feel Volkov's tension.

"Oh, excellent," she says with a smile. "I love surprises."

I get a text from my assistant, Chantelle.

> We have your information, sir.

I nod to Aleks to open the door.

"This weekend," I promise her.

"What's this weekend?" a higher-pitched, clear feminine voice sounds on the line. Polina.

I can hear the contempt in her voice when she addresses Volkov. "Oh. Who let *you* in?"

I blow out a breath and speak loud enough for all to hear.

"My wedding, *sestrichka*."

CHAPTER SEVEN

Aria

I WAKE from what feels like the deepest sleep of my life with a start.

Where am I? I blink at shadowed furniture and drawn shades. Tatiana's living room. I'm still fully clothed, my glasses askew. I must've fallen asleep on her couch. How strange. I never do that.

It was quite a day, though.

I push my glasses back on right and stumble to my feet. Last night, I came back to Tatiana's and told her everything. She assured me we'd find another way, but I could tell she was nervous. I don't blame her, really. I basically put a big ol' target on her residence.

I knew I had to find another place to go since she's at risk now that I've outed myself like an idiot to the Romanovs.

We had a drink together...and I guess I fell asleep.

Disoriented and bleary-eyed, I drag myself to the guest room, strip down to a tank and panties, then brush my teeth and splash water on my face before I turn and face-plant onto the bed.

I close my eyes, but memories of that truly embarrassing interaction with Mikhail Romanov plague me. I can still see his cold, calculating gaze. His heavy hands, resting casually on the desk, marked in ink. I can still smell the scent of pine and leather, unapologetically masculine. If I ever smell that scent again, I'll forever see large, calloused, inked hands resting on a gleaming desk. Hands that have no doubt committed unspeakable crimes.

Then why can't I stop thinking about them? About *him?*

I can't shake the feeling that Mikhail Romanov is a man that would stop at nothing to get what he wants.

And then the sharp, cold way he dismissed me like I was dirt on the bottom of his shoe. I told myself it was only business, but I'm still not truly immune to the biting sting of rejection. I guess that's something you don't outgrow.

I'm so tired I can't think of that now, though. I flop around in bed, my eyes closed, and finally manage to conjure up sleep when something startles me fully awake.

I blink in the darkness. What was that? I swear I heard someone breathing right in this room beside me.

Was that in my mind or dream state or...is there someone here?

I sit up straight, my heart tripping against my ribcage.

Did Tatiana hear that? I wait so long in the silence, my eyelids heavy with sleep, that I convince myself I imagined it, or it was some sleep-induced delusion. Still, my heart's racing.

I go to roll over when I'm struck with the sudden feeling I'm not alone in this room.

"Is somebody there?" I whisper, my voice husky and my mouth dry. How much did I drink last night?

My head feels as if it weighs twenty pounds. In my state of fear and confusion still tinged with sleep, I imagine I smell... pine and leather.

Oh my God.

I clear my throat and sit up in the darkness. I clutch the blanket to my body even though it offers little protection. "I said who's there?"

A shadow moves in front of me. I open my mouth to scream, stricken with fear, when a rough hand clamps over my mouth. I scream in terror but the rough, heavy palm against my mouth muffles any sound. A heavy body pins me to the bed. I'm paralyzed with fear, my heart racing and my breathing shallow. I'm shaking, my fight or flight instinct triggered.

Strong, iron-like arms swing around me, effectively immobilizing me when moonlight hits his face. It can't be.

Am I dreaming? Is this a nightmare? Have I conjured up in vivid detail the most terrifying man I've ever met?

His mouth to my ear, the words are clear. "You're coming with me, little hacker. If you try to resist, I'll punish you.

Please, give me a reason. I've thought of nothing else since you left my office."

Pain pricks my neck. A strange sense of grogginess and loss of control spiked with terror-soaked adrenaline courses through my veins. I try to fight, but it's useless.

I'm vaguely aware of how easily he picks me up, as if I weigh nothing at all. How the way he holds me is almost gentle as he walks to the open door. He doesn't even attempt to use the window or something more discreet, just bodily carries me out the door.

I scream in my mind but can't seem to make words come out of my mouth. I stifle a dry sob and lift my hands to push back, but I'm completely incapable of defending myself.

Why hasn't Tatiana heard him? I imagine he's as quiet as a mouse, the only sounds magnified in my state of fear, but... The front door is wide open. There must be a dog, a surveillance camera, *something*, but I quickly realize there's nothing at all between us and the wide-open space.

I'm being...*kidnapped*. Like you hear about on the news. Only then...those people very rarely come back.

My mind reels with this realization.

As he steps over the front threshold, the chill of the night bites my skin. I'm half-naked, groggy, and disoriented, and I can't fight him. My senses are dulled. I can barely comprehend where I am or where we're going, except I know that it's cold, and we're outside.

My mind reels with fear. What's he going to do to me when he gets me alone? Why is he taking me? The last time I saw him, he was unceremoniously kicking me out of his office and being a total prick about it.

And yet now he's surprisingly...tender. Holding me to his chest as if to shield me from the wind. When we get to the car, the door opens as if by magic. I find myself laid down in a warm interior, the seats cushioned, and a thick, velvety blanket pressed over me. I vaguely wonder if he'll gag or bind me, but it seems he doesn't need to. I can't move or speak.

I'm so tired, I can barely keep my eyes open. I try, but my head falls against the padded seat. Tires rumble beneath the car.

Help I try to scream, but the words never leave my lips.

CHAPTER EIGHT

Aria

WHEN I WAKE, I don't know where I am.

The room is dark, but I know my abductor is nearby.

I can smell that scent.

I can still feel his strong arms about me, and even though I knew I was in danger, I had a strange sense that I wouldn't be accidentally hurt.

No. If this man hurts me, there will be nothing accidental about it.

I'm still too drugged and disoriented to really appreciate where I am. I know that it's a large room, with very few windows. It's definitely not a cell, or underground, or really hidden anywhere. The faint touch of blue hints at sunrise out the window.

The smell of coffee and toast makes my stomach rumble.

Asshole. No one should turn the smell of morning coffee and toast into a negative thing.

"You're waking up."

I know that voice. I hate trying to piece things together like a toddler with a puzzle, but I can't help it.

I'm too drugged. Too disoriented.

I open one eye. So it definitely wasn't a hallucination or a dream. Mikhail Romanov didn't send one of his henchmen, either, but apparently took it upon himself to keep guard over me.

Dressed in faded jeans and a black shirt rolled up to his elbows, he's leaning forward, looking at me.

"It will take a little while for the effects of the drugs to wear off." He says it so casually, as if it's not terribly wrong.

I shiver uncontrollably, unsure of what's going on. "Wh — where am I?" My teeth chatter, and a full-body tremor makes my teeth clang together.

"You're in my home," he says.

His home. He took me to...his home? Why am I here?

"Are you cold?" he asks when I shiver again.

"Fr-freezing," I chatter. The fact that I can't speak properly makes me want to scream. I take pride in having complete control over myself.

"Hmm," he says thoughtfully. Leaning forward, he lifts a second blanket from the foot of the bed and tosses it over me. "Coffee?"

I shake my head because I don't trust my voice. What is going *on?*

"While you're not yet capable of talking fully and you're still disoriented, I'm going to catch you up to speed, little hacker." Because he has the decided advantage right now, in every possible way.

Little hacker. That's right, he said that when he first took me.

Took me. Mikhail Romanov *kidnapped me.*

I swallow, my throat tight. He knows. He knows I manipulated his online scheduling system so I could get in to see him. I've been so foolish.

If he knows I hacked into that, what's to stop me from hacking into damn near anything else?

Nothing.

He walks over to the side table and retrieves something slender. My heart beats faster when I realize he's holding some sort of silky rope. With effortless ease, he reaches for my wrists and begins to casually bind them. I hate that I can't stop him.

I push through the fog and try to protest. "What did you do? Who do you think you are, taking me like this?" I wish I could threaten that when someone — some unnamed, mysterious someone who actually cares about me — finds out I'm gone, there'll be hell to pay.

But it isn't true. It would be a lie, and he'll call me on my bluff.

Leaning back, Mikhail scowls at me. I noticed he was unnervingly skilled at binding my wrists.

"The punishment for violating security in my family is execution."

My heart nearly bursts through my chest. I look down at myself, still barely clothed, and realize how vulnerable I am. How easy it would be for him to torture or kill me.

But if he were going to do that...wouldn't he have done the job already? Why bring me here first?

"You broke a rule that in my world gets you punished." Casually, he opens a drawer and pulls out a gun. He strokes it lovingly before he places it on the bedside table. "I've killed men for far less than that."

I believe it's true. Based on what Tatiana told me about him, I know he isn't lying.

My heart is in my throat as I look at the gun. Hear the casual way he talks, as if this is just the way things go. You did X, therefore Y. As if things like *my world* and *punishment* and *execution* aren't wildly wrong. As if the casual admission of having killed people just makes sense.

Tatiana warned me. *They stop at nothing to get what they want.*

"You offered me your services. You demonstrated such services, and I won't lie — it's impressive."

I watch him like a hawk, as if he's going to strike at any moment.

He looks so different than when I saw him before. When he leans forward, his biceps stretch against the black fabric of his shirt. If I wasn't afraid this man was a psychopath, I'd find him hot. It's not my fault, though. I mean, any woman would.

Everything about him exudes raw, masculine strength and virility — the muscles that bulge against the tee, the definition in his shoulders and arms. Tattoos scatter across his neck and look like they go down his back, a stark reminder of his allegiance to the Romanov brotherhood. His perfect, ruggedly handsome face that would be model-perfect if not for the coldness in his eyes.

He's crazy, though, and he kidnapped me. So while he may have rules in *his* world, in mine? He's insane.

"So you drugged me," I say, my words still slurred as if I had an all-night bender with my sorority sisters. I rarely drank in college, so the effect is quite insulting. *And you think that's okay?* I want to ask him. It doesn't seem like now's the time to question him.

I wonder briefly if there's *ever* a time to question him.

With a shrug, he tips a finger under my chin. "I did. It made my job easier, for now."

When his phone beeps he looks at the screen with a scowl. Swiping it on as if it personally offends him, he rasps something out in Russian. The voice on the other end is plaintive and apologetic, but he cuts them off and hangs up. I don't even know Russian, but you can tell a lot from someone's tone of voice and body language.

I shiver. He isn't just a leader. He leads other men just like him.

My heart beats faster. Adrenaline surges through me when he leans in closer.

"I have questions for you, little hacker."

Apparently, we have a pet name. How cute.

I tremble. I'm pissed that I'm shaking. I walked into his office with my head held high and I want to be on equal terms again. "Hard to — talk — when I'm drugged."

"Mmm. I see," he says, as he sits on the edge of the bed before he reaches for me and lifts me up, placing me on his *lap*.

His. *Lap*.

I can feel the tightness of his thighs beneath mine, and I'm painfully aware that I'm nearly naked. I'm wearing nothing but a tank and thin white cotton panties while he's fully clothed.

I couldn't think of anyone more unlike me in this moment — him, muscled and strong and powerful. Me, damn near scrawny. Him, rich and powerful and fearless. Me, running for my life without a penny to my name. Him, a leader in the Russian mafia. Me...a nobody.

It seems like the most logical response to anything he asks me is to tell him the truth. I can barely talk, much less defend myself. And yet...I won't roll over and let him have what he wants. Yes, I hacked into his goddamn computer base, but that doesn't thereby give him carte blanche over me.

I gasp and flinch when he reaches for me. His fingers stab into my hair, effectively pinning me in place. I remember his admonition before I left his office about not leaving my hair pinned up.

He's been waiting to do this.

I clamp my teeth together and look into his cold, merciless eyes. I bet if he had a man in this position, he'd be treating him very differently. Still, it's unnerving how easily he dominates me into submission.

"Yes or no answers will suffice. A simple nod or shake of your head will do."

I clamp my lips together. I won't tell him anything. He won't break me.

"Did you or did you not hack into our database and break it so my secretary couldn't access it?"

I clamp my teeth together and look away. His fingers in my hair tighten. A warning.

"Answer me."

I stare stoically ahead. I know who I'm dealing with but I won't be bulldozed by a goddamn man.

"No one says *secretary* anymore. Join the modern age, you Neanderthal," I mutter through clattering teeth.

To my surprise, he shakes his head and gives a cold chuckle before his grip tightens to painful. "Answer me," he whispers in my ear. "Answer me now before this becomes a lot more painful for you."

I grit my teeth and refuse to speak.

He pulls my hair and I gasp. I freeze, unable to move.

"I have other methods to make you talk," he says in a voice that reveals no emotion. "But I won't use them yet. With the plans I have for you, it would be better if you and I weren't enemies out of the gate."

"Fuck. *You*," I seethe. As if he can just take me from my bed and manhandle me and expect us to not be enemies?

The pain worsens as he holds me in his grip. If I move, I'm fucked.

I feel his fingers against my aching scalp and his mouth to my ear. "Did. You. Do it?"

"Of course I fucking did," I manage to rasp out. "I needed to talk to you. All I did was make her calendar disappear for a little while, so I think you're *way* overreacting."

"Am I?" he asks. He sighs as if pained as he reaches for his gun and cocks it. "We could try traditional methods if that's what you truly prefer."

Fear spikes through me and I'm suddenly wide awake. I wonder if I've imagined that he's drugged me. My mouth feels dry.

"Her calendar should be back now," I say, my voice sounding strange to my own ears.

"That isn't the point, and you know it."

His tone of voice — cold and indifferent, as if I'm nothing more than a specimen pinned on a card — scares me more than anything else he's done. Why did I ever go to him to begin with?

Again, his fingers stroke through my hair, as if to remind me that if I behave, he can be very nice. But even drugged, I know that's a lie. I wince when his grip tightens.

"I'm going to ask you another question. Think before you speak, Aria." So we're heading into first name territory, are we? Excellent. Something tells me familiarity with this man will be a huge mistake.

His mouth to my ear makes me shiver from the closeness and intimacy. The difference between warm and cold makes me uneasy. One minute, he's holding me tight and the next, he's switching on a dime.

"Fine," I say, my teeth chattering.

"Did you hack into any of our other systems? Tell the truth now."

I don't respond at first. So maybe I did. Maybe I found it as easy as opening up a can of soup to get into her calendar, and...maybe I was curious. I wondered what I would find. Sometimes when I discover a hidden passageway or open door, curiosity kills me.

This time it actually might.

"I peeked," I say through gritted teeth. "I touched nothing. Downloaded nothing. I barely even looked."

This time when he pulls my hair, I feel as if it's coming out at the roots. I scream but it doesn't stop him. He knows exactly what he's doing, hurting me in a way that makes me vulnerable and won't leave a mark. Tears spring to my eyes.

"Tell me what you saw."

There's no point in holding back at this point. "I found the names of the men in your group. Contact information. Addresses. Some financial transactions. Contracts and identities I didn't understand."

Another lie. They had informant identities clearly marked and categorized. The contracts were drawn up with agreements and arrangements with other groups and individuals. It was very civilized, honestly. He needs better fucking cybersecurity, but it's probably not the wisest thing to *tell* him that right now.

"Very good. Some truth." To my surprise, he strokes my hair, almost gently, another reminder that he'll play nice if I do. "My brother was right."

About what?

I look away from him when he finally releases me.

He pushes me off his lap. I wobble on my feet.

"Get in bed," he says, turning away from me. "You're here now. Sleep off the rest of those drugs and when you wake, we'll talk about the consequences for what you've done."

Wordlessly, I stare at him before he scowls and turns me to face the bed. Gripping my arm, he smacks my ass, hard. "Bed, *now*. You'll learn very quickly that I won't tolerate disobedience." He punctuates his words with another sharp smack.

My cheeks flame with embarrassment. My heartbeat races as I climb into bed like a chastened child, afraid of what he'll do.

While he watches me, his arms crossed over his chest as I lift the blanket with my bound hands and slide under it, a part of me wonders if he's human underneath that stern exterior. Or is he so used to getting his way he doesn't know how to be human anymore? He manhandles and dominates me with such ease, it seems it's part of his character.

When I'm tucked into the bed, exhaustion hits me like a freight train. I'm vaguely aware of him swiping something on his screen and talking in a low voice in Russian before he turns away.

I can't sleep. I won't sleep, I tell myself, not when he's watching me and holding all manner of threats over my head.

I'm relieved to find I'm able to process my thoughts more clearly. I've lost everything — the few friends I have, a safe place to stay. A place to call my own. But the absolute worst of it all would be losing my ability to *think*. A cognitive impairment sounds to me like a punishment worse than death.

So when my thoughts begin to sift through what happened — what I did, and what he did — I realize with a sigh of relief, I can still *think*.

It feels like an hour or more later as the adrenaline finally crashes and the aftermath leaves me spent. I tell myself I won't fall asleep, that I'll stubbornly refuse to do what he tells me. But the bed is warm and it's quiet in here. I have no idea what the day ahead holds for me.

I should maybe sleep while I can.

I close my eyes and drift off, waiting for him to come get me at any second. I dream of codes and computers in a darkened room, but this time my hands are bound.

CHAPTER NINE

Mikhail

I WATCH ARIA CUNNINGHAM SLEEP, her hair tossed around her head like a halo. I wonder if she has any idea how beautiful she is. It seems someone who knew she was walking perfection wouldn't dress in drab clothing and hide behind scratched glasses. I want to unwrap her like a precious gift.

I will.

But I have business to deal with first.

Minutes pass as I watch her sleep.

My phone buzzes with a call. Aleks.

"What?" I snap.

"They're making a move."

I'm on my feet, pacing toward the window wordlessly so I don't wake the little hacker. I flick open the blinds.

"Detail all security you have in place and everything you know."

I expected this. Hell, I half wanted it. I told my mother I had a surprise for her in Volkov's presence for a reason. I don't want him thinking I'm being complacent. I want him counting down the minutes until he can make his move. But he's no fool. He knows I'm ready to make a move.

I look at the woman sprawled on my bed as Aleks runs down all the details.

"Safehouse ready. All bodyguards on twenty-four-hour alert with shifts switching every three hours. Kolya let it slip when he was having drinks that you're heading to Moscow, and I've ensured all private intel is encrypted. Lev ran a sweep an hour ago."

My youngest brother Lev, affectionately termed "The Shadow," moves in and out of places with ease. While Aleks is our group surveillance expert, Lev is our best strategist. He works very closely with Aleks. "He recommends we have a decoy."

I clench my fists. "For whom?"

"Both of you."

When I hesitate, Aleks pushes on. "I know, I know. You don't want to hide. Leave it up to you, and you'd personally beat the shit out of every one of Volkov's men and leave no one but Volkov standing, bound and gagged, while he watched you take your wedding vows. We know."

I growl. "Not a bad idea."

"You should listen to Lev, though, Mikhail. He's an expert at this. Yeah, we all want to destroy them, but we have to do it in a lasting way that doesn't bring blowback we don't have the manpower to handle."

I know he's right. I speak in a low voice when Aria shifts on the bed behind me. I suspect she'll lose her mind when she hears the word "wedding."

"Fine. Decoy. Get those in place while we get the wedding prepared." I blow out a breath. "Make sure their families are compensated." It could be a death sentence. It helps to play nice with the locals.

"Of course."

I hang up the phone and think. For some reason, it's easier to do with the little hacker softly snoring beside me.

I dial Polina.

"What?"

"Didn't anyone ever tell you how to answer the phone politely?"

I can hear the eye roll in her voice. "Didn't anyone ever tell you the fact that I answered the phone at all makes you lucky? I don't answer phone calls, Mikhail. People text in the modern age. Spit it out. What do you need?"

"A wedding dress."

She's actually silent for a few seconds before she squeals. "I get to play wedding planner! *Yesssss.* I knew you wouldn't let that moratorium pass. I *knew* you wouldn't. I was so damn excited when you said wedding. Yes, of course, what size? What should it look like, and how much time do we have?"

I don't miss the note of pride in my sister's voice. The weight of responsibility hits me. The future of my entire family rests on my shoulders.

"She's about your size, but a few inches shorter," I say, letting my gaze rove lazily over the sleeping form of my future wife. It doesn't matter what she wears. She'll look gorgeous.

In a few short hours, she'll be wearing this dress and taking her vows to me. "Surprise me with the style, but do *not* make it too revealing." The thought of any other man's eyes on Aria's naked skin makes my hands curl into fists.

"Jesus," she mutters. "This isn't the Dark Ages."

"And we're not going to a night club. This is my wedding," I snap. She's wrong. This very much *is* the Dark Ages, in more ways than she knows.

"Fine, fine, full-length dress, long sleeves, no dipping neck-lines or sheer panels. Whatever. I'll get it. Shoes?"

"Yeah."

"What *kind*?"

I grimace. "How the hell do I know? Nothing too high-heeled, probably." She wore flats into my office.

My phone's buzzing with text updates from security about Volkov's moves. He's sent a plane to Moscow with several of his men on board.

"Are you even listening to me?" Polina asks.

"Of course." Something about shoes and accessories. "The details don't matter as much as the speed does. I need everything here as fast as you can so we can move on. I don't want to waste time looking over specifics when it doesn't really matter."

"Mikhail," she says, pleading. "I know you've been raised to believe that. I know you don't want to hear anything else. But this stuff *does* matter."

"Which is why I called you. I trust you to handle this."

She blows out another breath. "Why thank you. I'll call you within an hour."

"Thank you."

My fingers are flying over the phone. Aleks is monitoring security with the impending attack. My house is the safest place to be, but we can't stay here forever, and news of our wedding will be spread far and wide. Strategically.

Lev's set up the decoys, and Kolya's arranging everything else. Aleks is working on plans and Polina has the finer particulars under control.

Everything is working like a well-oiled machine.

I eye the beautiful woman lying in my guest bed. In a matter of hours, she'll be my wife.

CHAPTER TEN

Aria

WHEN I WAKE, I keep my eyes closed. I'm aware enough to know it's wise to assess my situation before I make a move.

I'm in Mikhail Romanov's residence. He's taken me and I'm not sure what he's planning on doing with me, since all he's told me is "we'll talk about the consequences for what you've done" and threatened to kill me.

I don't know what I'm going to find when I open them, but I can barely think beyond the pounding in my head. It hurts so badly I feel nauseous. My stomach rolls, and my mouth feels as if someone's stuffed it with a T-shirt.

I do a quick mental assessment. I can wiggle my toes and my legs. Good. I don't feel any pain, so I don't think I was hurt in any way, which I guess is a good thing. I try to remember what happened. I was definitely drugged so I'm not sure I can trust my memory.

I finally venture to open my eyes then quickly shut them. It's blindingly bright in here and it hurts my head.

I usually get up at the crack of dawn to go to school.

School.

They'll be looking for me. There was an attack at the school, because they were trying to find me. Dammit. Despite my definite dehydration, I feel tears prick my eyes. What has happened?

I open my eyes again, and this time the first thing I see is the gun he left on the bedside table. I try to sit up, but it's surprisingly difficult to do when your hands are secured together.

"You're awake."

My heartbeat spikes at the sound of his low, husky voice. He's fully dressed, sitting on a desk chair a few feet away from me, leaning on his forearms. He likes to roll up his sleeves, I note, as I look over his corded, tattooed forearms.

My skin prickles in response. I swallow and nod, leaning into false bravado. "Obviously, yeah. Now do we want to talk about what the fuck happened last night?"

"No," he says, quirking an eyebrow at me. "Use that tone of voice with me again and I'll teach you to watch your mouth."

He says it like he's half hoping for a chance to school me. I stare at the challenge in his eyes, meeting him with a challenge of my own.

But now isn't the time to push him, not when I'm at a disadvantage like this.

"You're dying for a chance to show me, aren't you?" My voice doesn't sound as brave as I hoped.

His eyes narrow as his lips twitch. "You have no idea. You'll see soon enough, little hacker."

His voice is tinted with a Russian accent. A mild accent means he's been here a long time, because the older someone is when they immigrate, the stronger the accent. He came from Russia, then, and Russian mafia. It seems he's the old-fashioned sort.

"I'm just trying to sort out what really happened and if my mind's playing tricks on me. After the whole drug thing."

My eyes fall to the gun on the bedside table, and I realize I probably didn't imagine much of what happened last night, if anything.

Clouds shift outside the windows, nearly blinding me. "You hacked into my computers. You came to me for assistance. You're on the run because you found out information that had nothing to do with you. Your life is worth nothing, because not only are you on the run from every major organization in this country, you also decided to pull one over on *me*. Your life belongs to me now. I could kill you, but that would be such a waste. I need more than your dead body."

I open my mouth to speak, but I quickly shut it because I feel like I'm going to be sick.

"What is it?"

I shake my head and cover my mouth with my hands, which I hope is the universal sign for "I'm going to vomit."

"Are you sick?"

I nod and try to sit up, but it's awkward covering my mouth with two bound hands, and my ankles are tied together, which he must have done after I fell asleep. He unravels himself like a coiled snake, rising to his feet. Damn. I forgot how big he is. How *strong*. "We can't have that. Not today. It's a special day."

I watch him walk away.

A...special day. Why does that make me shiver with nerves again? What's he planning to do with me?

A moment later he comes to me with a glass of water and three pills in the palm of his hand. I turn my head away. I don't want to be drugged again.

"Open your mouth and take these. They're pain relievers. The small round one is anti-nausea."

I shake my head again. "No more drugs."

Leaning forward, he puts his mouth to my ear. I feel stubble against my cheek, the smell of pine and leather lingering in the air. "I warned you, little hacker. If you disobey me, I'll punish you."

I clamp my lips together.

He sits on the bed with ease and reaches for me after setting the pills and glass down, and I realize he's going to put me over his lap like he told me. I'm humiliated when I remember how he spanked me last night.

"Fine! Fine. I'll take them! What are they again?" The thought of being treated like a child makes my cheeks burn.

"Pain meds and anti-nausea," he snaps, but he doesn't ease

me off his lap. "I don't trust you to obey. You have three seconds."

I am absolutely going to end up over his knee. *God.*

I put the meds into my mouth and swig the water.

"Careful. If you're nauseous, too much water will make you sick."

He says it like he cares. Liar.

I obediently take a small sip.

"Lie back down until those meds kick in." To emphasize his point, he lays me back down on the bed. This time, his advice makes sense, so I do what he says. This is definitely a "pick your battles" kind of situation.

"Are you hungry?"

I don't really want to talk about things like food when I'm waiting to hear what he's going to do to me. Again, I wonder...if he were going to rape me, wouldn't he have already done it?

Or...no?

If he were going to hurt me, would he be giving me pain meds and offering me food?

I may be a prisoner, but this is a very civilized setting. I'm sure if he wanted to, he could easily put me behind bars or in a basement or handcuff me in a...cage or something.

I shiver.

I'll need my energy for whatever the day brings, though, so I finally answer. "I'm starving."

"Here. Sit up." I don't understand why he's being so gentle with me. I wonder if he's trying to trick me, to lure me into some kind of Stockholm syndrome thing where the victim bonds with the captor because they're the only one that fulfills the victim's basic needs.

Stockholm syndrome is real, and this is exactly what happens. The human brain is naturally wired to attach to people who feed them when they're hungry. Even abused animals will turn to their abusers when they're fed and their basic needs cared for.

When I shiver, he wordlessly lifts the fluffy blanket at the foot of the bed and spreads it over me. I wonder where he slept last night because I'm at his place. Is this his bed? I look around. This is either a guest room or he's a minimalist.

I watch as he walks into another room and comes back with a plate of food on a tray. My mouth waters. Scrambled eggs. Thick slabs of buttered bread. French toast, pancakes. Berries with whipped cream, half a grapefruit with sugar, and a small bowl of creamy oatmeal sprinkled with cinnamon.

"I didn't know what you liked, so I got you a little of everything."

"I'm surprised you didn't have a private detective figure all that out."

"I did, but all he came up with was a cereal bar for breakfast."

My eyes go wide. "I was...joking." I shrug and snort. "And yeah, it's a cereal bar or donuts, so...yeah."

"No protein? You need real food in you."

Interesting that the man who kidnapped me cares about nutrition.

I gesture to my wrapped wrists. With a nod, he lifts a forkful of eggs and brings it to my mouth. I open my mouth and eat them, my eyes riveted on his gaze. This shouldn't be...so intimate. My tastebuds explode with flavor. I swallow the buttery, creamy eggs and eagerly take another bite when he offers.

Halfway through, his watch vibrates on his wrist. With a scowl, he shuts it off and continues to feed me. "Easy," he says patiently. "Not too much, now."

After the fifth vibrating text, he curses and unfastens my wrists, allowing me to feed myself while he steps away for a moment.

In his absence, I feel strangely...bereft.

I take a bite of the buttered toast, and some more of the eggs. The berries with whipped cream are delicious, and by now the meds are starting to kick in. I sigh in relief. I won't admit it to him, but I'm feeling loads better.

When I lay the fork down, he returns.

"Good. Now we need to bathe you next."

We?

Since when is there a "we" involved in bathing? I consider telling him I'm pretty capable of bathing myself, but then decide that's probably not going to get me very far.

I look again at the gun on the bedside table. It hasn't moved, but it doesn't need to. It's there to remind me that I'm a prisoner. To remember why I'm here.

I fucked with the Russian Bratva, which is arguably worse than the situation I was in that led me there.

He lifts me, likely because my ankles are bound. Something white flashes in the corner of my vision, but I can't make it out. Are we alone in this house? It's the first time I've considered the fact that we may not be.

"Why haven't you killed me?"

"That's still an option."

I swallow and lick my lips. He tells me that, but I can tell that he doesn't actually want to kill me. What I don't understand is what he wants from me.

He brings me to the bathroom I used last night and slides me to the floor in front of him. Holding me against him with one hard arm wrapped around my body, he starts the shower. While the water heats, he bends and deftly unfastens the restraints on my ankles. Though he doesn't say anything, the look he gives me dares me to try anything stupid.

Bent down like this, he's in a vulnerable position. I could kick him in the balls. Knee him.

And then what?

Even if I did somehow get away from whatever security measures he has here, where could I hide from the Russian Bratva when I'm *already* in hiding? It isn't possible.

Even if I escaped, I'd be right back in the same predicament I was in that drove me to him, only this time I'd have a larger target on my back. I wouldn't last twenty-four hours.

But why hasn't he killed me?

"Good. I like that you're behaving yourself."

I swallow and look away. I don't want him to know that I... like his praise. I have to remember to hate him.

I watch as he reaches one of his thick, inked fingers to test the temperature of the shower. When he seems satisfied with the temperature, he begins to strip.

Strip.

I mean, what did I think we were doing in the shower?

He's getting into the shower with me.

He's...*coming in the shower with me.* Like we're...*lovers.*

I swallow.

I'm going to see him...naked.

And worst of all, when he's done...it's my turn.

"Mikhail," I whisper. But when he looks at me, I don't respond because I honestly don't know what I want to say. Instead, I watch as his clothes fall to the floor. I look away, my cheeks flaming.

I've never seen a man like him this close, and definitely never naked. I steal a glance back and quickly note heavily inked arms, rippling with strength. Golden skin, and a sculpted physique that speaks of a man that's never fully at rest. A man who's trained to use his body like a weapon, laced with so many tattoos, I know they must tell a story.

Broad shoulders flex as he pulls off his tee, revealing more tattoos and defined abs. When he tosses his tee into the hamper, it hits the side and slithers down. I watch the muscles ripple in his back, showcasing another intricate map of ink, but he turns before I note what it is.

And then his boxers. My cheeks burn hotter as I stare into his eyes because I am *not* looking there. Nope. I need to get into that shower, so…I guess it's…my turn.

I've never stripped in front of a man before. While I'm not exactly a virgin, the sex I've had was in the dark and absolutely forgettable. Something tells me that sex with *him* would be scorched into my mind for eternity. I mean, if I survived it.

I reach for my tee when he narrows his eyes at me, spins me around, and claps his hand against my ass.

"Hey!"

"You do not undress yourself."

I swallow and stare over my shoulder at him. "What?"

"You heard me, little hacker," he says in that low drawl of an accent. "That job belongs to me and you will not take it from me."

Standing there fully naked, he turns me to face him and reaches for my top. He rests his hands on my hips for a brief second before he lifts my top over my head. My breasts swing free. Next, he reaches for my panties and drags them down my legs.

My cheeks heat with embarrassment and I turn away when I'm fully naked.

I feel his hand on my chin.

"Why do you look away, Aria?"

Aria, not *little hacker*.

"I'm naked," I say. Isn't it obvious? I'm ashamed of standing front of him with nothing to hide me.

"You're beautiful," he says in a matter-of-fact tone. "You have nothing to be ashamed of. You belong to me now, and you will not hide what belongs to me."

I. Belong. To him.

Is that my...punishment?

"What does that mean?" I whisper, my voice trembling.

"You will see."

I'm so nervous. Wordlessly, he balls my clothes and tosses them into the hamper in the corner of the room.

"Ten points for Russia," I murmur.

His eyes melt into an almost-smile before he takes my hand in one of his massive hands, sliding his other down the length of my body.

"Ten points for America."

I swallow the feeling of pleasure his praise gives me.

It isn't real. This isn't real.

I watch as he steps into the shower. The steaming hot water slides down his belly, rivulets cascading down the contours of his muscles. Every inch of him speaks of power, strength, and almost...majesty. A part of me's still in awe.

This bathroom is enormous. The shower is one of those huge ones that you would imagine football players use, because they need to accommodate big men.

"Medication can make people shaky sometimes. Do not let go of me."

He stands a full head taller than me so I stand right at his collarbone.

I want to ask him what he means about me belonging to him, about the expectations he has for me. It's confusing and unnerving and I'm afraid of what it really means.

He'll use me as a prostitute? His slave?

Until he thinks I've paid my dues?

I watch as he takes a pink loofah and squirts white body-wash on it. "Turn around."

I turn to give him my back. When he steps closer to me, I feel his hardened length pressed up against me. Oh, God. This is it. This is where he's going to take me.

I'm not sure how I feel about that.

The suds and exfoliator feel so good on my back and shoulders I stifle a moan. One of his arms snakes around my body and holds me flat against him. His hand spans the length of my abdomen, his thumb pressed up against the underside of my breast, his fingers reaching down... much, much lower. I'm dizzy as I feel his erection between us and the familiar way he moves his fingers over my body.

Is it getting hot in here? Because all this has me feeling a little dizzy.

He bends down to talk in my ear. "People have different definitions of consent, Aria. And I'm going to tell you this now. You belong to me now. You betrayed my family. Your life is forfeit to me." He pinches my ass. "When I want to fuck you, I will. On my terms. Do you understand me?"

So that's what is going to be done. I'm going to be a little sex toy?

I give a barely perceptible nod because I feel lightheaded. "Listen well, little hacker. If it's the middle of the night and I want your pussy, I'm going to take it. If it's broad daylight out and you're in the middle of something, if I ask you to sit on my face, you fucking will. If you wake in the morning with my cock in your mouth, you will obey me every fucking minute and take every drop. If I want to eat your pussy for breakfast, I will. When and how I want to."

Ho-*ly* shit. *Now* we're getting somewhere. Now we're getting to the real purpose of me being here.

But he's not done yet.

"I will have you anywhere and everywhere I want. There's a reason I'm waiting right now, but you'll see. Do you understand me?"

I nod, speechless, my mouth dry. He continues, the loofah forgotten. His arms are wrapped around me like bonds as streams of hot water bounce off both of us. "You don't have to give me permission not to rape you. Do you have any idea how lucky you are that I haven't fucked you yet? That I haven't tied you up and taken my belt to your ass to punish you for what you did? That I didn't whip you before I licked your pussy and brought you to the edge of coming, and left you tied to my bed, sore, dripping with my come while you begged for your own release? While I have my reasons for not treating you this way, remember, Aria. The threat is there."

I'm trembling against him, when he tips my head back and runs hot water through my hair. Pours shampoo in the palm of his hand and massages it into my scalp. If I didn't feel like I was going to pass out from what he just told me, this would feel nice, but it doesn't. I know he's just doing this to make me complacent.

With my head tipped back to rinse the suds, he places his finger under my chin and bends me further back. Before I realize what he's doing, he drops his mouth to my breast. I tremble at the pink of his tongue flat against my hardened nipple. A tremor of arousal overtakes me and I let out a whimper.

"Fucking gorgeous," he whispers against the underside of my breast, running a thumb along my other nipple. When he grips the back of my neck, I fear he'll try to kiss me.

I turn away. I don't want to kiss him. I haven't brushed my teeth, I don't trust him, and kissing is so...intimate. You'd think showering with someone is intimate, but nothing like a kiss. You can't hide from a kiss.

But he doesn't kiss me. He runs his fingers through my hair and rinses the shampoo out while his phone rings again, and again.

"I've left toiletries and things you'll need. My sister picked up a few things for you."

His sister. Oh thank God there's a woman somewhere in the mix. I breathe out in relief.

Will she like me? Will I like *her*?

"There's pen and paper on the desk. Write down anything you need." Pausing, he leans forward and tips a finger under my chin. "And remember, Aria. I'll be watching even when I'm not here." In other words, don't do anything stupid. Got it.

Of course I won't. I watch him step out of the shower and towel off, seemingly oblivious to the fact that he's sex personified, a god in human form. Wrapping a towel around his waist, he reaches for his phone and steps out of the bathroom.

When he's gone, the first thing I do is brace myself against the wall and breathe. I let the water flow over me, cleansing me, and breathe in the invigorating, warm air. When my heartbeat finally slows, I explore what he's left for me.

The pink loofah's obviously mine, as well as some nice toiletries. Shampoo and conditioner, a bottle of moisturizer. Definitely not the stuff you'd find at the dollar store.

My heart leaps when I find a razor — one of those fancy five-blade deals with a lubricating strip. Great for shaving the legs, but not so helpful if you're looking for a weapon. I give it a long look and remember what he said about watching me. With a sigh, I use it to shave and nothing else. Thoughts of escaping come and go, fleeting thoughts of what a normal person would do in a situation like this.

But I'm not normal, and neither is he. It's better if I find ways to make this work. Make it tolerable. Keep my own sense of self while under the control of another.

I finally exit the shower to find a fluffy towel and robe waiting for me on a small table beside the vanity. I dry my hair and body, then take a moment to use the lotion before I slide into the robe. It's soft against my skin and makes me sigh in contentment.

I'll enjoy the small luxuries when I can. I'd imagine this is exactly what a luxury hotel is like. I could relish a touch of luxury for a moment.

But it doesn't last long. When I open the bathroom door, I pause, my mouth agape. Staring at the dress that's hanging in front of me.

CHAPTER ELEVEN

Aria

SATIN AND LACE, shimmering in the sunlight. An A-line silhouette that's classy and gorgeous, accentuated with more delicate lace at the edges of a sweetheart neckline.

It's a...white dress.

A *wedding* dress.

I'm wrapped in a robe staring at the dress, my mind reeling with my options. Or...*lack* of options.

Why is there a wedding dress in this room? A gentle knock sounds at the door, immediately followed by harsh voices. I look around the room for Mikhail.

It's happening. I'm looking for him for comfort and security.

I can't let myself go there.

"Who's there?" I ask.

No answer.

The voices rise and fall on the other side of the door. Still wearing nothing but a robe, I walk to the door and peek through the peephole.

I wish I knew the layout of his home. There's a little hallway in front of me, and three armed men. I'm kind of honored they consider me so dangerous I've got security like *that*.

But standing right in the middle of them is a young, beautiful woman with long blonde hair that hangs all the way down her back. She holds her chin high and talks to the men fearlessly.

"Hello?" I say tentatively.

She snaps at them when she throws her hands up in the air. "I fucking *knew* you had her in there. You monsters. Open the fucking door. Now."

The first shakes his head. "If your brother finds you came up here —"

It's his sister. Oh thank God.

She defiantly sticks out her chin. "If you don't open that door, I am calling him myself."

I'm...standing in a robe. Still, she's a woman, she seems like she's on my side, and I'm in severe shortage of people on my side right now. I go to open the door a crack. "Hello?"

She presses her face to the opened crack of the door. "I'm your almost sister-in-law, open the door and let me in, please. We have a lot to do."

He didn't tell me not to open the door, but I know in my gut obviously he doesn't want me to do it.

What will he do? Kill me? It's his sister.

I open the door amidst curse words and warnings from the security team. Yeah, whatever. The second she's in, I hear one of them call Mikhail on his cell. We don't have much time here.

She comes in, spins on her heel, and slams the door behind her.

Wow. This woman is stunning. Her long, flowing, platinum-blonde hair hangs down to her waist, and her ice blue eyes are framed with long, thick lashes. She's graceful yet athletic, standing a few inches taller than me. With fair skin, she almost looks delicate, but there's something about the way she holds herself that tells me that's only an illusion. I get the distinct feeling she's like tightly wrapped dynamite. A gymnast or ballerina or something.

She takes one look at me in my robe. "Hi, I'm Polina, and there will be hell to pay for me coming in here, but honey, we have to get you ready. The wedding's in an hour."

I grimace but need to ask her. I need confirmation. My voice sounds as if it's coming from somewhere else for the pounding in my ears.

"Whose...wedding?"

She stares at me, unblinking. "He didn't *tell* you?"

I shake my head. "He told me a lot of things, but I don't remember the word wedding coming into play. I'm guessing it's...mine? The wedding? The..." I gesture toward the dress. "The dress?"

The impending sense of doom?

She whistles. "Yeah, honey." She waves her hand at the dress and then gestures to a pile of accessories neatly lined up beside it that I didn't notice before. Shoes, a small satin bag, a gauzy veil. "My brothers can do a lot of not-so-nice things, but this is pretty low. Wow. Alright then. We still have to get you ready." Rubbing her hands together, she blows out a breath.

I should've known this. I should've pieced it all together. He'd said I'd be punished, that I belonged to him now. How else would I belong to him?

Marriage to a cold, heartless criminal? I remember how he touched me in the shower, detached and cold, as if I were his...property.

Property.

Polina looks from me to the dress and back again. "At least I have to say I did pick one that's going to look gorgeous on you."

"You bought that?"

"I did good, huh?" she says with a twinkle in her eye. "I'm really good at things like *this*. Explaining why my brothers do what they do? That, I'm not so good at."

"But can you tell me what's happening? Where am I?" I open my mouth to ask her more but can't bring myself to do so. *What happens after we're married?*

There's a commotion outside the door. Voices rise and fall.

Uh oh.

Mikhail is back, and he's furious.

Polina seems to realize this the same time I do.

"Hold your ground," she hisses, just as the door opens. "He isn't as scary as you think."

Oh, really?

"Out, Mikhail!" She shouts. "Do not come in here. It's bad luck for the groom to see the bride before the ceremony."

He storms into the room, ignoring her.

"Who the fuck told you, you had a right to come in here?" His voice is a growl. I notice he's lost the towel and has changed into a tux.

This is happening. We're doing this. We're going to get married.

"I asked you a question," he growls at his sister.

"I did!" I stand between him and his sister. If I'm going to get married to this beast of a man, the least I can do is use that to my advantage. "I need a woman to help me get ready for this wedding, which, I'll have you know, I didn't even know was happening!"

He turns the full heat of his gaze on me, and I have to concentrate hard not to wither under his glare.

Instead of responding to me, he turns back to Polina. "I specifically told you not to come near my captive. You were told not to talk to her."

She stands her ground, her hands on her hips. "She needed help and you were nowhere to be found. Do you really want to get married with her wearing a robe?"

He responds with another growl.

"And by the way," I say, asserting myself in an attempt to keep him on his toes. "When were you going to tell me about this wedding? On our honeymoon?"

"Very cute you think you're getting a honeymoon."

"Like I want a honeymoon with *you*," I mutter. Polina stifles a snort.

"Watch it, Aria," he says in a warning tone. "You think I won't pull you over my knee in front of anyone? Try me."

I look away, my cheeks flaming.

"You are going to spend the rest of your life with this woman, Mikhail," Polina says candidly. "I suggest you treat her nicely. You know literally nothing about makeup and bronzer and highlighter, you have no idea how to style her hair, and correct me if I'm wrong, but wasn't it you who told me there'll be photos we'll have to publicize? It would behoove you to prepare her."

"*I'll* help her."

"You will not see your bride before the wedding, Mikhail! It's bad luck."

One of the guards stands tentatively in the doorway, another hovering at his shoulder. "Boss, I'm sorry, there's a situation."

Mikhail shoves me behind him. *Shit.* I forgot I'm still wearing a robe.

"Get the fuck *out*. If you look at her, I'll fucking kill you."

Polina's widened eyes tell me this is no bluff.

They scurry out of the room like terrified mice. Mikhail blows out a breath and turns to Polina. He says something in Russian that makes Polina flinch before he speaks again in English. "You help her get ready. But this is not over. There are consequences for disobedience, and you know it."

He leaves, the scent of sandalwood and pine lingering in his wake. When the door shuts, she sticks her tongue out at it. Despite my pounding heart and shaky nerves, it makes me smile.

"I wish I could say he was all bluster, but he's not." With a sigh, she shakes her head. "He actually is quite terrifying. He's lucky I love him."

"What did he say to you just now?"

"Oh, it was just a string of curse words and promises to exile me to Siberia if I interfere. It's fine, we're good."

Definitely not soothing my nerves.

"Are you in...trouble?"

I'm confused about these family dynamics, but I do know one thing: Mikhail is the one in charge of damn near everyone.

She rolls her eyes, but I can tell it's only forced bravado. A part of her is scared.

"What will he do?"

"Oh, to me?" She reaches for the dress, her back to me, and waves her hand in the air. "Don't worry about me."

I do, though. I feel somehow responsible.

She quickly changes the subject. "Listen, I don't know why you're getting married, but I know why Mikhail is. You're going to find this out soon enough. If he doesn't get married, my entire family is fucked. That's the short story. You're getting married today. He's all strung up and on high alert because there are people who very much want to prevent this from happening. You are in danger. That's why you have like basically an entire squad of bodyguards outside the door. The last women he—"

She suddenly thinks better of telling me this and shakes her head. "Never mind. We have to get you ready."

"I see."

Quirking a brow at me she tips her head to the side. "What did you do?"

I give her a wry smile. "I came to them for help and protection and just sort of...maybe hacked a bit into their database and, uh...maybe breached a little security."

She turns to face me, a trace of a smile on her lips. "Wow. Seriously? That's the most badass thing I've ever heard in my life. But didn't anyone warn you what you were dealing with?"

Maybe?

"Girl, I could tell you stories..." She shakes her head. "There's something he likes about you, which is the only reason you're getting off easy."

I stare at her as if she's speaking a foreign language before I respond. "Listen, Polina, first, I hope to God he likes me because we're getting married. And in what universe is getting married to a man like him getting off *easy*?"

Obviously, they live in a world that operates within a much different set of rules than I do.

"Aria, they let you live," she says finally. "I know, you're obviously normal and not related to a bunch of psychopaths, and this is all hard to understand. But I'm so excited. I *knew* you were brilliant. You and I are going to be very good friends. You'll see. Now, let's get you ready. He'll probably be back here in like two minutes breaking the damn door down." She rolls her eyes but doesn't completely cover up her fear.

In a whirlwind that makes my head spin, I lose the robe and don the most luxurious undergarments known to humanity. She tones and moisturizes and primes my face, helps me into my dress, then applies makeup with expertise. I let her take the lead since I'm sort of in a state of shock and she knows what she's doing.

"Wow," I whisper, staring at my reflection. "You're a genius."

"Makes two of us," she says with pride. "Oh, you look amazing. If my brother doesn't swoon for you, I'll marry you myself."

"Now wouldn't that be a plot twist," I murmur. But I'm staring at myself in the mirror. I turn my head to the side, the logical side of my brain trying to make sense of the fact that this woman in the mirror is...*me*.

My almond-shaped eyes look mysterious without the shade of glasses, the deep brown almost black. My high cheekbones are tinged with pink, my lips a glossy rose. My long, jet-black hair flows past my shoulders with none of the frizz I've grown accustomed to.

"They say you can't buy beauty in a bottle, but..." I murmur.

Polina snickers. "Girl, you can't. You can enhance it, though. No wonder he got one look at you and made his move."

My heart beats faster. I feel as if I'm an actor in a play, and I'm not sure what the next act is going to bring.

A fist pounds the door so hard we both jump.

"Time to go."

"We're not ready!" Polina says, even though we totally are. Apparently, she doesn't like being told what to do. That makes two of us.

I give her a ghost of a smile, because I'm not sure that isn't Mikhail, and if it is...

"You have three minutes or I'm coming in and taking both of you out of there myself."

"*That* was Mikhail," she says. "Something happened. Let's finish getting ready. I was going to style your hair, but it's gorgeous down. We'll leave it down. Dear God, you really are stunning."

That actually makes me laugh. It feels good to laugh. "How do you survive with all this testosterone?"

"Well, it's a little bit of a secret. I might be Mikhail's favorite." She leans in. "Though something tells me you'll be top of his list."

I open my mouth to protest. He hates me. And I'm not even sure I *want* him to like me. But she leans in and kisses my cheek. "I can't believe I'm going to have a sister," she whispers. For one brief moment, I don't regret hacking into the Romanovs' databases.

The door opens and Prince Charming himself storms in. Polina groans. "For an otherwise superstitious people, it's shocking to me that you don't seem to believe in bad luck."

"What I believe in is Volkov's revenge," Mikhail says in a tight voice.

He takes me by the hand and suddenly seems glued in position.

"What? What's wrong?"

"There's nothing wrong," he says. "You look...beautiful."

"Mikhail! You can't look at her right now! I know, I know, you don't trust anybody else to protect her. Guess what, we have an entire army of men ready to kill anybody that threatens her. Okay?"

I needed protection. Holy shit, I *got* protection.

It feels like forever that I've lived day by day for survival, letting go of anything and everything that had meaning for me. Here, I have a chance to start over. I can go into this kicking and screaming. Or I can put a smile on my face and make the best of it.

I'm safe for now. For the first time in my life, I actually feel like I can breathe.

"After the ceremony, I'll touch up your makeup for the pictures."

"Pictures?" I feel myself blanche. What will happen when

my face is shown far and wide as the bride of Mikhail Romanov?

Polina goes on. "Mikhail is going to have to prove that he's married. The pictures will go literally everywhere. We haven't had a marriage in our family since my parents'."

"Polina," he says in a warning voice.

How strange. Don't they have siblings or cousins or something?

"And if I don't want my picture published?"

Maybe I do? Do I?

"Don't worry, little hacker," Mikhail says in a low voice. "I've got it under control."

Does he even know what worries me, though?

The last time I was outside of this room was before I was carried into the house, drugged and nearly naked and completely passed out. So I definitely don't remember the sweeping staircases, the elegant flower arrangements on every table, or the lingering scent of vanilla in the air.

We're on the second floor of what appears to be a huge house. I want to explore this house and see it with my own eyes. When I was a little girl, my mom had an extended family that was rich. We used to have holidays at their house, until there was some kind of falling out about money or something.

Oh, I loved that house. I'd never seen anything like it before. A sweeping garden out front, a three-season porch, a formal dining room, and an eat-in kitchen where the fridge made ice cubes and their stove had six burners. There was a large pantry filled with all sorts of snacks that I was allowed to eat, as much as I wanted, a study near the living room, and a finished basement downstairs.

Some of my fondest memories are of exploring that house, pretending that I was a princess and I lived in a mansion.

The touch of nostalgia hits me now. This house is much more modern than the one that I remember from my childhood, but there are nooks and crannies, carpeted rooms and hardwood floors, ceilings that reach to the heavens, and so much warm, bright light.

I walk down the stairs, and even though I'm not here of my own accord, even though I know this is part of a political act, a move that will advance Mikhail or whatever it is they do in their world...I kind of like feeling like a princess.

At the foot of the stairs, there's a sprawling living room with a large, wraparound sofa in navy and a modern fireplace.

There's a priest and only a small handful of people here. Polina sits beside an older, regal woman with silvery hair. Is that her mother?

Music plays, but the tension in the room is palpable. So tense, I feel the tension in my own body, and I find I'm practically holding my breath.

Outside this window, I catch a glimpse of the Manhattan skyline. Yes, we're still in The Cove, nestled between Coney Island and Manhattan. His eyes follow mine, and he drags me across the room, planting us in front of the priest. No one speaks.

"Begin the fucking ceremony," he growls to the priest.

Wow. So he just went there. No respect for the cloth?

I hear the sound of a thump and a cry. I stifle a gasp, but no one moves. Another thump and another, followed by a muffled scream.

Someone...someone's getting beaten out there. Maybe even killed. I glance out the window and see not one but three men on the ground outside the window, about twenty feet from where we stand in the living room. Blood pools on the concrete. I stare, stricken.

Oh my God.

"Aria." Mikhail's voice snaps like a whip. I look back at him. "Keep your eyes on me."

I swallow, my heart pounding in my throat, but I do what he says. My adrenaline pulses so hard I feel dizzy. I stare into the depths of his dark brown eyes beneath slashes of angry brows. I stare at his eyes on me, unwavering, as he stands over me and reaches for both of my hands. "Nothing else matters," he says in a low voice. "Nothing but keeping your gaze on me."

I'm not going to be able to take these vows if I see people being murdered right outside. Polina told me what was at stake — if we get married, their enemies will revolt.

Even the priest's hands shake as he goes about the ceremony. I stumble through my vows. I've never been to an Orthodox wedding, but this one is definitely an abbreviated form.

"Are you here freely of your own accord?"

Mikhail narrows his eyes. "That's not part of the ceremony and you know it."

The priest holds my gaze.

He's trying to save me. He knows exactly who these men are and the chances of me being forced to do exactly what I'm doing.

The truth is, I could probably walk...and then deal with the aftermath of my choice.

Yes, I'm being forced to marry Mikhail, but do I truly have another choice?

"Yes," I say in a breathy whisper and for a moment, it doesn't quite feel like a lie.

Mikhail goes quickly through the vows, likely meaning them as much as I do, until we both get to "I do." I half expect the priest to say that he may kiss the bride, but Mikhail doesn't wait.

Right outside the window— as in *right there*, I hear a sharp cry and thud as Mikhail leans in to me. I can hardly process that *he's going to kiss me*, right while someone's being maybe murdered right outside this window. He presses me to him, one arm wrapped around me so tightly I can't move. He yanks me closer with his right arm and with his left, drags me to his chest, effectively drowning out the rest of the world. Then tips my face, bends down, and claims my mouth.

My knees wobble from the intensity of the kiss. I feel vulnerable, as if he can feel the beating of my heart when we're connected like this. I feel windswept, bared to him, unable to think beyond the feel of his lips on mine.

When he turns us around to face everyone, my hand fisted in his with triumph, I'm suddenly aware of all the photographers. Flashes blind me, seemingly coming from all directions. I'm trying to smile, but it feels forced, of course. I look at the cameras and remember what Polina told me. *These pictures will be posted everywhere.*

In my peripheral vision, I see two men in handcuffs right outside the door, another bloodied, and another one on the ground unconscious. Dead? Alive? And still, the cameras flash, a reminder that what you see in a photograph is only a very small part of the whole picture. The priest is behind us, wiping his sweaty brow when I turn to look at him.

Outside the huge plate glass window, it looks like a battle scene. Weapons are drawn, there's still one man prostrate on the ground, his leg twisted at an odd angle. Another man holds someone still fighting, and while I watch, he slumps to the ground as well, choked out.

Whoever his enemies are, he has many, and they are vicious.

Mikhail leans in close. "Are you alright?"

I blink. I look up at him, and then comically look over my shoulder, wondering who he's talking to.

"Aria," he says sternly. "I asked if you're alright?"

I shake my head. "It's all a little much. But yes, I'm fine."

"I know." He reaches for my hand and gives it a little squeeze. Why is he being...nice to me now? Is he? He's been downright mean and borderline abusive, but now...

Leaning forward, he whispers, "You do not leave my side today. If something unnerves you, gesture. Tell me. You're mine now. We've made this legal and defeated Volkov."

I don't know what it means, but I can tell that something's shifted in him.

He keeps saying things like...*You're mine.*

"We're heading out for the reception. I do not want Volkov to think I'm bowing to him or hiding. It's just my family, nothing big. The most important part is behind us."

I barely know where I am, or who he is, so I'm totally fine not traveling to some exotic location with this man that I hardly know.

"Why were there people who tried to attack us? I don't understand."

"I'll explain everything later. For now, we're eating dinner with my family. I know you may not have an appetite right now, but it's considered rude for the bride not to eat on her wedding day, so do the best you can."

Who is this man and what has he done with the grumpy caricature? Is it just the relief he feels having defeated Volkov? Or is it something more?

After a short drive, we arrive at the restaurant. He pulls a chair out for me at a table, and I sit down. "I feel like I need a bib or something," I mutter to myself, looking down at my pristine white wedding gown. I don't want to splatter food on it.

"You're fine. I'll send it to the cleaners. Eat if you're hungry."

I look to see armed men, not even bothering to hide their weapons, standing at each entrance to the restaurant.

"Welcome, Aria."

Beside me sits a man a bit older than Mikhail, well-groomed and intelligent looking with graying hair and glasses. He has gray in his beard and keen blue eyes. Like the others, he's fit and healthy.

"Aria, meet Kolya, an old family friend."

"Old? Touché, Mikhail." He shakes his head and lifts a glass. "To the new couple! To the new era of the Romanov family." There's a solemn feel at the table, in the room, like we've just come to the end of a battle.

This is my exchange for protection and safety?

How naïve and foolish I've been, thinking that they only wanted my skills. They wanted much, much more than that.

The new era for the Romanov family.

That will involve...babies.

Of *course.* I mean, did I really expect I'd be married to him and not have his babies?

Everybody clinks their glasses solemnly.

"My mother, Ekaterina, and of course you already know Polina." Ekaterina's a timeless beauty with silver hair gracefully swept into an elegant up-do. Even her eyes are a steely shade of gray, reflecting strong, yet graceful features. She sits ramrod straight but gives me a warm smile.

"Welcome to the family."

There's something about her that tells me this woman has experienced deep, abiding pain. How could she not have? Was she married like me, against her will? How did her husband treat her?

"These are my brothers." Mikhail continues the introductions. "Lev, the youngest." A quiet, unassuming, very attractive guy some years younger than Mikhail nods his head and raises a glass. His eyes are sharp and though he's seated, I can tell he's got an athletic build. Short, dark hair like Mikhail's and deep blue eyes.

"Nikko." An enormous man, heavily tattooed with a rugged, primal appeal to him, who appears to carry weapons. His large frame and menacing scowl make me want to hide.

"Ollie." Ollie sits tall. Startlingly handsome with a beard and piercing green eyes, he exudes a rugged disinterest. His leather-clad appearance makes him look fully the part of the bad boy.

"Viktor."

A hulking, muscular man with a shaved head and a scar running down one cheek who appears to favor black leather jackets. A hulking, heavily tattooed man, also with a rugged charm. His strong, scarred features and imposing physique exude a magnetic appeal.

"And you've met Aleks."

Aleks glares at me but looks away when Mikhail gives him a look.

Oh, right. I circumvented his shitty cybersecurity. Aleks maybe doesn't like me.

"Now that introductions are over, let's eat, Mikhail," Ekaterina says. She gives me a smile. "My first son to get married won't rob me of our family traditions. We'll eat our traditional foods, son."

It's a midday meal, but still, waitstaff enter with a variety of finger foods and appetizers, pickled vegetables and dumplings. There's caviar and salad, stuffed savory patties they call "shashlik," and a creamy stroganoff served over thick noodles and roasted greens. I eat, but my appetite's waning after all the festivities. My head is pounding and I want a nap.

"Are you alright?" Mikhail asks, concern etched in his brow. I'm almost touched he actually cares.

"Just a headache," I whisper back. How much longer do I have to perform? Even though there's only a small crowd here, I'm putting on a show and socialization is so not my thing.

"We'll leave after dessert."

It's honestly refreshing that he doesn't care about being polite. I never did like having to follow social conventions. It's so fake.

Like this marriage?

And yet...what will happen when I'm back home with him? What's next? How exactly will we...begin the next era for the Romanovs?

CHAPTER TWELVE

Mikhail

I KNEW Volkov would try to sabotage my wedding.

Of course he would. He was, of course, unsuccessful. So when I get my bride in the back of our limo, driven by one of my men, I open the small bottle of champagne left on ice.

My bride.

We did it. We circumvented Volkov's attempt to destroy my family.

His first, anyway.

"Champagne? It's traditional in Russian weddings to celebrate with champagne."

"I would've thought vodka," she says lightly, belying the fear in her eyes. Good. If she fears me, she'll obey.

"You want vodka?"

Shaking her head, she looks away. "Where are we going? Where are we?"

I hand her the half-filled flute. "Do you know anything about The Cove?"

She shakes her head. "Not much. I know that there's a beach, and...well, your family." She takes a sip and sighs appreciatively. Kolya knows how to buy the good stuff.

"Yes. We're in The Cove, where I run our operations. My father died just over a month ago, so I've taken over. As we're driving, we have begun a controlled leak of our wedding photos. A strategy to allow information to leak to the right channels, so that everyone knows we married. We won't reveal where, or who you are."

"So you have an informant." She misses nothing, her mind as sharp as a steel trap.

"We have many."

"Media coverage?"

I shake my head.

"Do you have counterintelligence in place?"

"Of course. Right now, secrecy and security are paramount. We need word to spread to our rivals and enemies. They knew it was happening, which is why they tried to attack. So the leak will spread that word."

"I see."

She doesn't.

"We have our traditions," I say, intentionally leaving her hanging. I don't want her to forget that our marriage is also punishment. She's surrendered all control to me. "You'll see when we get back to my house, Mrs. Romanov."

Light filters in from the window and highlights her widened eyes. I stare at my bride. She's so beautiful. My heart thumps with the knowledge that I own her. That she's mine, irrevocably.

I'll enjoy every goddamn minute of despoiling her.

I crook a finger at her.

"Come here."

Aria gives me a wary look but only hesitates a few seconds. She's learning. When she nears me, I bring her onto my lap and lean her against my chest, my mouth to her ear.

"Do you know what it means now that we're married?"

I imagine her tied to my bed, taking my cock, over and over and over again. I imagine her on her knees, subservient to me. I can already hear her screams of pleasure and pain. She'll learn to love them both.

"I'd guess...sex, but I don't want to assume," she says in a whisper before she swallows. The blush on her cheeks tells me she's curious.

I tuck her closer to me on my lap, not an easy feat with miles of fabric. "You and I will get along very well, little hacker, if you can remember a few things."

"What's that?" she asks, in a throaty whisper. I rest my hands on her flat belly, my thumb pressed against the other side of her breast.

"As my wife I'll expect complete obedience. Everyone in this family obeys, especially you."

She nods. "I figured as much."

But she didn't say she would...

"We have old-fashioned principles. You will have an allowance, and limited freedom. You'll have to earn my trust. You came here asking for protection, and I granted you that, but everything comes at a price."

She nods. "I know."

"No one will hurt you. No one will threaten you." I put my fingers on her chin and push her gaze to mine. "Except for me."

Aria holds my gaze unblinking. Brave, foolish little hacker.

I glide her dress up the length of her legs and slide my hand beneath it. I palm her pussy, the silk fabric of her panties already damp against my palm. *Christ.*

"Remember what I told you in the shower," I whisper into her ear. I slide my fingers past the silk panties and push the strip of fabric to the side, stroking her pussy as we pull to a stop. I withdraw my fingers and lick them while holding her gaze.

"Jesus, I can't wait to taste you tonight. When we are with family, you will be respectful and obedient. Anything less than that, and there'll be punishment. And don't forget that when I have you naked in my bed tonight, it will begin with you over my lap. Am I clear?"

She swallows. "Crystal."

Of course she won't obey me. That would be so boring and damn near vanilla.

I realize at the same time as my phone buzzes with a text that we aren't where we're supposed to be.

We had been ten minutes from my home where my staff waits for us. I should see the Manhattan skyline or the depths of the Atlantic Ocean outside these windows. I see nothing but high-rises.

Aria sits up straighter, her eyes taking in every detail. I tap my phone.

> Lev: Your driver was found dead. It's been hijacked. Get out of the car. We're trying to locate you.

Fuck.

I take my phone and open a blank message. I type and hold it up to show her because anything we say can be overheard.

We were hijacked.

Aria's eyes widen and her nostrils flare. She thinks for a minute and doesn't lose her shit. Wordlessly, she takes the phone from me and taps back, her hand trembling.

I can help. But you have to distract the driver. Can you trust me?

Can I trust her? Of course I can't trust her. But we need more than brute strength, which I'm happy to supply.

She types again.

If you can distract the driver, cars like this have an ECM I can access remotely.

The electronic control module supplies fuel. If she can disable the engine...Jesus.

I confirm with another text.

So what you're saying is, I distract the driver while you disable the engine. But if you do that, we could crash.

She nods.

I'm aware. Seat belts? We'll be attacked when we do, you have weapons?

Oh I fucking have weapons. I nod.

I'll need your phone to do this.

I have to trust her. We'll have to work as a team.

Okay.

"This dress — ugh, I need to be able to move," she whispers.

She points to a few loops at the bottom and shows me how the train part is detachable.

Slowly, carefully, she detaches the train and shoves it under the seat. "Glad I said no to the heels," she whispers. "You ready? He's getting suspicious. We should look normal."

I lean in and bend her back, holding her to me while I kiss her. At first, she struggles, surprised, but soon melts against me. "How's that?" I whisper in her ear.

"Very good. You win an Emmy. You ready?"

"So fucking ready."

We share a look. I nod, slide her my cell and we both buckle up. Her eyes light up as her fingers dance across the screen. I watch as she sends our location signal. My brothers will get that. Next, she skillfully taps into a screen I've never seen before, her tongue sticking out of her mouth as she concentrates.

"I'm in," she whispers with a gleeful smile. She's in her element. It's so fucking hot. "Let's go."

The car's speed drops dramatically at the same time the privacy screen lowers. The driver grasps at the wheel, but Aria's effectively overridden the engine and brakes.

"What the fuck," the driver mutters in a panic.

"Brace yourself," she whispers with a grimace as she taps a button and we come to a screeching halt. We spin out like we're hydroplaning. The driver's thrown against the steering wheel, but we were prepared. Aria bangs her head but quickly sits upright, ignoring the flash of red on her temple.

"Go!"

I unbuckle my seat belt and lunge forward. I seize control of the wheel and slam us into a roadside barrier. Glass from the windshield rains down on us. There's a pop as tires explode and sparks fly as we come to a sudden, violent halt.

"You alright?" I ask her, as I wrap my hands around the neck of the fucking driver. I hold him in place and look to her.

"Fine. Wish I had a weapon."

I grit my teeth. "You don't need a weapon." I hold the driver in a choke hold. I've got three to four seconds, max, before he's out. I'll beat the shit out of this son of a bitch, but not until we have answers.

"Get on the floor," I order Aria as I exit the vehicle and quickly scan our surroundings. Another car's only a few car lengths behind us. They accelerate and I don't hesitate. I pull the trigger and shoot their tires. They spin out.

Liquid fire courses through my veins. I grit my teeth and pull the trigger again. I hit the other driver in the shoulder and his accomplice in the neck. One will survive, and that's all I'll need. He fumbles with the car door to try to run when he sees me advancing on him, but he's too late.

I yank that driver out of the car and slam his head into the concrete. "You fuck with me on my wedding day?" I kick him, ribs cracking, and he screams.

"I didn't know you were married already! Volkov said to stop the wedding!"

"Volkov's a fool and you're a bigger fool for following his orders." I put my gun to his head. Aria screams when I pull the trigger once, twice, three times. He slumps to the ground, in a pool of his own blood and battered flesh.

When I turn to Aria, she's staring at me wide-eyed and pale.

I put the gun away and take a step toward her. To her credit, she doesn't flinch when I reach my hand to her cheek and cup her face. "You alright?"

She nods, but she doesn't speak.

I'm so proud of her. I grip the back of her neck and give my wife a kiss while we stand over the bodies of our enemies. In my mind, it's the most romantic fucking thing I could've imagined. I release her too soon, eager to get her alone.

I whisper in her ear. "Take a picture of us with my phone and make sure the bodies are in the background."

With trembling hands, she obeys, a pained expression on her face, but her eyes are bright.

I take the phone from her and send the picture to Volkov.

> We're already married, you fucking douchebag. You know what this means. They attacked after our wedding. We'll get retribution.

Headlights blind me.

"Don't shoot, it's your brothers," Aria warns me.

I don't even ask her how she knows. She seems like she's one step ahead of me.

Lev pulls up and stares at the two of us. I know what he sees. Her torn wedding dress and bloodied forehead. My tux is wrecked. Two dead bodies and one unconscious.

"Get in, lovebirds."

Aria stares, wide-eyed. When she turns to the car, her dress hangs off her shoulder.

"One look at her and I'll beat the fucking shit out of you," I warn Lev. He yanks his eyes away from the sight of her bare skin. I shrug the torn tux coat off and place it over her shoulders.

"Be nice, Mikhail," Aria whispers. "He came to save us."

No one ever tells me to be nice. I grunt in reply and turn to Lev.

"Take us home."

CHAPTER THIRTEEN

Aria

WE SIT in the same living room where just hours ago, I took my vows. My hand shakes holding the shot glass. When Mikhail pressed it into my palm and ordered me to drink, I drank. I didn't see any reason to push back, not now. Not when I *wanted* something to soothe my nerves.

Not when he's told me explicitly what his expectations for obedience are. What's he going to do if he drugs me again? We're...married.

Doesn't mean he couldn't take advantage or get creative, but...

Maybe I'm more naïve than I thought.

My dress is torn and my temple throbs. I'm trying to forget the sight of blood mixed with brains on concrete, but it's not easy.

I could probably use more than a stiff drink.

"Mr. Romanov." One of his staff stands nearby, likely waiting on the next instruction.

"Out," he snaps in a tone so harsh I flinch. "Everyone's dismissed for the night. Exit through the back door immediately."

He's...dismissed his staff for the night.

Interesting. They leave quickly with hushed voices, doors opening and shutting behind them.

He's in worse shape than I am, but it doesn't stop him from walking to the downstairs bathroom and retrieving a first aid kit.

I sip the vodka he promised me we'd celebrate with. God, this stuff is liquid fire. I let it hit my lips as he curses in Russian, filtering through the first aid kit until he comes up with a bottle of saline and some white gauze.

"Head back."

I tilt my head back and grit my teeth. This will hurt.

I brace for the sting of pain, but it doesn't hurt as badly as I anticipate. "Vodka's an excellent anesthetic," he murmurs as he dabs the gauze on my cut.

"Good to know."

I'm sitting in an overstuffed leather chair, my arms barely reaching the armrests, my feet lightly gracing the floor. Mikhail kneels in front of me, glaring at the cut on my head as if it personally offends him.

"So," I say. "Want to tell me what happened? Who were they?" I ask. He doesn't answer at first, but after a quiet moment he blows out a breath.

"We have many enemies. My father's cousin is our greatest. Fyodor Volkov's notorious for having no use for modern conveniences like mobile phones. I sent him on a wild goose chase with decoys which delayed him, but he found us out. Since the men that were to report to him that we were already married are being buried as we speak, I'm guessing he didn't get that memo. He sent his henchmen to fuck us up."

I'm filled with sudden pride.

"And we fucked *them* up."

A smile plays on his lips. "You were fucking brilliant, Aria."

I feel my jaw drop in surprise, but I don't speak. I'm afraid if I do, I'll ruin this moment.

Praise from Mikhail Romanov? Be still my heart.

"It was nothing," I say with a modest shrug even as my chest swells with pride.

"It wasn't nothing." His scowl makes me look away as I battle conflicting emotions. "I wouldn't have been able to do what you did. It came so swiftly and naturally."

I swallow and nod, surprisingly emotional about his praise. I'm not sure how that makes me feel.

It seems simpler...*safer*...if only I could continue to hate him.

"Well," I tell him. "I'm good at what I do. You could've

benefitted from my skills as a hacker probably way more than you'll benefit from my skills as a wife."

The bold, predatory look he gives me makes me draw in a breath and I wish I had somewhere to hide. I'm practically sweltering under the heat of his gaze.

"Maybe you should reserve your judgment on that," he says in a low drawl I feel way, way, low in my belly.

My jaw drops. Did he just...go there? I set him up for that, though, and walked right into it.

I'm not good in bed. I have no idea what I'm doing, and we barely know each other. If he thinks — *no*.

"Maybe." I swallow as he continues to doctor me with surprising patience.

Our voices echo in this enormous room. I haven't been here long, but it's already a little unnerving, not hearing any sounds other than the two of us in this enormous estate.

He presses damp gauze to my forehead and finally nods, as if satisfied.

"Now it's your turn," I tell him, rising and pointing to the seat.

"I'm fine."

I snort. "You're fine compared to who? I'm no doctor but I think it's probably best you prevent...I dunno, infection or something by cleaning these wounds. And maybe we should...get some clean clothes."

"Fine," he finally agrees. "But we won't be needing clothes."

Je-SUS. Ack.

My injuries were superficial and his likely are, too, but I need him to take these clothes off.

"Does this sort of thing happen a lot?" I ask, as I turn my back to him so he doesn't see the way my hand trembles when I put saline on the gauze.

"Yeah."

So this is the world I'm in for. "Do you have a family medic or someone you trust?"

"Not yet. We will. Polina's studying nursing."

Interesting.

Armed with what I need, I turn to face him. "Alright, sir. Off with the shirt, please."

The heat of his gaze skates across my skin. There's stubble along his jaw that wasn't there this morning. I have the sudden, compelling need to reach out and stroke it. I want to feel the rough prickle against my fingers.

"We only took vows a few hours ago. Already, you're undressing me?" he says as he reaches for the buttons on his shirt.

I have to pretend the sight of his skin bared to me doesn't make my belly dip. "Of course I'm undressing you. If I'm going to perform my wifely duty, you'll have to perform your husbandly duty."

I can't believe I just said that. *Why did I just say that?* The sudden vision of me naked, flat on my back on his bed makes my cheeks heat— wait, there's *no way* this man's vanilla and favors missionary sex. My cheeks burn even hotter.

The sound of his chuckle hardens my nipples. Oh God, I haven't heard him laugh before. A part of me wondered if he even knew how. His laugh is deep, dark, and wicked, as golden as his skin.

"My husbandly duty is teaching you your place, woman. Keeping you in line. Making sure you learn there are consequences for disobedience."

"That's old-fashioned and chauvinistic, you Neanderthal."

"Your point?"

As he talks, I help him out of his shredded shirt, trying to steady the trembling of my hands fruitlessly. It doesn't help that I'm met with the vision of his temptingly naked skin.

"We've gone over that," I say with a haughty toss of my head.

Small talk helps distract me from the fact that he's getting naked in front of me.

I stare at his flawless arm, the sculpted biceps and sturdy forearms with visible veins beneath his tanned skin. His rugged hand rests casually on his knee, fingers strong and fingertips calloused.

When he shrugs out of his second sleeve, his ragged shirt falls, a tiny shred still tucked into his pants, but his back on full display. I stifle a gasp.

"Wow." A stunning image stares back at me, taking up his entire back. Unlike his arms, this is the only tattoo on his back, somehow making the bold lines of his muscles look more intimidating. I stare at the distinct features — bold orange and black with accents of amber. Indomitable eyes, powerful muscles, vertical stripes meant for camouflage. The background of snowy mountains and a full moon accentuate the brightness of the focal point.

"It's a...tiger," I say, as I walk around him, intentionally keeping my eyes averted from the tapered waist and little dimple in the small of his back.

"It's a Siberian tiger. My father called me the Siberian tiger when I was kid," he says. I sometimes forget he has a Russian accent, but it comes back in full force when he talks of his family. "It was my first tattoo."

I gape. "First? Your first tattoo takes up your entire back."

"It does."

I swallow and pretend this doesn't awe me. With a gentle tug, I take off the remains of his shirt and toss it. I stand awkwardly in front of him, pretending I don't want to stare at him. I remind myself why we're here.

I have to take care of his injuries.

He only has a handful of cuts, though, so it's quick work.

I dab antiseptic on a cotton round and make quick work of cleaning him up. "This will sting," I warn, when I get to a particularly angry looking scratch on his left shoulder. He doesn't respond.

I note a few tats I'm not familiar with and suspect they have something to do with him being Bratva — stars on each shoulder, barbed wire on his neck, a spiderweb on his elbow. I note the crosses on his fingers as well and wonder what that's all about. He's not what I'd call a particularly religious or spiritual sort.

When his back and arms are cleaned up, I stand in front of him, and do what I've longed to do — reach my fingers to his chin and tip his head to the side.

He'd almost seem vulnerable sitting here in front of me like this, if not for his sheer unbridled strength. His presence alone fills the entire room, even when he's silent. When I stand directly in front of him, I'm completely dwarfed by his shadow.

"Mm. Little bruise on your cheek but no cuts. I'd bet the other guy looks much worse."

It's a stupid attempt at a joke, but he doesn't smile. My heart sinks. I'm trying to make the most of this situation but he —

His hands span my waist, effectively anchoring me in place as his eyes bore into mine.

"They were fools for coming after you. If any of Volkov's men step foot near you again, I'll beat them with my bare hands until they beg for mercy. Then I'll bind them and make them spend their last minutes on earth watching me fuck you. Then kill them so no man has a memory of you but me."

A shiver makes its way from the base of my neck down the length of my spine. "I'll make an example of any of his men who even thinks of breathing the same air you do."

"I know," I say honestly, because I *do* know.

Siberian tiger indeed.

The largest cats in the world, the adult male can weigh up to six hundred pounds. Powerful predators, they're nimble and quiet with an exceptional sense of sight and hearing.

Sometimes I wish I didn't have a photogenic memory of everything I've ever read. I swallow and nod, trying to pretend I'm not freaking the fuck out.

I married a fucking *tiger*.

Still staring into my eyes, his voice lowers. "I want you naked, Aria."

By now, I know the low tone of his voice doesn't mitigate the command for immediate obedience.

The mention of his duty and mine ring in my ears as I step toward him. I feel an immediate rise of my ire when he tells me what to do, but I know I have no choice.

He's going to strip me.

With deft movements, he holds me with one hand and pops the pearly buttons off the back of the dress.

"This was a nice dress!"

"There are nicer ones. I unwrap my presents the way I like. Are you criticizing me? Go ahead, Aria. Give me a reason to put you over my knee. I've barely stopped thinking about it since you left my office."

My pulse thunders in my ears and my belly swoops. A wedding night spanking may not be the best way to make memories.

I stand still as he continues to undress me.

He mutters under his breath, shaking his head when he sees something he likes.

"What?" I say in a small voice. If he doesn't like me — if I've made it this far and have to stay wedded not only to this brutal monster of a man, but have to stay with him knowing he finds me homely or something —

"I won't allow you to wear things like this often, but they suit you." He runs an appreciative hand across my silk-clad ass. I squeeze my legs together at a sudden rush of arousal, just feeling him palm my ass.

I won't...allow you to wear things like this...

"Do you have something against ivory or silk under-garments?"

"I have something against anything that prevents me from seeing my beautiful wife."

The dress pools around my feet. The warmth of it straddles my ankles as he reaches for the dainty panties and rips them.

My beautiful wife.

"I liked that, too," I say with a little pout.

That earns me a growl.

I want a little push and pull. I'm not someone who's ever rolled over and obeyed anyone, much less a man. And I reason now that we're married, he won't exactly — hurt me — will he?

I want to see what happens when I push a little. I want to know why my heart beats so fast when he threatens me. It isn't just fear...is it? What is a spanking really like? I mean, I don't spend *all* my time on computers and in classrooms. I know there's a whole world out there that's unexplored. Hell, there are romance books about these things.

"Stand still. Turn around and let me see you."

Honest to *God*.

"You think you can just tell me what to do now that we're married? We don't really *know* each other yet, you know. I think we should —"

I'm swept off my feet so quickly the breath whooshes straight out of me. My pulse races when he lifts me straight into the air and yanks me to his chest. "Do you really think I'll go soft on you so quickly?" he says curiously. "Or are you testing me?"

"I—don't—" I clamp my mouth shut because I realize pretty quickly that was a rhetorical question that may not really require an answer.

With ease, he arranges me over his lap so I'm staring at the floor. I squeal when he pins me in place with one of his rough, calloused hands, because I know what's coming. So much for avoiding a wedding night spanking.

My heart leaps into my throat and I'm frozen in place, bracing for the first smack of his palm. Will he hurt me? Why did I push this?

"Look how gorgeous you are. *Khristos*." He runs a hand over the curve of my ass. "To think, just a few days ago, little hacker, you hadn't even come into my office. And now here you are, earning your first punishment." He draws out the word *punishment,* accentuating each syllable.

When he palms my ass I squeal, surprised and afraid because I expected the first spank. "You're so high-strung. Have you never been spanked before?"

"I have not," I say in a voice that doesn't sound like my own.

He continues to palm my ass roughly. "Then why did you practically ask for one?"

I shake my head, mortified. "I didn't."

The first slap of his hand across my ass sounds like a gunshot. "Ow! God!" My skin's on fire, and he's only given me one.

"Do not lie to me." Another sharp smack follows the first. I'm whimpering and squirming by the time the third one falls. "If you ever lie to me again, I promise you much worse than you're getting now. You'll earn the strap for lying, Aria."

Oh dear God. Another smack follows another. It's such a strange sensation, pain mixed with pleasure as my body aches for another. After three sharp swats, he's back to palming my ass, but it hurts like hell.

"It was —" I decide against talking back to him and qualifying my lie when I'm completely vulnerable and over his knee, my ass already on fire. "I—I wanted to know what it was like. It sort of...intrigued me. But I was stupid, it hurts!"

"Does it? Does it sting?" he asks as he lifts his palm and slams it across my ass again. "There are methods, you know. Methods that will teach you to learn how to crave my discipline."

And that's exactly what I'm afraid of. If I cave to him, and I start craving literally *anything* from him — attention or affection, or anything even close to sex — he'll have me exactly where he wants me. I will not cave to any man.

Still strewn over his lap, I kick my feet. "I don't know how anyone could ever want something like this."

"You little liar," he says, palm pressed to my back as he smacks my ass again. "Your body's begging me for more." The rough back of his hand spreads my legs. I squeal when he strokes the inside of my thigh. "I can feel your arousal here, painted on your thighs. You make me crazy, Aria. I want to tie you to my bed and use you. Lick your pussy until you come on my tongue and beg me for more."

My pulse races as he details the wicked, carnal things he wants to do to me and I realize with sudden alarm — I want that too.

"Is that my...wifely duty?" I'm trying to distract myself from the absolute base things he's doing to my body. More accurately — how they're affecting me.

He pauses, his hand mid-raised to give me another spank. "Are you mocking me, Aria?"

My heartbeat throbs.

No. Tell him no.

I want to protest and tell him no, but that would be a lie. And he's already told me what happens to liars.

I seem to have lost the ability to speak, though. My body's one big throbbing ball of arousal.

When I don't answer, his palm slaps against my ass again. The sound of him spanking me seems to take up every inch of this room. Thank God his staff isn't here.

"Tell me you'll obey me, Aria," he says in a growl, his hand poised over my ass.

I nod and try to open my mouth, but nothing comes out. With a sharp *crack* his palm slaps against my ass again.

"I'll obey you!" I manage to cry out, even as my mind rebels against such a concept. Right now I'll do anything to stop the spanking. But when he slows down and begins to finger my pussy, I spread my legs.

"Look how eager you are, you beautiful little slut," he whispers in my ear. "Go ahead, take my fingers. Open your legs and take what's yours."

My cheeks burn but I open my legs, my eyes screwed tight. I know what I need and in that moment, it seems he's the only one in the world who can give it to me.

The feel of his hot, rough palm on my inner thighs. The stinging burn on my ass. My throbbing clit and aching breasts. Every primal cell of my being screams to be dominated by him, to follow this large, alpha beast of a man who I know will ruin me.

His fingers tangle in my hair with the first stroke of his touch against my pussy. The bold flare of sensation makes me whimper. Before I know what I'm doing, I'm moving my body for more of his touch, pushing my pelvis against his hand.

"Such a bad girl. Got a spanking and now wants to turn her punishment into pleasure. That's not how punishment works, Aria," he tells me even as he continues to stroke my pussy and make me lose the ability to think.

His hardened length presses against my belly. He likes this as much as I do, probably more.

My hips jerk. I'm going to lose my mind.

"Don't you dare come. If you come before I tell you, you're in so much fucking trouble. It's our wedding night. You'll come with me. We'll come together."

I would think it weirdly romantic if I wasn't so consumed with warring thoughts of fleeing and surrendering. It seems as if my entire body, mind, and soul are wrapped up in the throbbing between my legs. I can't speak or think beyond my need.

When he stands with me, I'm half-delirious. A throw rug and blanket lie before a roaring fire, warming my naked skin. Flames flicker and I feel so warm and cozy except for my sore ass pressed against the soft blanket.

Mikhail's eyes bore into mine as he presses his weight against me and pins my wrists above my head.

"Tell me you liked your spanking, little hacker."

I open my mouth to protest, but realize I don't want to lie. I hold his gaze as I give him the truth. "I loved my spanking. That felt fucking amazing."

The dark flame in his eyes warns me before he spreads my legs with his knee. My wrists are immobile, my body pinned beneath his.

"Good," he says in a low growl. "I'll let that language slide this one time, but you'll watch your mouth. Finally some truth out of you. I knew you'd come alive under a firm hand."

Oh, did he, then? *Ahhh!*

I feel his hot, thick cock at my entrance. Panic sweeps through me.

"Birth control. I don't use birth control." Why would I, when my sex life has been as dry as the Sahara? "Mikhail," I say haltingly. "Wait. Please."

"Yes?" He bends and kisses the hollow of my neck.

"Would we...do you...I don't have birth control."

He growls and bites my neck. I hiss in a breath when he lowers his weight on me, effectively pinning me in place. "There will never be a barrier between us. *Ever.* Marrying me was your first payment to me. The second will be bearing my child."

Why have I not suspected as much? I've barely had time to think this through, to formulate a plan.

No birth control.

Children?

"Are you a virgin, Aria?"

I shake my head and hold his gaze. Will he dislike that I'm not?

"Believe me, it was nothing special," I mutter.

Narrowing his eyes, he leans down and presses his chest to mine. "Good. That will save me having to hunt him down and erase the memory of you. There will be none after me, Aria. None."

I'll give him anything if only he'll take me to where my body longs to go. There will be none other than him.

I moan in pleasure as he finally slides his cock in my pussy. I'm so full I can't breathe as he stretches me and my pussy hugs his cock.

The first stroke feels like magic, as his hips thrust and my body's engulfed in flame. The scent of pine and leather. The flickering warmth of the fire against my skin. The sound of my heavy breathing and his in the stillness.

He glides in and out effortlessly. I wish I knew Russian because I'd give anything to know what he's saying now.

"You come with me," he says with another firm thrust. "Are you ready to come, Aria?"

I nod my head and say something that sounds like an affirmative, but's really not much at all. I can't speak beyond the way my pulse races and my needs are firing.

"Tell me you'll obey me," he says with a hard thrust.

"I'll obey," I say, the first wave of pleasure rippling through me.

"Tell me you're mine," he growls with another savage thrust.

I don't want to cave so easily, so I clamp my lips together. But when he stalls his thrusting, hovering above me waiting for my response, I nearly lose my mind. It's worse than any spanking he could give me. I want to climax. If I don't, I'll lose my mind.

"Aria," he warns, pressing my wrists more firmly. "Tell me."

I'm craving his cock like I'm dying of thirst in a desert. I finally cave. "I'm...I'm yours," I whisper. The next thrust sends me spiraling into ecstasy, and he's claiming that. Claiming *me*.

His breath catches as he thrusts again with a low growl. Every nerve in my being culminates in this. Ecstasy floods me. I'm completely swept away, empowered by his own guttural growl of ecstasy. His hot come lashes in my pussy as pleasure wraps me in a hot, tight cocoon. Again and again he thrusts, as both of us ride the waves of perfection together.

CHAPTER FOURTEEN

Mikhail

SHE'S ABSOLUTELY WRECKED.

I can't remember the last time I felt this pleased over anything I've done.

We lazily clean up with our ragged clothes. I lift her to my chest. She leans against me, boneless, her head on my shoulder. My beautiful, feisty, brilliant little hacker.

My wife.

I brought her to my home and made her mine. She gave me good reason. But now that she's here...now that she's mine...

No. I have a duty to perform and so does she. If I let myself have feelings for her, I'm leading myself to a dark, dark place.

"I instructed my staff to leave us food. We'll eat, and then settle in for the night."

"Mmmph," she mumbles incoherently against my chest. "Your home is lovely. I can't wait to explore it. Tell me I'll get to explore it or will you..."

"You may explore my home because it belongs to you, too. I kept you prisoner at first because I did not know what you were capable of." I know now, though, that if she wants to escape in any way, she's written her own death sentence, and not just from me.

Her circumstances keep her captive better than any cuffs might.

"But first, you'll eat and get some rest."

"Food sounds good right about now."

I lay her on the couch and drape a soft white blanket around her body. I love the way she sighs in contentment. I quickly pull on a pair of boxers and go to the kitchen then check my messages from my brothers.

> Lev: Volkov's men have retreated. He won't say it but he knows he fucked up. Unlikely to be retaliation right now.

Right now, when she's only minutes past being fucked in my living room.

When I've gotten her pregnant, that will be another story.

> Kolya: Congrats, my son. Your father would be proud.

I wish he'd leave my father out of this. Still, I send him a message back. He means the well wishes.

The next message is from Aleks.

> She did an excellent job. It's honestly
> pretty impressive. Don't fire me, will you?

I snort to myself. He's actually admitting she has superior skills. As someone who prides himself on being the best, this takes some humility.

> I won't fire you but don't count on your
> Christmas bonus

> That's fine, I wasn't going to get you
> anything anyway. You inherited an entire
> clan of badasses, what more do you need?

> Lucky me

I drop my phone on our food tray.

I actually wish I'd kept staff on so I wouldn't have to leave her and could instruct them to bring us our food. I don't like leaving her side. I make quick work of retrieving what they left, and when I come back, her eyes are half-lidded.

"Aria."

She only mumbles to herself and shifts, pulling the blanket up to her chin.

"Food," I try again, but I already know it won't work when I hear a light snore.

I set the tray of food on a side table, snag my phone, then and bend and lift her. She doesn't wake, but nestles against my chest and whispers something incoherent.

I walk into the master suite to the scent of jasmine and roses. My first time ever bringing a woman into my bedroom. I instructed staff to make my bedroom less... austere. I wasn't really sure what they'd do, but the flowers are a nice touch.

I lay her on the bed and brush the hair out of her face. Traces of makeup from earlier linger on her skin. Does she have a...nighttime routine or something? Not so sure what to do about that.

I text Polina.

> Aria is asleep but she hasn't gotten ready for bed yet. What do I do about...the makeup? Hair?

> I am SO screenshotting this for future blackmail. This might be the sweetest text you've ever sent.

> I control your phone access. I can delete your screenshots. And what's sweet about it? Maybe I don't want makeup smeared on my pillowcase.

> You are SO overbearing, ugh. I take it back. There's a small blue rectangular package in the bathroom with the things I bought her. It should say micellar water. Use those. They're cold so they'll probably wake her up

> Thanks

> You're welcome. And Mikhail? She's a good one. Don't be mean to her. I LIKE HER

I roll my eyes and toss my phone on the dresser. Whatever.

I find the little package and take out a wipe. Smell it. Shrug. It doesn't smell like much, but it's cold. I press it between my palms until it's warm. I sit on the edge of the bed and brace Aria's face with my hand. "Sorry to wake you," I mumble, then lean over and wipe her face.

She opens one eye. "What is that?"

I shrug. "No idea. Thought I'd help you get ready. Now go back to sleep."

She closes her eye and obeys for once in her life.

I toss the wipe and use the bathroom, then take my laptop into the office outside this door so I don't wake her.

I have work to do.

Tonight was only step one.

CHAPTER FIFTEEN

Aria

I HAVE no idea what time it is when I wake, but the bed is empty. It feels like the middle of the night, inky black still outside the window.

Mikhail is nowhere to be found. My mouth feels dry and my stomach aches. I have a vague memory of him offering me food, but I was exhausted and just wanted to sleep.

I open one eye and look about the room. I see his cell phone plugged in on a nearby table, and a second phone beside his with a little note beside it. His script is firm and bold, in slanted lines with no frills or whimsy.

Of course.

Aria,
This is your new phone, monitored by me.

All online access, including social media, is restricted and recorded.

You may reach out to your friends — women only. They'll know you've been married by now. Make up whatever story you need to.

You do not talk to men other than my brothers without my express approval.

You have a credit card under your name and may buy whatever you want, but if I buy something for you, I expect you to wear it.

You will post nothing or tell anyone about our life or my family's. I expect loyalty. In return, your needs will be provided for.

You will only socialize with people I approve of.

There will be no working outside the home. There is no need, and I will not have you unnecessarily in danger. You will, however, be asked to work for me. We need your skills. You will be well compensated.

We'll discuss what you are doing and when. You will not be allowed outside of the home or to travel without my express permission.

You know what will happen if you disobey any of these rules.

—M

Some of this — the phone, social media, where I go and when — doesn't surprise me. Overbearing? You bet your ass. But overbearing is his middle name. I don't expect he can have a wife putting any of his family or herself at risk. The socialization thing is laughable. I have no friends and love being alone.

The online access is tricky, though. I love what I do and crave to feel the power of a laptop under my fingers. I actually give myself a little time to pout over that one. I sigh and read it over again. I mean, fine, I'll wear whatever he gets me, yeah. And a credit card? I've been living off ramen and dollar store toiletries, so that sounds pretty sweet. But if I don't have access to doing what I love...

I slide the note to the side and touch the screen on the phone. It jumps to life in vivid detail.

2:23 *a.m.* Why isn't he in bed?

I settle back into bed with my new phone, holding my breath at how fast it operates, how easily I'm able to glide from one task to the next.

Maybe...I can get a laptop?

My laptop. I sit upright in bed, my heart pounding. What happened to my laptop? What did they do with my possessions?

Ugh. It's gone. Lost. There's no way I can recover that now.

I have to get something to eat.

I push up out of bed and feel an ache across my ass. Oh *God.* He did that, didn't he? He totally went there.

I remember what it was like being over his lap. I remember I came so hard I couldn't breathe when he was done.

Yeah, I am in so much trouble.

To think I was afraid of getting close to him. Now I'm half a breath away from calling the man Daddy.

Gah.

I look around the room for something to wear. He said something about clothing on that note...He doesn't need to tell me that walking around his house naked isn't a good idea. I got that memo *loud and clear.*

There's a closed door to what might be a closet, so I turn the handle.

I cover my mouth with my hand. This is the biggest closet I've ever seen in my life. I could set up an entire office in this closet.

Will he let me?

Shoes and handbags, dresses and jeans. Tees and all sorts of leggings and skirts...wow.

Why does he have so much feminine stuff in here?

Did he buy this stuff? Wait. Is it...for me?

So am I expected to wear it?

On a small hook by the door hang several lovely robes in the softest material, beside matching fluffy slippers.

Well, then.

I wrap a soft blue robe around my body and slide my feet

into slippers. I feel a little like a princess, and we're just warming up here.

My stomach rumbles again with hunger. Where is he? I don't much care about what he's doing so much as I'm not crazy about the idea of stumbling into him unawares. He's a tiger, after all. He'll definitely bite.

I open the door and try to get the layout here. His room is on the second floor, and from here, much like the guest room I was in before, I can see the moonlit view of the Manhattan skyline. It's gorgeous, with high-rises and moonlight glinting over the brilliant blue of the water.

From what I've seen and what I've pieced together, I can tell this is a luxurious, high-end home nestled prominently in The Cove. Expansive glass windows and modern architecture give it a striking, minimalist appeal with clean lines and vast rooms.

Even with only moonlight illuminating what I see, I can tell already we're right on the water. It looks like there's a terrace and garden out front, with soft, ambient light strips along the stone pathway and interspersed throughout the garden. It lends an elegant aesthetic to the home that might be too harsh without the touch of green and light.

And yet...it's past two o'clock in the morning. Does the house not sleep, much like its master?

I think back on the note he left me. I'm allowed to roam this house, I'm just not...how did he put it? *You will not be allowed outside of the home or to travel without my express permission.*

I start toward the top of the stairs and breathe in deeply. This is the next stage of my life. I came here under duress and I wouldn't be here if I truly had a choice.

With every step I take, I can feel the punishment he administered earlier tonight. I can't help but wonder how this is going to work between the two of us. How will I maintain who I am — my identity, my autonomy, my self-worth — while married to a man that's stripped me of everything?

He's spared me my life...but at what cost?

I hear the faintest sound of music playing. I stand still and close my eyes so I can concentrate. Where is it coming from? It's not on this floor, but the main one.

I pad noiselessly down the gleaming hardwood stairs in my fluffy slippers and cinch the belt on my robe a bit tighter. My stomach growls, reminding me of my errand. First, I want to know what the music is. It's something hauntingly familiar.

The night feels enchanted, bathed in moonlight, the quiet broken only by the music that gets a bit louder as I walk down the stairs. The view outside the windows looks solemn as the world sleeps, but when I get a little closer, I can see the earth is frosted in ice.

Now that's why I have the robe and slippers.

On the main floor, I take in my surroundings. The living room that already holds quite a few memories for me — where we took vows, my momentary life as a princess. Then later, lying over his lap while he gave me the first spanking of my life. Our wedding night consummation.

I wonder idly if his group demands consummation. If so, we have nothing to worry about. I know hardly anything about organized crime, but I do know the basics. Those within the group are bound to secrecy and loyalty. There's a hierarchy, and my husband's at the top. They are wealthy and own property, business, territory. From what Tatiana told me, they own all of The Cove.

But there are other basic tenets of mafia life I've already seen firsthand. They use intimidation and violence to get what they want. They break the law. Those in charge demand complete obedience and will not hesitate to enforce rules.

I find I'm following the sound of the music even as my heart beats faster and I have the strange feeling I shouldn't be up and prowling about this house. I'm curious what Mikhail might do when he finds me. Or, more accurately...when I find him.

As I walk, I mentally catalog the layout. It's gorgeous here with clean, vertical lines and a sense of tranquility. It's a little surprising that for someone who values secrecy and privacy, his home has oversized windows that bring in natural light during the day and moonlight at night.

It's an oasis in here. Past the living room, an open doorway leads to a sitting room. There's a doorway to a bathroom and another to what looks like the kitchen. I don't explore, though, because I'm drawn to the music.

It's a piano. Someone's playing a piano. Since we're the only ones here, it must be Mikhail.

He has a piano.

I want to leap for joy.

When I find it, I almost turn away. Will he be upset if I interrupt him now? He doesn't have the friendliest personality, one might say.

But as I stand in the doorway, I'm haunted by the music. I close my eyes, trying to remember where I've heard it before. It's...Russian, yes, I remember. While Tchaikovsky is likely the most famous of all Russian composers, there are so many lesser-known composers that were arguably even more skilled. At least in my opinion. I've always been one to root for the underdog.

Lobanov, Roslavets, Feinberg. Yes, I remember it now, Feinberg Piano Sonata No. 12, Op. 48: II. Intermezzo...his piano sonatas are hauntingly beautiful. I took one course on composers years ago to satisfy a prerequisite for my degree. I never forget anything.

I lean against the doorframe, lost in the music. The rise and fall of the notes, expressive and hauntingly beautiful, makes my heart ache. I feel sad yet hopeful, energized yet calm. They say that the sound of a composition is impacted by the person playing it.

While I stand here, effectively intruding on his playing, I feel as if I'm dancing through myriad emotions. I'm walking on the beach, dancing in moonlight, the waves lapping on the shore...yet not alone. The melody, like an untamed cat, begs to be stroked before it pounces away.

I quickly take in the room — an elegant design of simplicity like the rest of his home. A baby grand piano sits as the focal point in the center of the room. The piano, a stunning matte white, lends a contemporary air.

Shades of white, gray, and black create an atmosphere of calm and tranquility. The walls feature a handful of framed prints I can't see in the dimmed lighting. The floors are polished hardwood, the furniture sparse — a coffee table, a few end tables, a few elegant armchairs, and a simple white leather sofa.

The last notes of music fade.

"How long have you been there?"

He doesn't turn around to look at me. I adjust the belt on my robe, viscerally aware that it's an exercise in futility.

"Long...enough." My words are quickly swallowed up in the expanse of the room. He doesn't turn to look at me. I stare at his naked back. The tiger's eyes stare back at me. A shiver of awareness runs down my spine at how strong he is, even bent over the piano, showcasing every inch of his chiseled back.

My pulse spikes when he turns to me, and his eyes meet mine.

"Come here, Aria."

My heart leaps in my throat. I'm not sure why. He's only asked me to come to him. I haven't done anything that would make him want to punish me.

Have I?

I walk to him, powerless to disobey. Has he conditioned me, this quickly, that I leap to his command?

As I draw nearer, my body responds to the deep tone of his authoritative voice. The way his eyes watch my every move. Halfway to him, he rasps out a sharp command.

"Lose the robe."

The robe is warm and comfy, but his gaze warms me more thoroughly.

I lose the robe. The gorgeous little garment likely costs more than my weekly salary, and yet it falls to the floor like so much wrapping. I step away from the warmth of the robe at my feet. He didn't tell me to lose the slippers, so I walk toward him stark naked save for the fluffy white slippers.

Have I imagined that crinkling at his eyes? The slight twitch of his lips?

Shaking his head, he chides me in that deep rasp that drags over my skin and makes my nipples pebble. "Testing me, Aria? You haven't learned any lessons at all yet, have you?"

"What? Me?" I ask, holding his gaze, the picture of innocence. "You told me to lose the robe."

"Fair enough. Lose the slippers as well."

With a belabored sigh, I step out of the fluffy slippers.

He crooks a finger at me.

When I'm close enough for him to touch me, he reaches for me and draws me onto his lap. He's still wearing boxers, but nothing else, so when I sit on his lap there's only a whisper of fabric between us. His large, rough hands slide across the small of my back and lace behind it.

"Why are you up?"

"I couldn't sleep. I'm starving. Why are *you* up?"

"I don't really sleep. Haven't for years. Did I wake you?"

I shake my head. It's almost sweet that he cares. "No, not at all. That was beautiful. Feinberg?"

His eyes widen and his brows rise. "You know Feinberg?"

"I do. I studied composers for a prereq in college."

"You studied composers years ago in college and yet immediately identified an obscure Russian composer," he concludes, disbelieving.

"I didn't just identify the composer. That was Piano Sonata number twelve...Opus forty-eight, no?"

He blinks.

I shrug. "I'm not just good at coding. I have an excellent memory, which is partly what makes me so damn good at coding and hacking. I have perfect recall."

"Really," he says, a statement, not a question. He's thinking this over.

"I told you I had skills you could use, and I wasn't exaggerating," I say with a not-so-modest shrug. It's nice to actually be admired for something for once. "How do *you* know Feinberg?"

Holding my gaze, he seems to be mulling things over. With every question I ask about him, I'm delving deeper into his background — who he is, and how he became this person. Revealing personal details makes him vulnerable, and it doesn't take a rocket scientist to figure out that Mikhail Romanov is hardly someone who allows himself to become vulnerable very easily.

"When I was enlisted, I was under the command of an officer who was obsessed with Feinberg. Whenever we had the chance, he played the music over and over again. I became obsessed, too. It was my lullaby and my comfort. There's something about Feinberg's music that makes me...I don't know how to describe it."

"Feel emotion?" I whisper. Could it be that he understands this?

He stares at me for a long minute before he finally nods. "Yeah. You could say that."

I swallow. "Me, too."

He gives my hand a gentle squeeze. "Do you play?"

I don't answer at first. Do I play? Well, yes, I do, but not well. I always wanted to, but my parents couldn't afford classes.

"Why the hesitation, little hacker?" he asks softly, then holds my chin and brings my gaze back to his when I look away.

"Hesitation?"

A corner of his lips quirks up and he mutters something unintelligible in Russian.

"That isn't really fair that you just randomly speak a language I don't."

"You're brilliant. You could learn Russian if you want to."

Maybe I like the sound of enigmatic words in his some-times-harsh mother tongue.

I shrug. "Maybe I will. I don't play much, no. My parents couldn't afford piano lessons, so I used to sneak into the back of the school gymnasium so I could listen in on piano lessons some of the kids took after school. I did my best to listen and then practice when no one was there, but it's a hard habit to hide, and the other kids eventually found out." I want to change the subject. The memory of my shame when I was discovered still burns. "So you enlisted, then?"

"I did."

No further elaboration. Interesting.

"How long?"

"Twelve years."

Whoa. Twelve years. That's a long time.

"Are any of the tattoos you have related to the army?"

His accent thickens. "None. These are all Bratva."

Bratva.

The way he says it makes me shiver.

"Can you tell me what they mean?"

"Eventually, maybe."

As he talks, I'm aware of his hardened length pressed up against my butt, and my own body tightly coiled with arousal that snakes around my belly and pulses between my thighs. Once wasn't enough.

"I didn't know you were in the military."

A hint of ice flickers in his gaze. "There are many things you don't know about me, little hacker."

I do what I've longed to do — reach my hand to the stubble on his chin and cup his jaw. Though he stiffens, he allows it, and I don't need him to tell me this is an allowance he likely affords no one else.

"There are many things I don't know about you, yes. But there are many things I do."

The roughness of the stubble on his chin bites into my palm, sending awareness and a pulse of need between my legs. I wonder what it would feel like if that stubble scratched my thighs...

"I know you can be ruthless. You have no qualms about violence and taking human life if you feel it's justified. You're skilled with weapons and not just the ones you hold – you've conditioned your body to be used as a weapon, too. You don't like clutter, lies or disorder. You have routines and systems in place because you run your family like you'd run the military. You are direct with your words and instructions."

I swallow. "You take care of what's yours." I look away, suddenly bashful. "I mean, your home is beautiful."

"Thank you."

I have the sudden desire to lay my head on his chest. For just a little while, to stop carrying the burden of my constantly churning mind, fear of what happens next, and the ever present need to be on high alert.

"Am I wrong?"

He shakes his head. "No."

Encouraged, I continue. "You are courageous and deter-mined. Action-oriented with little fear of the aftermath. You are a natural-born leader. Assertive. Resilient. Protective and likely resourceful as well."

He narrows his eyes but doesn't respond. I take a bold step and brush the pad of my thumb across his full lower lip, my voice a whisper now. "You struggle with vulnerability. You can be aggressive and impatient, and I'd hazard a guess you're total sh—absolutely terrible at obeying those in authority over you."

He grunts. "Very good censoring your language."

I shrug. My stomach gives an audible growl.

"You need food, Aria."

I do need food, but I like sitting here with him. It's quiet and intimate, a magical time when no one can interrupt us or remind us why we should hate each other.

"Mhm."

Another growl. Do tigers growl?

"Is there something you'd like in particular?"

I laugh. "It's like three o'clock in the morning, nothing's open."

With a shrug, he shakes his head. "That doesn't matter."

Wow. The power he yields. I'm sure he has his grip on much more powerful things like politics, economics, corporations, or the media, but the fact that he could wake up the local owner of a pizza parlor to make me a pepperoni pizza in the wee hours of the morning is a bit impressive.

"Something simple might be nice?"

"Simple we can do."

He lifts me off his lap and stands me in front of him.

"The only problem is, I don't know exactly where your kitchen is."

Quirking a brow, he gives me a piercing look. "I don't recall telling you you'd join me. While I'm gone, I'd like you sitting cross-legged on this bench with your hands resting on your thighs. Wait for me in that position."

I frown. "What if I have to use the bathroom?"

"Do you have to use the bathroom?"

"Well, no, but I might have to."

"I won't be long."

"What if there's an emergency?"

"There won't be an emergency but if there is one, you'll call out to me."

Huh.

I sit obediently with my legs crossed and my palms on my thighs as instructed. "And if I don't?"

CHAPTER SIXTEEN

Aria

"YOU KNOW the answer to that question, little hacker. And if you don't, why don't you try me."

I watch him walk toward a doorway in the corner of the room. So that's how you get to the kitchen from this room, whatever it is. Interesting.

While he's gone, I do what he says. *Why do I push himmmmm?*

I've been like this as long as I can remember, with the strange need to push my boundaries, challenge authority, question the status quo. *Why* do twelve-year-olds go to seventh grade? What if they're ready for ninth? Who decided there was a hierarchy to things like governments and churches anyway, and why do dumbass people who don't deserve power have it? Who decided traditional gender roles dictate how people dress, what jobs they perform, and what's expected of them?

But while I sit on the piano bench, my legs crossed and my palms on my legs as he told me, I find it's nice to quiet the incessant questioning for a little while. My body begins to still, and my breathing slows. I listen for sounds of him getting food or whatever he's doing, but it's silent in here.

Play the piano.

I want to lean over and play it. I want to feel my fingers stroke against the keys. I'm curious if I remember how.

I turn and stare at it and consider my options. If I disobey him, he'll punish me. And while punishment might lead to something deep and dark and deliciously sexy...getting there won't be.

I don't ever sit still. This is a challenge for me.

I close my eyes and breathe in deeply, allowing the air to fill my diaphragm. I do a quick mental assessment of my body. As usual in Mikhail's stubbornly sexy presence, I'm definitely aroused. Sitting here naked enhances that. There's something wanton and risqué about it. I swallow and try to focus myself.

Breathe.

Breathe.

A wave of hunger hits me, followed by a wave of nausea. I'm starving and need food *now*.

I focus on using all of my senses. The feel of the leather seat, warmed from Mikhail, against my naked legs. The scent of Mikhail that lingers in the air, the faintest whiff of pine. The smell of toast and something savory, making my mouth water.

The sound of a door opening and closing. I open my eyes and Mikhail walks in with a wooden tray of food.

"Ah. Very good, little hacker. You've earned your dinner."

In the dark, I can't tell if he's teasing or not. Would he really deny me food? A spanking would be mild in comparison.

He walks with such elegant grace and strength, I sit and watch him, half-struck with admiration. Wordlessly, he walks toward me with the food.

"You may get up and come sit on the sofa," he says with a nod toward it. "Join me here, please."

He settles himself on the sofa and watches me as I uncross my legs and rise. The way his eyes rove over my body and he takes everything in makes me feel like a *queen*. I stand tall, my shoulders back. I don't miss the robe. It's strange how comfortable it feels being naked when I know the only person who sees me loves my body.

I sit next to him and look at the tray he's set on a small table. A few sandwiches wrapped in wax paper sit beside a small plate of cheese and crackers. Small, golden-brown pastry shells are nestled on a second plate, beside thick, pancake-like cakes.

"Wow, this looks amazing. And...interesting." I give him a curious look.

"I'm not sure what you like to eat, and it would please me very much if my wife would join me in eating the traditional food of my homeland."

Fortunately, I like a large variety of foods so I'm game to try

Mother Russia's spread. "Alright, then. Let's give it a go. Can you tell me what they are?"

He points a fork to the pancake-like things first. "Syrniki. They're like pancakes but made with cottage cheese. Breaded then fried." Next, the golden pastries. "These are pirozhki. Pastries that can be savory or sweet, depending. These are savory, filled with potatoes, onions, and meat."

"Interesting. Let's go."

I look to him and wait to see if I'll be allowed to feed myself this time. He gives a subtle nod and looks pleased. I'm catching on.

I reach for the fork and cut a small wedge of the pancake first. It's crispy on the outside with a crunchy breadcrumb edge, but the inside is mildly sweet and creamy. "Mmm. Delicious. Did you cook these? Right now?"

"I heated up the food I had staff leave us. I'm pleased you like it."

The nod of approval and hint at a smile make my heart flip in my chest. The warning bells that were clanging to warn me of impending doom if I seek his approval are getting harder and harder to hear. I...I like pleasing him. It's so rare that he isn't scowling, I feel as if I've won a major battle. The words *I'm pleased* don't often escape his lips.

Next up, I take a bite of the savory pirozhki. Flavors explode in my mouth. "Mmm," I say involuntarily, reaching for another bite. "Mmm, these are delicious. I've never been much of a sweets person."

"Me neither." He joins me and we quickly polish off the food.

I sit back against the couch, my belly full. Finally, my eyes are sleepy again.

"Oh, God, I just realized I have my makeup—"

I reach for my face. No, wait. He helped me clean up last night, didn't he?

Did he?

"Everything alright?"

"Did you...help me get ready for bed?"

With a shrug of his massive shoulder, he reaches for the last pirozhki and eats half of it in one enormous bite. "Of course. I told you I take good care of what's mine."

"True," I say, changing the subject because this is dangerous territory for me.

Another casual shrug. He knows I didn't miss his point.

I stifle a yawn. "I'm exhausted."

And...naked. I can't forget I'm absolutely buck naked. And I'm sitting next to a man twice my size who's claimed me as his. My...husband.

He's my *husband*.

It's still so hard for me to swallow all this.

"We will go to bed. Tomorrow we have some work to do to prepare you to live here with me."

CHAPTER SEVENTEEN

Mikhail

ARIA ADAPTS MORE EASILY to life here with me than I'd expect her to. I don't blame her, when I think about it. She was on the run long enough, not even knowing where her next meal would come from, it only makes sense that she appreciates having a roof over her head.

She won't like living with me, I can guarantee that. But I don't need her to like it. I need her to stay.

It's strange that when I look at her phone over the next few days, I notice no unusual behavior. She's a hacker, after all. I half suspected she'd be downloading software, communicating with her friends, or at the very least researching and learning about my family and what she's gotten into. She doesn't so much as open up an app.

Does she have no friends?

I have a large volume of work to catch up on over the next

few days, so I stay home and work from my at-home office while she gets accustomed to life here.

On the third day, she comes to my office wearing a pout.

"Alright, I'm bored out of my *skull*." She crosses her arms on her chest and glares at me.

Ah. This is what I was waiting for. She can only behave for so long before her true personality will shine.

"Oh?" I ask. "Maybe download a game on that damn phone you hardly touch."

"I don't want to crush candy, Mikhail."

I continue perusing the spreadsheet Lev gave me and don't turn toward her.

"Do I detect a recalcitrant tone, little hacker? Have I taken such poor care of you?" My voice is deceptively low.

She heaves a huge sigh. "You call me little hacker and yet you don't give me a chance to actually, like, *hack*. Or do anything other than sit around and look pretty and then eat food in between...well, you know, sex. And while looking pretty and eating good food are nice things, I don't want that to be all I do every day."

I turn and give her a curious look. "Did I tell you that's what I want you to do?"

"No, but you haven't given me any options, either."

I lean back in my chair. "Haven't I?"

She narrows her eyes at me. "Wait. The letter said I had a credit card and that I could leave, I just have to have your permission. Right?"

"Yes. And the answer is no, you may not leave. Not now. It isn't safe right now."

Her face falls, but only for a second. "But I can buy a computer with the credit card?"

"You can buy all of goddamn Apple with that credit card. You could hire someone to come here and build you a computer from scratch and someone else to bring a small menagerie of animals to entertain you while he did it. Go for it."

She bites her lip and shakes her head. "I have no use for those products. Apple? *God,* are you even serious right now?"

She's fucking adorable. "Let me guess. You want to build your own computer with open-source software so no one can track you?"

She throws her hands up in the air. "Of course! Jesus, tell me you're not using a MacBook."

I show her my own laptop, custom-built by Aleks. "Of course not."

"Good, they're fine for like normal people, but people like me and you need privacy and security," she says with a serious nod.

"Right. People like me and you. So get yourself some equipment already."

"But I can't go in person?"

I think it over. I could send her with one of my brothers or security guards. While Volkov's sent an apology, we did indeed get our retribution, so I have no doubt he's ready and able to strike again, and soon.

"No. Not this time."

With a labored sigh, she sits back in the chair. "Alright, so I can work with you?"

"Of course. I'll expect you to. The credit card has been loaded into your phone so you may buy what you need."

She eyes me suspiciously as she takes her phone out and swipes on it with her fingers. "No *way*. Well, fancy that. Whoa." She quietly swipes across screens for a few minutes. "Do you have any idea how risky that is? You should definitely not have this loaded on a phone."

"Really? Interesting."

"Unless you don't care about losing a few grand before your credit card company realizes." She pauses. I continue to read the data on the spreadsheet I need for a meeting later today. "Wait. Like you *don't* care about a few thousand dollars?"

"I do care about a few thousand dollars, yes, but it's more important to me that you can easily buy what you need rather than bother about details. Just buy what you need, Aria."

"Alrighty then." Another few minutes of quiet swiping. "You sure I can't grab a ride to Coney Island? It says here—"

"No. You may ask Aleks to pick up anything you need. He's the best man for the job."

She gives a little grimace. "Yeah, pretty sure he hates my guts."

He'd better fucking not "hate her guts." I go still.

"What gives you that impression?"

"Oh, only the way I made him look like a douchebag in front of all of you because he's shit at cybersecurity and he thinks I'm threatening him or something." She clamps her hand over her mouth.

I slowly close the laptop and turn to face her.

"He doesn't hate you, but you're not exactly his best friend. Has he been rude to you in any way?"

My voice is deceptively calm. If he so much as looked at her sideways...

"Well, no. It's just a *vibe*."

"Ah. I see. A 'vibe.' Don't think I missed the curse you said, Aria."

My dick throbs at the look she's giving me. Pure, unadulterated defiance. Her chin juts out and there's challenge in her eyes.

My little hacker needs attention, it seems.

"You're not allowed to curse. I don't want to hear those words coming out of that pretty mouth of yours."

"Oh yeah?" she asks in a low voice laced with resistance. She tips her head to the side. "Would you object to my mouth wrapped around your cock?"

I reach for my belt and unbuckle it. My cock throbs. "Let's test that theory."

CHAPTER EIGHTEEN

Aria

OH, shit.

So what if I was a little bored? I'm not a "sit around the house" kind of girl. I like action and I want to be involved in things. Yeah, I used the exercise equipment in his huge home gym, but that only takes so long and it got boring being there alone. Mikhail's been super busy catching up on work.

Apparently I've occupied him.

And now I've stepped right in it. I stare at him, dressed in a dark blue Henley that showcases every one of his gorgeous muscles. I stifle a hum of need. He's so damn hot. What's he doing to me? We have sex literally daily, and it's never enough.

"What are you doing with that belt?" I ask, suddenly nervous about pushing him. Is this really the type of attention I wanted?

"You know exactly what I'm doing with this belt." He lays it across his knees and begins to roll up his sleeves.

Oh *fuck*. My belly swoops at the sight of his golden skin adorned with ink, those corded muscles and bulging veins.

Fisting his belt, he stands and points to his desk with it. "Bend over my desk."

I'm internally losing my shit. *Ahhhhh!*

I don't dare disobey him. Cursing is a milder offense. Refusing to take my punishment? That's not the type of line I want to draw with him.

Shaking, I bend over the desk and do what he says, my arms resting on the surface.

I shiver when I feel his warmth behind me, practically pressed to my back. He bends his mouth to my ear. "You're getting five lashes for those naughty words, Aria. Then you'll make it up to me by showing me how well you can use that mouth."

Ahhhhhh!

I swallow and nod, unable to speak. I screw my eyes shut tight, my heart threatening to burst. He's only ever spanked me with his hand and when he's done...

"Count them."

My eyes fly open as the first whistle of the belt warns me before the strike. It hurts, a sharp, intense pain, quickly taken over by a burning sensation. I swallow and choke out, "One." My cheeks flame with embarrassment. I can't believe I'm —

The second lash falls hard. I flinch. "Two."

It hurts, but not as badly as I expected. Mikhail could flail me with his brutal strength and a length of leather, but he's carefully moderating each strike. Still, it's no tickle. The burning sensation intensifies. Arousal pools in my belly when he palms my stinging ass with his free hand. "Good girl. That's a girl."

I hardly remember to count the third, and by the time the fourth lash lands, I'm practically blissed out. Oh, fuck, this is incredible. It hurts, but the best kind of hurt, the kind that clears the mind and senses and grounds you fully in the present. My clit throbs, and my pussy aches to be filled by him.

"Last one," he says in a harsh tone. "Count."

The hardest smack falls. "Five," I say in a whisper because it hurts so damn much, and I want so much more.

"Let me see," he says as he reaches for the clasp of my jeans. I intentionally chose low-cut flared jeans that I think make my ass look amazing. But at times like these..."Let me see my handiwork on your gorgeous ass."

His massive hands circle me as he deftly unfastens my jeans and pulls them down. My body flushes with heat as he bares my ass to him.

"*Khristos.*"

I guess the tiny pink thong he bought me looks better than he thought it would. I thought so myself.

I moan as he comes up behind me and grips both of my hips, grinding his erection against my ass. "You look gorgeous. I can't believe what seeing you wear my stripes does to me." He continues to praise me in Russian, the sweet sounds more welcome with every day that passes.

My husband likes what he sees, and that makes me feel like the sexiest woman alive. "I want you, Aria," he whispers in my ear. "My beautiful, sexy wife. I want your pussy hugging my cock. I want to hear you scream after I've whipped your ass and fucked you against my desk. I want to remember the sound and feel of you when I work."

Spinning me around, he lifts me and yanks the jeans and panties off. "Spread your legs for me."

My heart's in my throat as he kneels in front of me. I hardly know what to do with myself until he places himself between my knees and has me straddle my legs around his face.

"Such a good girl," he says in a whisper, before he rubs his cheek against the sensitive skin of my thighs. The prickle makes my pussy throb. Nestling my feet on his shoulders, he spreads my thighs further apart. "You deserve a reward for being a good girl." His accent's thickened.

With a deep breath, he inhales my scent and mutters in Russian. He leans in and first kisses the inside of one leg, then the other. "I can taste your arousal already and it's making me wild." With a low growl, he bites my inner thigh. I scream and jump, but he holds my legs fast. "Stay right there."

With the flat of his tongue, he licks where he bit, sending mixed vibrations all through me. I feel half wild with need and fear, the two emotions so irrevocably entwined I can hardly think straight.

"So sweet," he whispers again, dragging his stubble along the sensitive skin. "You taste so sweet. Spread your legs and stay right where you are."

With trembling knees, I obey. He grips my aching ass, leans in, and inhales my scent.

The first tentative press of his tongue to my clit feels like heaven. I gasp and jerk. No one's ever done this to me before, and I'm already half-drunk. It's so personal, so private, and yet—

So is being in his bed.

So is being over his lap.

So is riding his cock and obeying him.

I'm in so deep there's no escaping.

He ravishes my pussy with his mouth, suckling and licking, nipping and fingering. I'm whimpering with need with every stroke of his tongue. Holding my gaze, he suckles my throbbing sex before lazily dragging the flat of his tongue along it again. Just when I think I'm going to soar into climax, he lifts his mouth. My eyes fly open and meet his.

His voice is a low drawl thick with his accent. "Tell me you'll watch that mouth of yours, Aria."

I nod crazily. "I will, I promise, I will."

The warmth of approval in his eyes makes my heart thump madly. "That's my good girl. That's what I want to hear. Such a good, obedient girl you are. Now beg me for your climax, sweet girl."

"Please, Mikhail. Please don't stop," I beg in a breathy whisper, my voice unrecognizable to my own ears. My entire world is centered on the need for the release he could grant me. My voice diminishes to a plaintive whisper. "Please."

"Please what? Who am I?" He gives another lazy stroke of his tongue that makes my hips jerk with the first spasm of orgasm. He bites out his next words. "Say it."

"Please, Mikhail."

The sharp rasp of his teeth against my thigh makes me scream. I bite my lip.

"Say it."

I want to scream and fight this, the claim over who I am to him, but the desperate, carnal need for release trumps all rational thought.

"Husband. Please, husband."

A wicked grin spreads across his face and he holds my eyes. "Good girl. I'm so pleased with you, *moya zhena.* Ask permission before you come on my tongue. You do not climax until I tell you."

What?

I reach for his hair and grasp it. "Mikhail, you made me call you husband and I did!" He damn near tore it out of me. "I can't — you can't —*ooh.*"

With a groan of pleasure, he buries his face between my legs and licks me again, a sensual stroke of his mouth to my clit. He's already made me call him husband, he *won't* make me ask for permission. *I won't.* I let myself go, powerless to stop.

The first wave of pleasure hits me. I can't hold myself back, no matter his instruction.

The next stroke of his tongue sends me soaring into ecstasy. I let myself go again. "Oh, *God*," I moan, half delirious with pleasure while a small voice whispers a warning in the back of my head. I disobeyed him and he won't like that.

If he stops—

But he doesn't. He takes one quick second for a guttural groan and curse before he's back at my pussy, riding me through wave after wave of perfect bliss until I finally sink back to the desk, wrung out like a rag doll.

He presses a kiss to my still-throbbing pussy.

"Beautiful. You're fucking gorgeous when you come." Another kiss, followed by a rough growl. "Even when you're a naughty, disobedient little wife."

Uh oh.

"I couldn't stop myself! You were the one who was pushing me there!"

Why is he still kneeling between my legs? I don't trust that look he's giving me.

"You dare to compound disobedience with talking back?" His accent is in full swing as he shakes his head at me. "That won't do, little hacker. Not at all. It seems I haven't fully demonstrated my demand for your obedience."

Ah, that might not be the issue. He's absolutely demonstrated his need. I'm the one that's not so sure this is for me.

I bite my lip, my thundering heart slowing only slightly. Slowly, he rises. I forgot for one brief moment when he was kneeling in front of me how tall and muscular he is. Now, lying on the desk with his full height looming over me, I am very, very aware.

My heart kicks up again. Will he spank me again? Use his belt again?

Or...something worse?

With a frown and subtle shake of his head, he bends and places me over his shoulder.

"Where are we —"

The sharp crack of his hand against my ass silences me. *Yeowch* that hurts when he spanks me over the sore place he punished earlier, like a slap over a sunburn.

"Quiet. You disobeyed, Aria. I warned you against that."

He did indeed. It doesn't mean I was determined to exactly obey, though, and he ought to know that.

Does he? Was that a test?

That was absolutely a test and I failed it.

Was he looking for a reason to punish me?

Over his shoulder, I'm a little disoriented and unsure of where we're going next. By now, I know the layout of his home so well, I know he's heading for the bedrooms. His bedroom — *ours*, maybe?

He walks with firm, steady footsteps. I realize he's dressed again when his cell phone rings in his pocket.

"Not now. I have important business I'm working on. Can it wait?"

Important business.

"I'll talk to you when I'm done. Instruct the others not to interrupt me."

The voice on the other end asks a question.

He barks out a reply. "Until I'm finished."

His pace accelerates. I wait for him to lecture or to tell me something about what I've done, but our march is in utter silence. When we reach the bedroom, he pushes the door open with his foot and brings me straight to the bed.

"On your hands and knees, chest down, ass up."

My belly quivers. I nod wordlessly against him, half terrified of what he's going to do to me.

I roll over onto my belly and do what he says, ass up, chest down. My arms lay straight out in front of me. Since this is a massive bed, I have plenty of room. This is the first time he's had me in this position, though.

My mind races with possibilities. Why this position? He could spank me again with something, he could fuck me from behind. He could take my ass, or...*gah*. He could do damn near anything he wanted.

I shiver in anticipation. Was chasing that climax worth this? At the time, I was pretty sure it was. Now? I'm not so sure.

"I'm disappointed in you, Aria." His voice sounds distant and a bit muffled. Is he in the closet? "I planned on giving you the best orgasm of your life. Waiting until I tell you to come means building to a better experience. And I thought I'd emphasized already the utter importance of your obedience."

I nod into the bed. You did. Yup, you did, nothing to see here, folks.

The only way I know he's enjoying this is because his accent has thickened. "And now, instead of one perfect orgasm, you'll be punished instead."

With my ass in the air and head on the bed still, I nod to him.

I can hear him gathering things behind me but can't see what they are. I'll have my answer soon enough.

I try to talk myself off the ledge, to quell my churning nerves. *He hasn't beaten you. He's heavy-handed but very protective of you. If he were going to hurt you wouldn't he have done it by now?*

My aching ass is a vivid reminder that he hasn't exactly coddled me.

I hear the echo of his footsteps as he draws nearer to me. I shiver when his mouth brushes my ear. "You look so beautiful lying on our bed wearing my stripes. So beautiful."

Somehow hearing him call the bed *ours* makes my heart melt a little.

Gently, he gathers the hair at the nape of my neck and swoops it over my shoulder. His lowered voice is the tone I've come to recognize as dangerous. "You wanted an orgasm, Aria. You'll get exactly what you wished for." I stifle a gasp when he nips my ear and pay close attention to the way he makes his way down my spine until he reaches my ass.

Wait. He's going to punish me with an orgasm?

Framing my hips with his massive hands, he bends down and brushes his lips to each hot, flaming cheek.

"Beautiful."

Something cold hits my inner thigh, and my hips buck.

"You're so skittish, little hacker," he says in a tone that could almost be described as teasing. I swallow and nod.

"Maybe a little."

The rough feel of his palm against my ass makes me hiss in a breath. Again, the warmth of his cheek to mine, his mouth to my ear. "You should be. I thought you'd know by now that disobeying me wouldn't be a very smart choice. It seems I haven't done my duty as your husband, have I?"

While a very small part of me wants to protest and push against him, reminding him that these aren't the Dark Ages anymore...my body teems with need. I crave the utter weight of his dominance and command with a raw, visceral need that quickly trumps all logic. I swallow and lick my lips before I finally nod.

Yes. Yes, he hasn't done a very good job with his husbandly duty, has he?

Gah!

I clench the bedspread in my hands and try not to imagine what torturous device he has pressed up against my hips.

When he pushes it higher against my folds, the hint of vibration and cold makes me shiver.

"Your body is mine, Aria Romanov. *Mine.*"

He slides the cold object between my folds, onto my clit. My hips spread wide of their own accord, as I'm helpless to protest. I crave the vibration and pressure...right...*there*.

Oh, God.

He made me come only minutes ago, so the sensation is intense, too much. My hips jerk and I cry out. "It's too much. Mikhail! Please, it's—"

"The consequence of your disobedience," he finishes in a harsh rush of words, a thrill in his voice.

I try to move away from the vibration against my clit, while at the same time feel myself moving closer and closer to orgasm already. I can't do this, I'll—

"Oh, *God*," I moan as my body clenches, on the edge of coming.

"You wanted to come, my dirty little wife. Didn't you? You wanted to come before I granted permission. Come, then. Come until you've had your fill."

His fingers spread me wide, and he glides something in. It hits the walls of my pussy and vibrates while pleasure explodes. I shatter into a second orgasm, so intense I clench every muscle in my body before I lose my mind. I scream and try to get away from the intensity but I can't.

Mikhail grips my neck with his massive hand and turns my head to his, claiming my mouth in a kiss at once so sensual flames erupt across my skin. I can't think or move or speak as every nerve in my body electrifies. Sharp spasms of plea-sure course through me, my blood pumping through my veins like molten lava. We're fused together, my breath his, our heartbeats matched.

I nearly cry when he breaks the kiss.

"Come, Aria. Come for me," he orders in my ear. "You have my permission now, my greedy little wife. Take it."

Still writhing with spasms of pleasure, I can't speak or even breathe. And still, whatever sex toy he slid in me vibrates relentlessly.

I come down from the orgasm and collapse on the bed, praying he doesn't keep pushing those little torture devices. For a moment, they stop. He pulls one out and shuts the other one off.

"Did you like your orgasm, Aria?" he whispers in my ear. I'm vaguely amused that he's using the singular. I didn't have *an* orgasm. That felt like twenty all rolled into one tight pack of dynamite.

"Mmm," I say, nodding. Did I? Did I really enjoy that or was it too much?

Too much.

"Good," he says, as he moves my body from the position he had me in on the bed and lays me on my back. "Now open your legs."

I peer up at him. What's he...going to do?

I can't disobey him, not again. I can't take another spanking or forced orgasm. I stare at him and open my legs with a stifled whimper.

"Good, just like that." With a frown, he reaches for my wrists and raises them above my head. Something clicks into place. I try to move my wrists, but they're frozen in place.

I...

"Mikhail," I whisper. "I'm sorry. What are you..."

My voice trails off at the sight of something short and whip-like in his right hand. He taps it idly against his thigh.

Bending down, he brushes my damp hair from my forehead. Brushes his lips to my temple.

"You ask me permission before you come."

I nod. Yes, yes, of course, I will definitely —

He takes my hips and swings me over the edge of the bed, kneeling in front of me.

"Mikhail—"

Looping my legs over his shoulders, he bends his mouth to my sex and presses a tender kiss. My hips leap off the bed, the sensation is so intense. If he— I don't think—my thoughts stutter as he parts my legs. I want to reach to him to stop him but my wrists are bound and I'm helpless to move. I strain against the cuffs.

"Please," I whisper. "Don't—"

He licks my sensitized, throbbing clit with the tip of his tongue. I hiss out a breath and bite back a scream. I'm so sensitive and swollen, the second stroke of his tongue makes me whimper, even as my body craves more.

How?

I lose his heat and wonder if I'm delirious. I open my eyes to see him wielding the whip-like object in his hand a second too late.

"Mikhail!"

He flicks it on my pussy with just enough pressure that the sting quickly melts into a pulse of arousal. I open my mouth to protest when he whips my pussy again and again. Four, five, six strokes of the lash before he leans on one hand and flips the whip around. I feel the handle at my core and my eyes go wide.

He wouldn't— my head falls back when he glides the hard length of it in me. It's smaller than his cock but unyielding and cold. I whimper as my sex clenches around it. "You like to come, don't you, wife?"

I nod and plead, tears blurring my vision. I'm half delirious when I feel the loss of pressure and his familiar warmth between my legs again.

He pushes his thick fingers in my core and circles as he licks my clit. It's frosted candy, blinding sunlight on snow, the clang of cymbals and trumpets at once. Too much. Too intense. I want to run from the onslaught of sensation, from the pleasure so exquisite it's almost pain, but there's no escape. "Mikhail," I beg, my cheeks wet with tears. "I can't — it's too much — *please*."

But he doesn't stop. Over and over, he licks my clit and fingers my pussy until I'm coming against his mouth. I scream until I'm hoarse, drowning in endless undulations until I finally fall to the bed with a whimper. And still, his tongue lashes at my clit.

"Please," I beg. "Oh, God, I need a break." I'd take anything instead of this — his belt, or worse, starvation. I had no idea pleasure could be so punishing.

"I'll decide when you need a break." His harsh voice cuts through the haze. "You've had enough when I say you have. *Breathe*, Aria. Trust. *Surrender*."

Helpless to resist, I draw in a breath that expands my lungs. Again, he licks my clit and this time, even though I'm so sensitive I'm on edge, I find it's...tolerable. Bliss to the point of near pain, but not...quite.

My mouth falls open when he spreads me wide, thick fingers in my channel opening me up.

"You taste like fucking heaven," he says in a growl as he licks me again, and again, and again. I cry out loud as my hips jerk against his mouth. Tears flow freely down my face. "Beg me. Beg me, you perfect, gorgeous little slut."

"Please! Please stop — oh, *God*. No," I moan, when I find I'm right on the edge of coming again. "Don't...please. Please, Mikhail. May I come?"

"Good girl. You please me so much. You may," he whispers against my thigh, taking one quick moment to scrape his stubble along the edge. I feel a prickle against my clit and just as I open my mouth to gasp, the softness of his tongue flickers where he just assaulted. The sensation sends me soaring into another climax.

I've lost count by the time I'm boneless. Ten? A hundred? A million times he's brought me to release, until every muscle in my body's spent and I'm hoarse from screaming, begging, pleading, riding the waves of pleasure and pain.

"Good girl," Mikhail croons in my ear. He seems like he's above me. Is he carrying me? I can't move or open my eyes. I can't speak. I'm boneless and spent as he lifts me against his chest. "You're the most beautiful woman I've ever seen," he whispers. "I don't deserve a woman like you, Aria."

I wonder if I'm half-dreaming the words he lavishes over me. I feel delirious and drunk, but mostly exhausted.

"Tell me you'll obey me. If you can't speak, nod, my love."

I nod. I'll obey. I'll do anything he tells me to. He commands the very beating of my heart with all he does, how he makes me scream with pleasure and cry in pain. I feel as if he's climbed into the recesses of my heart and made himself at home.

It's more than a little disconcerting.

Vaguely, somewhere in the distance I hear the sound of running water. "Where are we?" I mumble, surprised I can form words with my thick, heavy tongue. Every part of my body feels weighted and tired. Did he take me to a waterfall?

"You're taking a bath. Hold onto me, Aria. There. That's my girl. I'm so proud of you. You earned your punishment, little hacker, but you took it so well. So goddamn well."

I sigh with pleasure as warm water laps at my skin. The pain on my ass and inner thighs lessens with the warmth of the water. The soothing floral scent of roses calms my senses as Mikhail holds me to his body and pours the water over me. A soft cloth at my temple and face. He cleans me gently, with care and attention. I didn't know he was even capable of such tenderness.

And then the water is gone and I'm wrapped in something soft and warm. I sigh as I feel myself lifted. My head lays against his chest and I think to myself idly...it was worth it. The punishment and pain, every second of torture. If this is what he does when it's over...it's worth it. Laying my head against his chest feels like...belonging. Home. Comfort I've only ever imagined.

"Drink, *milaya*." He speaks in Russian, sweet words I can't understand but I don't need to. The tone alone — praise and adoration — warms me to the tips of my toes.

I open my mouth and feel a straw against my lips. I didn't realize I was so thirsty. I eagerly sip until he pulls it away.

"I'm still thirsty," I whisper, half-asleep, even as I've already pulled back and laid my head on his chest again.

"You can have more in a little bit. Easy, now."

Something warm comes over my shoulder and I'm already half dozing. I hear him mutter to himself in Russian. I can't help feeling he's hiding something from me. I blame my delirium.

Have I fallen for my Russian captor?

Has he fallen for *me?*

CHAPTER NINETEEN

Mikhail

"ARE you coming to the gala or what?" Polina's not feeling very patient.

I look at the sleeping form of my wife on the bed beside me. Her mouth is gently parted, her hair wild and crazy in waves around her. Pink marks on her bottom and legs. She wears my marks so beautifully I'm beginning to think she'd look naked without them.

I stifle a sigh. I did tell my mother I'd be coming to the gala and bringing my new wife. My family's eager to see her again.

It's risky, though.

For the past two weeks, Aria and I have spent nearly every waking moment together. The shipment of computers and monitors she ordered arrived, and she gleefully spends the days typing away while I work. Our nights are filled with nothing but reveling in each other.

It can't be like this forever, and I know it. But a part of me wonders...why not?

I don't like sharing and never have. I also don't want to scare Aria any more than necessary. She met my family at our wedding, but meeting them in person, full force...

Every year, my family hosts a lavish gala, a charity event with an elite guest list. It's the highlight of Polina and my mother's year, as they spend months planning the event. Last year's function raised 2.4 million dollars for the local children's hospital.

I do not want to take my wife. It's a worthwhile event, no doubt — hosting a gala of this magnitude allows us to maintain an image of philanthropy. We can maintain our front as legitimate businesspeople while skillfully forming alliances and networking.

It's a charitable front, but the real heart of it is a major power play.

If Volkov has the nerve to show his face...

"Mikhail, you *have* to take her. You can only hide her away in that lair of yours so long. No, no, wait. Tigers don't live in lairs, do they?"

Oh for Christ's sake. My *lair*. "Polina..."

"Where do tigers live?"

I blow out a breath. "Tigers are solitary animals and live in lots of places. Some live in dens."

"Your den! You can't hide her in your den forever. That sounds awful."

She's not making this any easier for me.

I don't ever go back on my word, though, and I told my mother I'd come.

"I told you I'd come to the gala. I will."

"Alright, *good*. Wait. Not just you, right? You weren't answering my texts so I was starting to get worried."

I roll my eyes heavenward. "Not alone. And you sent me ten texts about food, seating arrangements, and wine. I don't care about any of those things."

"It's important your bride likes what we give her, Mikhail! What if she hates us? What if I serve the chicken with walnut sauce and she's allergic to walnuts? What if I make a kale salad and she despises leafy greens?"

I make a face. "Tell me you're not serving kale salad."

"*Mikhail.*"

I shrug. "She'd politely decline and eat something else from the large array of way too much food you'll be serving us. Or she'll decline and come home here, where I have enough food for the apocalypse. Who cares?"

"*I* care. God, sometimes you're so fucking *male*."

I growl. My little sister has been spoiled. "And sometimes you are too forward, little sister. Watch that mouth of yours."

"You are not my father, Mikhail."

"Lucky for you I'm not. You wouldn't have gotten away with half of the things you do now."

"Tell me about it." I can see her now, her hands on her hips, her lips pursed.

"Enough, Polina."

She sighs. "I just wanted to see if you were coming," she says, in a much more polite tone.

"We will be there. I trust you'll make the right decisions with the details. If you have any doubts, ask Lev. He's the one that cares about this shit."

"Actually? He doesn't care. He's the only one nice enough to humor me when I ask him."

"Well there you go."

Aria stirs, one eye opening. "I have to go. We'll be there."

I hang up the phone before Polina has a chance to reply.

"Mmm," Aria says, closing her eye again. "I had the strangest dream."

"Did you?" I stroke my hand on her bare shoulder. "Want to tell me about it? Or are you hungry?"

"Starving. I had no idea rough, toe-curling sex burned so many calories."

"Rough, toe-curling sex...I like the sound of that."

Her eyes still closed, she raises her brows. "Oh, I know you do. No doubt. Anyway, in my dream you were talking about tigers and dens and galas. What's going on?"

I lean my pillows up against the headboard and reach for her, pulling her onto my lap. She curls in like a little kitten. I tuck a blanket around her.

"Every year, the Romanov family hosts this huge gala in the dead of winter. Why winter, I have no idea. Half the time it's snowing. It's called the Glacial Gala. Everyone comes to it. Makes us look good. We earn a ton of money and donate it and everyone thinks we're philanthropists. It's sort of Polina's passion."

"Ahh. So when you say everyone...who might that include?"

"Everyone who's anyone of influence. Celebrities. Business leaders. Politicians." I make a face. "Socialites."

"Yikes. You'd probably rather have your fingernails pulled off one by one, wouldn't you?"

"Hmm. That'd be a hard choice, but..."

Aria stills. Pressing a finger to her chin, I lift her gaze up. "What is it?"

"Those are the exact people I discovered, Mikhail. You know this, right?"

I nod. "I do. Why do you think I hesitated when talking to Polina? But she's right. You can't hide forever. Better parading in front of those who might want to pursue you while wearing your armor."

"My armor?" she asks curiously, her head tipped to the side.

I bend and take her mouth with mine, a kiss that's at once sensual and demanding. After last night, I suspected she'd be malleable and eager. I'm not wrong. "Me."

"Oh, God," she whispers when I move my mouth to the hollow of her neck. "What are you doing to me?"

"Worshipping you, obviously." I nip her ear and her back arches. I lick the sore flesh and suck her lobe between my lips. "I love how you taste. I love how you feel."

Rolling over, I pin her beneath me. "That's so sexy," she whispers in a low moan. "Calling yourself my...armor."

"What else would I call putting myself between you and anyone that threatens or hurts you?"

She smiles against my lips as I take her mouth with mine. I touch my tongue to hers and relish the way she moans and responds, her fingers stabbing into my hair as she wraps her legs around me.

"So fucking beautiful," I whisper in her ear. "I'd kill for you, Aria. I'd kill anyone that came between you and safety or happiness. Do you understand me?"

I want her to take me fully, as I am. I need her to know who I truly am. Finally, she nods, spreading her legs for me. A silent invitation for me to take her fully.

I plunge myself into her hot, slick pussy.

Her head falls back and she screams in pleasure, her arms wrapped around me. I take her wrists and place them above her head, lowering my full weight on her.

"I understand," she murmurs. "I do."

I bend and take her mouth. "Thank you," she says softly when I pull away.

I wonder if she'll be thanking me when she knows what else I have in store for her. Will my adoration and protection be enough?

CHAPTER TWENTY

Aria

I WAKE with a wave of nausea.

I toss my hand over my mouth and run to the bathroom just in time. I kneel over the toilet and retch.

Oh, God.

Something I ate? Maybe it was something I ate. We ordered DoorDash from some Russian bistro place he likes, and while it was delicious, I ate some foods I'd never eaten before.

God, no, I can't be sick! Not today.

Tonight's the night of the gala. Polina and I actually got to go shopping and pick out accessories. Mikhail picked out my dress and I'm excited to see it.

Wait — the night of the gala. The night when I'll be around all the people that want me dead.

Maybe I don't have to go? Conflicting emotions? Yeah.

I bend my mouth over the toilet a second time. When I rest my head on my arm, panting from the exertion, I feel Mikhail's warm presence behind me.

"I'm so sorry you're sick, love," he says with concern. I open my mouth to respond, when another wave of nausea hits me. This time, he holds my hair until I'm spent. I rest my head on my arm again.

"Maybe it's the food we ordered last night?"

I lean back against the wall. The cool tile feels good beneath me.

Mikhail crouches in front of me, his eyes a picture of concern. He's already hit the gym and showered, his dark hair damp, and he's dressed in business casual, so he likely has a meeting.

My throat gets all tight when he brushes my hair out of my eyes and places his large hand across my forehead. "You're not warm. How else do you feel?"

I wipe at tears in my eyes. "That's so sweet," I say, wondering what's come over me so suddenly. I'm not usually all sappy and sentimental. "I was just nauseous."

"You fell asleep so early last night." He rises and gestures for me to stay where I am before handing me a small cup of water. "Maybe you shouldn't have slept so soon after a meal."

If there's anything I've learned from being with Mikhail, it's that Russians are a *very* superstitious people. They knock on wood to ward off bad luck, have religious icons and art all over the place to protect them despite the fact that they are decidedly *not* religious, and I once saw their mother lose her mind when one of them was whistling indoors. Apparently, that brings bad luck. There's likely some myth or belief about eating before bed being related to illness.

"I don't...I don't know. I—" I swallow.

I pause because it suddenly occurred to me that my period was due last week.

He reaches for me before I slump over. "You look like you're going to pass out, Aria. Let me." I normally love his Russian accent and how he's all protective. The "come with me" is followed by him carrying me in his arms with gentility.

"Mikhail." My voice is just above a whisper, but it gets his attention loud and clear. "You have a meeting?"

"I'll call it off."

I remember Polina talking about the important officials coming into town for the gala. For all I know, he's meeting with the prime minister of Russia, and he's about to call it off.

"You don't have to. Really, Mikhail, I'm *fine*."

His growl tells me he definitely doesn't agree.

"Except. Well. Maybe..."

"What is it?" He lays me in bed and brushes a hand to my face, holding my eyes with his. "Tell me."

I can't be pregnant. God, no. But we haven't used birth control, and I'm in good health...

"We maybe need to get some pregnancy tests."

He comes to a sudden halt. "Pregnancy tests. Do you think you might be pregnant?"

"I just lost my cookies for no good reason, I fell asleep at like seven o'clock last night, my period is late, and I've been having very frequent unprotected sex with a man who's hung like a king of the forest. I'm not sure if it's science, but I'd hazard a guess that does something to your virility." I'm trying to tease him, but he doesn't smile. He stares.

I actually managed to convince myself that Mikhail Romanov doesn't *do* surprise or really any emotion that might stem from any apparent weakness.

Apparently, I was wrong.

"Here, Aria." He adjusts me on the bed as if I'm going to break. "Stay still. Do not move."

Pregnancy. Babies. No protection. I knew this was a possibility, but I somehow managed to convince myself that would be way, *way* in the future. Why would someone like me be so fertile when there are thousands and thousands of women that try everything for years so they can conceive?

What if I don't want a baby?

What if I...what if I'm not ready?

I'm not ready.

I curl up on the bed and he reaches for a handknit afghan his mother brought us last week. She said it was a late wedding gift because it took her longer than she thought. "He needs something very big to cover him fully," she said with a laugh.

He pulls it up over my shoulders and heads toward the bathroom. I stare at the intricate pattern of ivory and caramel-colored yarn.

He bought pregnancy tests. Is that cute or controlling?

Can it be both?

I don't. Want. To be. Pregnant.

I remember what he said to me weeks ago when we got married.

Marrying me was your first payment to me. The second will be bearing my child.

Payment to me.

The second will be bearing my child.

My child.

I've finally gotten accustomed to some of his ways. At least I think I have. I've finally made peace with the price I've paid for his protection. For taking care of me. And he does take excellent care of me.

But I don't want children. I never have.

I go through my reasons for not wanting children.

First, I don't have extended family.

Mikhail does, though.

Having been poor my whole life, I didn't want a child to experience poverty, either. It matters to me to be able to provide well for a family.

That's also not a concern anymore.

Before I can continue my list of objections, Mikhail comes to me. My mind continues to bring up every possibility and fear I can muster. I've never seen him look like this before, his eyes bright and excited. "Alright, so you need to use the bathroom, then we dip this stick..."

I pause, staring at him. I can't air my concerns. I'm here for complicated reasons, and if I decide not to have a baby... what happens next?

"Let me help you up," he says, lifting me in his arms.

"Mikhail, please," I say with a little laugh. "I can walk. I'm not injured or anything."

He scowls at me. "Are you talking back to me?"

"Well, no," I say with a pout.

"Are you pouting?"

"Doesn't a woman who's maybe pregnant have a right to pout?"

I wouldn't have chosen this, not on a bet.

"Then why do you look that way?"

"Nausea," I respond. "Doubts."

"Ahh. There's nothing to fear, Aria. No matter what, I will take care of you."

Easy for him to say. He isn't the one potentially carrying *human life in his womb*.

He stands reluctantly outside the door when I pee on the strip, then practically bangs it down when he hears me flush.

"Your impatience won't make the test result come any sooner," I tell him, but he ignores me, of course, and just walks into the bathroom and stares at it, as if willing it to reveal two pink lines. The timer on his phone ticks.

I'm a little scared of his reaction if it's positive. Will he wrap me in bubble wrap or confine me to bed?

I'm a little scared of his reaction if it's negative.

Will that mean I've failed?

One minute passes. I feel nauseous again at the second minute, and by the time the third minute's over, I'm swallowing hard to keep the remaining contents of my belly down.

I don't even know how to tell him I'm not sure what I want the test to say.

Pregnant? With the mafia lord's child? Destined to be raised wealthy, yes, and loved, absolutely, but — into a world of crime and violence?

Or...not pregnant.

Mikhail's fallen expression tells me my answer before I even look. "I'm not, am I?" I ask in a little voice.

He shakes his head.

I expect nothing but relief but I'm surprised to find I'm... also disappointed. I sigh. "I'm sorry," I whisper. Am I?

I don't ever remember being so conflicted over anything in my life.

Am I sorry that he's disappointed?

Wordlessly, we clean the bathroom. I toss the negative test into the trash bin and wash my hands. I try to conjure up a feeling of relief, but it's...mixed.

"How are you feeling?" he asks me.

"Hungry, honestly. Oh, wait, is that what you meant, though?" Does he mean emotionally?

"Yes, all of it. How are you feeling?"

"I'm...not sure."

Relieved? Disappointed?

"I'll get you breakfast. We need you better for tonight, because it's crucial we get you there."

It feels so good to lie down. A buzz sounds on my phone.

> Polina: Can't wait for tonight! You ready?

> Feeling not so great, honestly. Maybe something I ate?

> No! Oh, I'm so sorry. Make that brother of mine get you something to eat.

I snort. As if anyone could "make" Mikhail do anything.

He's already getting me something, though.

I bite my lip when he leaves the room to get us breakfast. Should I tell her?

Why not?

> Honestly? I just took a pregnancy test.

> OH MY GOD. Annnddd??

> Negative. I think...no, I know Mikhail is very disappointed.

> Oh, it will happen. Sometimes it doesn't show up right away on a test! Are you late?

> Yes.

> Test again tomorrow! I'll bring things for you tonight. Stuff that will help. My bestie is pregnant and I know all about it!

> Thank you! Good luck!

Sometimes it doesn't show up right away....

Yikes. I need to check again, and soon.

Pregnant.

Pregnant.

What would a baby with Mikhail look like? Would he or she have those deep, dark eyes and charming personality?

I actually manage to snicker to myself.

I sit up in bed, grateful for the food when Mikhail brings in a tray of buttered toast, scrambled eggs, thick bacon, and a fruit bowl.

"Eat, Aria. Try at least three bites."

I grunt. I'm not sure I want to. But the look he gives me dares me to push him, and I'm starting to become honestly... *pretty* aware of when he wants me to do something.

"Aria," he warns.

"Would you really force a pregnant woman to obey you?"

He doesn't miss a beat. "Yes. And you're not pregnant."

"Yet," I mutter, as I take a triangle of toast and bite the edge.

His eyes crinkle around the edges, a rare sight that does funny things to my heart. I swallow.

"You stay and rest in bed for a little while. I'll check on you and then we can make a plan for tonight."

I sigh. I don't want to stay in bed, but he has a point, and I know he won't budge, either.

"Can you pretty please bring me my laptop though?"

"Which one?"

It's a fair question. I've maybe gone a little crazy with that credit card.

"Hmm. The rose gold one, please."

I maybe had a little fun with that.

While he gets the laptop, I head to the closet to get something comfy to wear. I still feel a little guilty going into this closet. I never had anything like this in my life, and now I have more than I could've ever imagined. If my mother saw me now...I pull out a pair of soft white sweats and a hoodie when a garment bag catches my attention.

I peek at the dress hidden behind a blanket of plastic, hanging right in front. Is this...*oh, wow*. Okay, so this is the dress he got me for the gala. I lift the plastic to take a peek.

Wow.

Woooowwwww.

It's *breathtaking.* I reach a tentative finger out to touch the coal black, luxurious satin bodice. It's elegant and sophisticated, modest because he won't showcase me *too* much, but...sexy as hell. Spaghetti straps and a fitted bodice, accented with a panel of sheer lace at the waist and a cinched waistline accented with a thin satin ribbon. A full, A-line skirt, a narrow hem adorned with rhinestones.

Or are those diamonds? I've never worn anything like this in my life.

I let the plastic drop. My eyes fall on a few shoe boxes, each labeled in my size, and a hanger featuring the sweetest little handbag with a rhinestone clasp that matches the hem of my dress.

I'll feel like a princess tonight.

No, not a princess.

A *queen.*

An elegant, sophisticated queen.

But for now, I'm just Aria, certified hacker.

I hear Mikhail's footsteps. I join him in the room.

"That dress is stunning," I tell him as I climb back into the bed.

"Mm," he says with pursed lips. "If you go tonight. Let's make sure you are well."

I prop myself up on pillows and notice the wooden tray with tea and snacks on the bedside table. He had his staff bring them up. I swallow the lump in my throat.

"I should be fine. I really think it was just something I ate."

"Or," he says, lifting a brow at me. "It's just too early to test, like Polina suggested."

Why do I always forget he has access to my phone and reads my texts? I stifle a grumble.

"Right."

Is it, though? I don't want to think about that. Right now, I don't have any reason to believe I'm pregnant, and I'm perfectly fine with that. There's no positive test.

It's a bug. Something I ate. Hormones. Whatever.

"You have a job for me to do today?" I ask hopefully. In the past week or so he's given me various tasks to do. It's the highlight of my day, using my skills, even if what we do isn't exactly...well, legal.

"Yes, and it's time sensitive."

I fist pump. My *favorite*.

"I'd like you to find your way into border security. We have a shipment of goods coming in from Canada, costly merchandise we need for tonight's gala — rare artwork we are planning to auction. Should've arrived three days ago, but border agents found out they were being delivered to us in The Cove and they're being dicks about it."

I rub my hands together gleefully. "Oh, yeah," I say with a little chuckle. "That's what I'm talking about."

A corner of Mikhail's lips quirks up. "You're beautiful when you're in your evil genius mode."

I wave a hand at him, though my heart does a quick little thump of approval. "You say that about everything."

Leaning in, he captures the back of my neck and brings my mouth to his with a sensual kiss that makes my toes curl. I soften against him and sigh. It's not fair how quickly he does that to me.

"That's because it's true," he whispers in my ear before planting another kiss to the top of my head. "I'll be in the office. Aleks is downstairs to detail an attempted cyberattack from some of our rivals."

"Oh?" I ask with feigned nonchalance. Aleks and I do not get along. "Send him up if he wants a few lessons."

"Aria," Mikhail warns.

I blow out a breath. "Fine. I'll play nice. Go ahead, go soothe his ego while I get the real work done."

"Behave yourself," he warns as the door shuts behind him.

I quickly forget his admonition and my nausea and fears when I open up the laptop and come alive. This is where I shine.

I happily tap away, secure that I'm not being watched by anyone but him because of his excellent firewall and setup. It cost big bucks to get me this souped-up laptop, but it's a rounding error for him. Mere pocket change. My fingers dance over the keyboard so I can secure this shipment in time.

No one dicks around with my husband.

"One more...there we go...yeppers." *Boom.*

The digital access to border security appears on the screen. A wave of nausea hits me, and I automatically grab a square of toast and sip the tea he left me. Oh, nice. Spicy and a little sweet. Ginger?

"There we go, suckers," I say gleefully to myself. "That didn't take long at all. You guys really need to up your game."

Right in front of me I have access to everything — security cameras and electronic locks, a list of all imports and exports and addresses for where they're going. Personnel names and shifts.

Perfect.

Evil genius mode.

Who knew he had a sense of humor?

I smile to myself when another wave of nausea hits. I absentmindedly eat the food and drink the tea until it's gone while I navigate my way around as if I belong here. "There we go. Come to mama, baby," I whisper, as I navigate through the layers of safety protocols with ease. Firewalls and encryption barriers? *Zing.* See ya. I screw my face up in concentration as I look from one thing to the next.

Surveillance cameras are going down first. My fingers fly over the keyboard as I look for any hole in their armor, a vulnerable entryway for me to get into their camera systems and make sure I—

"Oooh, yeah," I say, like a teen furiously killing aliens in a game. "*Pew, pew, pew!*" I take them out one at a time.

I don't have audio access to the main guard station but can see the looks of consternation on their faces. That's right, boys.

What happened to your little security cameras? *I* happened to them. That's what you get for fucking around with my husband. If Mikhail Romanov wants to auction expensive, rare artwork so he looks like a philanthropist? That's what he does.

While they're likely occupied bringing the cameras back online for everything that's literally right in front of their faces, I move toward the electronic lock system.

Plink.

Plink.

Plink.

It's easy enough to do this remotely, as well.

Next up, I override their internal texting system and have a little fun. I give one of them the day off. Tell the second there's been a mistake and all held cargo will move ahead double speed because they were delayed. And the third's sent to do some busywork sweeping a holding cell near the main office.

"You didn't even hear me come in."

I nearly jump out of my skin to see Mikhail and Aleks standing in the doorway. Aleks, his hands shoved in his pockets, jerks his chin at me in greeting. He doesn't dare mistreat me in front of his brother, but I know he's seething below the surface.

"I was concentrating. Maybe you could knock or something to pull me out of evil genius mode."

Mikhail gestures toward his phone and narrows his eyes, a warning to watch my tone of voice. I shiver, suddenly aware of how hot he looks when he's staring at me like that.

"I could. Or you could answer your phone."

I swallow and nod. Yep. Yes, I could.

"I was catching Aleks up to speed but before I do, how are you feeling?"

"Much better." I gesture to the empty tray. "See? It must've been that food we ordered."

Mikhail scowls, unconvinced.

"What did you order?" Aleks asks Mikhail, not looking at me, of course, but at him.

"Moscow Morsels," he mutters.

"I'm telling you, those blinis were terrible. I swear they cook them from frozen," I chime in.

Aleks shakes his head. "They're the worst there." We suddenly realize we're agreeing on something.

I turn away. *Hmph.*

Still, a part of me remembers what Polina said about testing for pregnancy...

"Have you made any progress?"

I snort. "Have I made any progress? You bet your ass I have."

Mikhail gives me "the look" with a hint of a smirk. A warning. Not exactly a curse but I'm close.

I look at him with wide-eyed innocence. "I mean yes, sir, *of course* I have."

Aleks seems to forgive me momentarily. "Fill us in?"

I quickly tell them the progress I've made.

"It would be a lot easier if only I could hear what they were saying. I'm right there, right on the cusp of getting your shipment expedited but it's a bit tricky."

Aleks's eyes gleam. "I know exactly how we can hear inside."

Hmm. I'm not jealous at all. I narrow my eyes at him. "Yeah? Tell me."

"May I?" He gestures toward my laptop.

"No one touches my laptop." I glare at him. "Tell me."

Mikhail nods, so Aleks tells me, even though he's obviously not too pleased about it. "Voice over Internet Protocol. We intercept VoIP traffic and —"

"I thought of that," I interrupt impatiently. "We don't have time for that."

His lips thin. "Have you found any vulnerable devices? Security camera with a microphone, unsecured smart phones?"

He has a fair point. "Maybe not fully," I admit. Maybe not at all?

"I'd start there."

I'm already on it. In seconds, I've located *Jim's iPhone,* wide open for all to see. I quickly enable the audio function and hit the speaker volume on my laptop. I can hear them as well as if I were standing in the room next to them.

Point one for Aleks, but I won't admit it.

"Something's not right here," one of the voices says. "We should be able to access all video footage, and it seems…"

Their voices get jumbled for a moment.

"Our ten o'clock hasn't arrived."

I put my hand over the speaker. "Their ten o'clock hasn't arrived because I hacked their texting system and gave him the day off."

Aleks looks impressed. Mikhail, however, gives me a wary look and pulls out his phone.

"Relax," Aleks says, waving off Mikhail. "I have a firewall and MFA installed so no one can access our lines."

"MFA?" Mikhail shakes his head.

"Multi-factor authentication," Aleks and I say in unison. He glares. I narrow my eyes at him. Not sure if now's the time to demonstrate I can totally get by his firewall and MFA?

"You should conduct more frequent penetration testing," I tell him.

"Oh for fuck's sake, the network segmentation covers that," Aleks says with a near-growl.

"Hmm," I say, stroking my chin. I lift my phone. "Are you sure about that?"

Mikhail looks from me to him. "I can't tell if you two are getting along or fighting."

"Neither," we say, again in unison.

Aleks crosses his arms across his chest. "What's your favorite scripting language for penetration testing?"

"Can you stop saying *penetration*?" Mikhail mutters but I'm already thinking.

"God, that's a hard one. Ruby's a fave, but Python..."

"Infinitely more readable minus the simplicity of Ruby," he supplies.

"Mmm." I'm starting to warm up to him, but he can answer a question of mine now. "Best way to handle the aftermath of a data breach and compromised system?"

"Murder and bloodshed, obviously," he says with a shrug of his shoulders.

I laugh out loud. "You are so brothers. Okay, so murder and bloodshed aren't my methods, but of course they would be yours, after you lock down encrypted data and issue an alert. Real question. Protocol for if and when you encounter a WAF and have you ever successfully bypassed it?"

"Web Application Firewall," he says to Mikhail. "And yes, of course I have. My methods have, in the past, involved evasion through encoding and protocol tunneling, but there's no goddamn way I'm going to give you details on anything else."

"Hmm. Touché."

Apparently *Aleks* doesn't get in trouble for swearing. That is so unfair.

Mikhail crosses his arms on his chest so they now very much look exactly like brothers.

My computer dings. I pump the air.

"Your shipment is on the way via expedited shipping and will arrive on time. Your name is Gladys Anderson and you're a multi-billionaire old lady, if anyone asks."

Aleks snorts. "She got one right."

Mikhail reaches for my chin and cups it. "Well done, little hacker," he says. My chest warms at his praise even as my mind does a somersault.

Multi-billionaire?

God.

Mikhail's phone rings. Silencing it, he starts to shove it into his pocket when it rings again. He exchanges a look with Aleks.

What's going on?

Mikhail blows out a breath and answers the phone. "What?" He listens, his eyes darkening. "I'll handle it."

He'll handle...what?

CHAPTER TWENTY-ONE

Mikhail

I WATCH my wife get ready for our gala, a bit stunned that she's mine. I stare at her from a distance, sitting in my desk chair while she puts the finishing touches on her makeup.

Is she pregnant? I don't know, but I hope that it's just a matter of time.

It's not just that I need to secure my place as *pakhan* of the Romanov Bratva. It's so much more than that.

I want to solidify my relationship with the only woman I have ever loved. I need to make sure my family is secure, and establishing ourselves as a family unit with a solid footing in this world is the easiest way to do just that.

"You are a million miles away, Mikhail," Aria says with a twinkle in her eyes. The nausea from this morning has abated, due in no small part to her ability to spar with Aleks. He is excellent at what he does.

She's better.

Aria comes alive under the light of a monitor, her fingers flying as if she's dancing. She circumvents every firewall, every safety mechanism in place until she gets what we need.

If the FBI knew about a woman like her, they would pay top dollar to secure her. Or put her in jail.

But Aria Romanov is mine.

Finally, she places her lipstick on the vanity I've installed in here for her and walks over gracefully to me like a satisfied kitten ready to purr. I reach my hand to the back of her neck and bring her mouth to mine while I hold her body to me.

"Lipthtick," she mutters though her eyes twinkle at me. "Do you really want *Pretty in Pink* smeared all over those lips?"

I shrug and drag a lazy hand across my lips. "Take a part of you with me? Of course."

She places her hand on my shaven jaw, holding my eyes with hers.

"Listen, I know that we're basically swimming with sharks tonight. I further know that I'm basically diving in there with fresh blood on me. I know that they're prepared to attack, but I further know that you," she reaches for my tie and adjusts it just so, "will do everything within your power to stop anyone from hurting me." She holds her head high. "Let's show them who we are."

Pride surges through me and I press her to me. I don't want to let her go.

"The hair! First the lipstick and now the hair!"

I let her go with a teasing smack to the ass. "You're beautiful. Let them see smeared lipstick and mussed up hair and know you're mine."

I like to think we're untouchable, but past experience has taught me well. Still, I spin her around and place her in front of me, so we stand in front of the mirrored doors to the closet. Me, much taller than her, dressed in formal attire that I hate. My queen, dressed in luxurious black satin.

"They will weep with jealousy when they see you." And weep with pain if they so much as give her a dirty look.

The entire way to the gala, Aria chats excitedly about what she discovered today. It turns out being friends with my brother actually comes in handy. "I had no idea there was a potential entry point for exportation with that new software the government installed," she says, her eyes gleaming, as if someone just told her the best news she's ever heard in her life. "Do you have any idea what this means?"

Yes, of course I do. It means that she's going to be able to hack into more databases than we ever have, securing information for my family that we need. "Do you know what would be the funniest thing in the world? A CTF competition, with me and Aleks and whoever else you have."

"Aria, what the hell is a CTF competition?"

"Capture the flag. Honestly, Mikhail, do you know *nothing* about hacking?"

"Do you know nothing of the Russian language? My knowledge about hacking is about the same."

She gives me a smug little smile. *"Zdravstvuyte! Kak dela?* I've been practicing."

Sassy little girl.

When we arrive, Nikko's waiting outside with a joint pressed to his lips. He throws it on the ground and grinds it out with his heel when he sees me coming. While I don't forbid them smoking pot, I don't encourage it. Not when there's so much at stake. Tonight? I might ask him if he has another.

"Tell me again who that is," she says. "I remember everybody's names, and I do remember their jobs, but I need a refresher."

Is my little hacker wife admitting that there's a flaw to her perfect recall memory? She was under stress the last time she met everybody, when we were all together anyway. It was weeks ago at our wedding.

Nikko is our family assassin, but she doesn't need to know that.

"Nikko," I say affectionately. "When we were in high school, they joked that he looked like Superman."

"It's those rugged, boy-next-door good looks. I bet that comes in handy."

Sharp jawline, piercing eyes, tousled hair. What those girls who swooned over Nikko didn't know was how lethal he is when it comes to a hired hit.

"You know Aleks. And Lev." Lev often helps us because he's our team strategist. My youngest brother is also a trained fighter. With his athletic build, he's the one we send in to maneuver through tricky situations and defend himself if needed. He's confident, with a magnetic presence that women everywhere swoon over. He never dates, though. He's too occupied with other things.

"Do you member Kolya?"

"Of course I do. Your father's buddy, right? The older guy?"

He would cringe to hear her call him the "older guy." He's only fifty years old, but he's the only one with silver in his hair and beard, and he's more fit than men half his age. More like an older brother than father figure to any of us, our group mastermind oversees all operations.

"Who's the one that's always wearing leather, with those green eyes?"

"Ollie." We sometimes call him "The Lone Wolf" because of the wolf tattoo on his shoulder and his propensity for doing things alone. He likes to be alone.

"OK, so far we have Ollie, the lone one in leather, Nikko the scary weapon guy. And then there's the younger one, Lev, who looks like he power lifts on lunch breaks. He's the one that picked us up on our wedding night. Kolya, your dad's war buddy. Aleksandr, Polina, and your mother. What should I call her?"

"Ekaterina."

"Wow, that's a beautiful name. But you have one more brother, don't you?"

"Viktor. You've only met him once, at the wedding. The one with the scar on his cheek? Shaved head?"

"Ah, yes. I didn't think anybody was scarier than you, Mikhail, but he has you beat."

"Is that right? Is this a test? Do you need a demonstration?"

I love that shy little look she gives me. "It's just that scar on his cheek. Oh, and the fact that he's always wearing that black leather jacket. He's easily fifty pounds heavier than you, and he doesn't mind carrying weapons everywhere he goes. People scatter like scared little mice in his wake. What's his nickname?"

"The Iron Fist."

"You guys seriously do not fu – mess around, do you?"

I shake my head when we pull up to my childhood home, where my mother's hosting the gala.

This is the first gala we've ever hosted here in the absence of my father. No wonder my mother is so worried.

"You didn't tell me she lived in Manhattan! This place is beautiful." Her eyes shine as she takes it all in. It's a wintry feast for the eyes with ice sculptures showcased with spotlights and a well-kept winter garden. I happen to know for a fact that my mother and Polina have been hard at work making sure every single detail was perfect before tonight's event.

"Show me around?"

"Of course."

But before we even make it inside, a silver limo pulls up right beside me. *Jesus Christ.*

"Lemme guess," she says with a sour look on her face. "Volkov. I can tell just by the way your eyes look murderous."

"I also don't need to tell you not to look at him, or talk to him," I say, in a low, warning voice. "Right?"

"Yeah, definitely not."

Before we got here, I got a message from Lev detailing how he knows Volkov suspects that I am trying to get my new wife pregnant. Apparently, he's put bugs in place at every local OB's office, and even made sure that pharmacies that sell pregnancy tests are out of stock. Volkov's aging tendencies are beginning to show. First of all, we're not meeting an OB at any old office. And I would never buy a test from a fucking pharmacy.

Most importantly, though, he has to know that my wife *is* going to carry my baby, and there's nothing he can do about it. I've warned him, and he knows better than to cross me.

"Good evening, Mikhail." His oily voice mars the crisp evening air. I take Aria and hold her to my side.

"What have we here? Your beautiful wife. I have to admit, I didn't think she'd marry someone like you." He gives Aria a sardonic grin. "How much did he pay you, beautiful?"

"Ignore him," I say through clenched teeth, noting the pink flare of heat on Aria's cheeks. She turns away from him with a haughty expression on her face and begins to walk away.

"Don't you dare turn your back on me," Volkov snaps. "It seems Mikhail hasn't taught you manners."

In three steps I'm in his space, my hand wrapped around his scrawny neck. Three of his guards immediately come after me, when my brothers step out of the shadows.

Nikko holds a wicked blade. Lev, a pistol. Viktor stands with a towering presence, daring anyone to start something the night of the gala. He needs no weapons. I continue to hold Volkov by the throat and press him against his limo.

"I warned you, old man. You'll speak with respect to my wife. I don't care who you are, if you talk to her again tonight, you're going down. If your men try to defend you, we'll have a battle on our hands. Do you really want to do that right now?"

This gala is the Romanov family's night. If his family causes a scene at this event, it will have the exact opposite effect on the local people that us hosting it has. Where others see us as philanthropists, keystone members of the community, if he does anything to start violence against us, he will be blackballed and ostracized from the community.

There is only so much that money can buy.

He practically spits fire at me but doesn't respond. I continue. "The only olive branch you're getting is the fact that you're still breathing. Do you really want to play this card? So soon?"

This man is responsible for my father's death. This man made any woman who came near me a target. I know for a fact that he'll stop at nothing to hurt Aria, or our unborn child. I need to stop that before he even gets one toe in the door.

Other guests begin to arrive in limos and armored SUVs. There's a rush of dresses, the click of high heels, the scent of luxury in the air when I finally let Volkov go. He shrugs me off and brushes his clothes, as if removing any fragments of dust that cling to him from my hands.

Soon, I've forgotten Volkov and his insidious presence when I bring Aria to my mother. My mother glides across the ballroom effortlessly, engaging in conversation with anyone and everyone. Every time she sees Aria, she smiles, and at one point she blows a kiss at her.

"Okay, I love your mom." She eyes the wine on the table and then decides instead to drink water.

"Champagne, madam?"

She shakes her head, and I hold her champagne in my hand.

"The shipments have arrived," Lev says in my ear. Perfect. Aria's plan worked.

I turn to tell Aria when I realize she's doubled over in her seat, clutching her abdomen.

"What is it, baby? Are you alright?"

She shakes her head.

"Poor baby," a cold voice says over my shoulder. "Was it something she drank? Or something she ate?"

I have to ignore Volkov to tend to her. Her face is pale and she's in obvious distress.

"Something's wrong," she says in a whisper of a voice.

"Polina!" I hail my sister from across the room. She stares at me when she hears my tone. All eyes in the room come to me but I don't care. Polina runs to me in a rush of shimmery silver clothes.

"She said she's sick. What's going on?" Polina bends down and whispers to Aria. Aria clutches her abdomen. I've never felt so helpless in my life. Polina puts a hand to her head and asks her a few questions.

"Call an ambulance, Mikhail," Polina says quietly. "She needs to be seen immediately." She's kneeling beside my sister, her normally pale face even whiter than usual. She holds her hand. "Now."

CHAPTER TWENTY-TWO

Aria

"MIKHAIL, PLEASE. SIT DOWN."

I sip the glass of water Polina gave me and wish she could talk some sense into him. He's been ranting and raving and insisting on attention since we got in here.

"What's fucking taking them so long?"

Polina shakes her head. "Aria isn't the only patient. You threatening the doctors isn't going to make her better anytime soon."

Still, I can't help but find it a little bit endearing.

"That guy at the nurse's station? He decided he was going to eat dinner. Dinner — when my wife could be in danger. I saw him leave and come back with food!"

Polina's lips twitch, and her eyes quickly come to mine before returning to him. "A doctor is allowed to take a break,

Mikhail, especially when it's not an emergency. And Aria's stable and fine."

He might be complaining, but there are six doctors in the hallway and four nurses in the room with me. When a Romanov comes into the ER, it's all-hands-on-deck. They've been practically rolling out the red carpet since we got here. I don't blame them, really, Mikhail's as volatile as a ticking time bomb.

"You look familiar," one nurse says with a smile to Polina, probably trying to ease the tension in the room.

"I was in here recently. I had a clinical."

The nurse's eyes widen comically. She's just realized that Mikhail Romanov's sister is going into nursing. I don't blame her. This could mean a lot of things for the staff here.

I put a tentative hand out to her. "He can be really nice when he wants to be," I say quietly.

The nurse laughs. "I'm sure he can," she replies before she pats my arm. "He's not the first overprotective husband I've met."

Do I enjoy his overprotectiveness? Yeah, I think I do.

"The small talk is great," Mikhail says, his attempt at calming himself down laughable. "But where is the doctor? We're not getting anywhere."

"We are, sir," the nurse says with a placating smile. "We've ruled out poisoning, as you suspected. We've also ruled out abdominal distress. The doctor will be in momentarily to explain what's happening."

Of course, my husband immediately thought Volkov was responsible for my illness. Who could blame him? But I only ate the food Ekatarina herself gave me, and I've been socializing so much that I barely ate.

The doctor walks into the room, a tall, black woman with thick hair in a knot at the nape of her neck. She sees Mikhail and smiles. "Mr. Romanov, I believe we've met before?"

Mikhail audibly sighs in relief. "Thank fuck. Someone I can trust."

The doctor raises an eyebrow. "Language, Mr. Romanov. This is a family practice here. We see children on the same floor as adults."

Mikhail gives her a sheepish look. "I'm sorry." Polina and I look at each other. Someone giving my husband a dressing down? I need her name and number.

"I don't often get to say this in a situation like this, but I have good news." She smiles.

Mikhail stands by my side and holds my hand, looking positively stricken. God, the poor man. He's seen his father die, and I happen to know that he witnessed severe casualties when he was enlisted. I also know he was engaged before me, and the woman he was engaged to ended up mysteriously dead. It seems almost everyone in his life who mattered to him has been killed, so I don't really half blame him for being out of his mind right now.

"I could use some good news," he says on a growl. "What is it?"

"Your wife is having a baby." She smiles at me. I stare back at her.

A baby.

Mikhail stares at her, a dazed look coming over his face, another rarity.

I swear, for one second, I'm afraid he's going to cry. My husband — the most formidable person I've ever met in my life. Crying.

It makes tears spring to my own eyes, and a lump form in my throat. I feared this, even half hoped for it, but now that I have the confirmation, I'm not so sure how I feel.

"Then why the pain? Why the bleeding?"

"It's nothing to fear, Mrs. Romanov. You have what we call a subchorionic hematoma. It's a collection of blood between the uterine wall and the fetal membrane, honestly, pretty common during pregnancy. Sometimes it does cause abdominal pain, and it does cause bleeding, but it almost always resolves itself on its own without harming you or the baby. We'll have to monitor you closely to make sure everything progresses as it should, but I have no doubt you'll be in excellent hands." She nods to Polina and Mikhail.

She's not wrong. He may have the family doctor move in with us.

"Thank you."

Mikhail pales. He swallows and licks his lips, and when he speaks, his voice is a little husky. "So my wife and the baby are okay?" She nods and gives him a few more words of assurance. "There may be some discomfort, and I'll provide some recommendations, but she should be fine."

Now that Mikhail realizes that we're safe, the tension in the room finally lets up. He leans over and holds me.

"I'm sorry, doctor. I know I overreacted."

And now another apology? They say men don't change, but...

She waves a hand in the air. "I understand your concern."

As the doctor talks to Polina and Mikhail, I lay my head back on the pillow. I'm tired after the events of tonight. And honestly? Relieved that it wasn't something stupid Volkov's men did. I don't want to see my Mikhail preoccupied with revenge.

On the way back home, though, I start to freak out.

I'm...pregnant. I'm having a baby. I'm not ready for this. It's not just that I'm afraid I won't be a good enough mother, it's that I'm taking a whole other step of intimacy with Mikhail.

I feel like even though I've gotten to know him a lot better, we still have so much to learn about each other. And it's absolutely terrifying to me to imagine raising a child in this atmosphere. In this family. What if I don't want a baby?

I'm quiet on the ride home. I already feel like I am taking a next step I'm not ready for.

But my biggest fear of all? What if he only wants to be with me so I can be his baby mama? What if I am not enough?

My entire life, I've battled a fear of not being enough. And now, I'm nothing more than a woman who will bear his child.

But when we get back to the house, I have my doubts. Mikhail leads me in with such tender care, I can't help but feel maybe he really does love me.

When I first got here, I feared falling in love with the man that had captured me. But now that I know who that man is, a part of me – a very small part of me – can't really imagine being in love with anybody else. After truly experiencing the full blaze of a heated sun, I can't go back to the shade of who I was before. I might be burned standing next to my Mikhail Romanov, but I couldn't imagine my life any other way.

I take Mikhail's hand when he reaches for me. He leads me up to our house – our house, not just his – and brings me inside. I laugh when he helps me over the threshold.

"OK, Mikhail, when I am like nine months pregnant and huge, maybe then you can help me over the threshold or help me tie my shoelaces or whatever you need to do. But right now? I'm fine. Please."

"Just because you're pregnant doesn't mean that I'll take it any easier on you," he says with what is an attempt at a stern look, but he's definitely bluffing.

"Hmph."

"Are you hungry?"

Polina got me a candy bar from the vending machine in the hallway at the hospital, and while it was a quick fix to give me energy then, now I'm starving.

"Any cravings? Aversions?" he asks.

Okay, so he's being about as cute as Mikhail gets. "Um, I've barely wrapped my mind around the possibility of me being pregnant, and I don't know if I've quite gotten to the cravings or aversions part." I shudder. "Definitely *not* Moscow Morsels."

He grins. Actually grins, and it's so rare I let myself stare at him, fusing it into my memory for the next time he goes all overbearing asshole on me.

Maybe I am craving something. Something deliciously cheesy and crispy on the edges. My mouth waters. "Pizza sounds excellent right now."

"Good as done. Go lie down. I'll order the food, and I'll join you in a minute."

When we get to our bedroom, I kick off my shoes. He stands behind me and silently unzips my dress. When he bares my shoulder to him, he bends and places a kiss right there. Then he walks away toward the bathroom, still talking.

"I'll have to assemble a team of bodyguards to make sure that you're safe."

"Mikhail? I already have a team of highly trained bodyguards!"

He pierces me with a stern look and raises an eyebrow at me. "Are you talking back to me?"

My heart immediately thumps. Even pregnant, I have no doubt that he will still demand obedience and respect. He hasn't gotten a personality transplant, after all.

"I will stop at nothing, Aria. Fucking nothing to make sure that you and our baby are safe."

"I know you will. That's who you are. That's what you do."

He's experienced grave loss in his life, and he's dedicated to making sure it doesn't happen again. It's more than that, though. I remember what Polina told me about his having to marry, securing his family. I remember him telling me that my duty to him was to bear his child.

There's something more at play here. But tonight, I don't care.

Tonight I want pizza and a good night's sleep.

"I'm building you a safe room," he says over the sound of running water.

What is he doing in there? Drawing a bath?

"I'll have surveillance cameras and reinforced walls, so if there's any type of threat, you retreat there."

His home is already an absolute bastion of safety. But whatever floats his boat.

"Alright, honey," I say on a yawn.

When I'm in bed, I'm thinking over how quickly things can change. This morning, I was convinced I had food poisoning. Tonight, I was convinced Volkov poisoned me, and now, I know that one of my greatest fears has actually come true.

I'm pregnant. There's a baby knitting in my womb at this very minute and my overprotective husband is going to lose his *mind*.

I lie against the pile of pillows in bed and note that I'm practically floating on them.

"Mikhail? Are there more pillows in here?"

"Of course," he says over his shoulder, his accent thickening. "I called ahead of time and made sure staff put everything you need in here. There's a body pillow, pregnancy pillows, blankets if you need them, and a call button next to the bed if for some strange reason I'm not here and you need anything else."

Okay, so now he's getting out of control. But for now, I'm not going to argue because these pillows are quite nice.

"You move fast," I say with appreciation.

He shrugs. "It's what I do. What kind of pizza do you want, my love?" he asks from the bathroom. The scent of lavender fills the air. It smells so nice.

"Wherever you got that thin-crust one with the really crispy edges. Pepperoni, please."

"Anything else?"

"My husband here so I can snuggle with him a little bit?" I ask, testing the waters. He peers in the doorway, a boyish smile on his face, his hands anchored on his hips.

"A snuggle? Do I really look like the type that will snuggle?"

He is absolutely the type that will snuggle, we just can't admit that out loud.

He walks over to me, holding my gaze the entire time, and my heart does a somersault in my chest. When he comes to the bed, he leans down and kisses me. Unlike the usual kiss he gives me, with his hand gripping my neck and my entire body suffused in sensuality, this is a gentle kiss. Just a brush of his lips to mine.

"First, a bath. I want to erase the memory of tonight from your mind and mine." His voice has softened. What will fatherhood do to Mikhail Romanov?

I feared that I would fall for him, and now...

I love this man.

The realization doesn't shock me, as I'd think it would, because I've known for a little while now. I don't do anything in halfsies, and neither does he. My commitment to him, the intimacy we've forged under fire, the knowledge that who I am matters to him — all of it. I've not only fallen head over heels in love with a criminal...I'm having his baby.

I can't think of that now.

"Bath sounds quite nice, provided it's followed with—"

"Pizza. I know. It's already on its way, my love."

My love. It's new, this little endearment. And he also has little Russian phrases for me. I kind of miss *little hacker*.

The oversized tub is filled about halfway with suds and steam that smells like lavender. I sink under the hot water, submerging myself fully to my chin. "Are you going to join me?"

"You think I want to smell like lavender?" he asks, crouching beside the tub.

"As if you care. Ha!"

He smiles at me and tweaks a lock of damp hair. "I have a few things to do. I'll join you for pizza."

I hear him on the phone in the other room. He's making lists, barking out commands to his team, likely his brothers.

I don't exactly know what he's doing right now, but I hear the phrase, "the best doctors possible," and another phrase, "research the safest equipment." Equipment? I sink under the bubbles for a few seconds. When I come to the surface, my Mikhail is still talking on the phone.

I lie in billows of scented bubbles until I hear a knock on the door. "Our pizza has arrived."

Mikhail helps me out of the bath and towels me off. By now I am used to the way he likes to take care of me, as long as I know I can also take care of myself.

"You can have whatever you want, Aria," he says as he leads me to bed. "But I do have a team putting together the best dietary plans for a pregnant woman as well. I will make sure that our chef has everything that you need prepared."

I smile. "You're sweet."

He makes a face like he just ate rotten fruit. "I'm not sweet. Are you crazy?"

"You're right. You're definitely not sweet as a personality trait. But this is adorable."

He scowls at me. "Call me cute or sweet or adorable again and see what happens."

"You'd punish a pregnant woman?"

He holds my gaze for a heated beat. "Absolutely."

My heart flips.

When I stare at him with that sexy rush of panic I get when he threatens me, he finally laughs.

He has the nerve to *laugh.*

"What?" I ask.

"Time for pizza, little hacker."

I release a breath I didn't realize I was holding. I needed to hear him call me *little hacker* again. I probably need him to take me over his knee, too, because I need some normalcy in my life when everything else is a swirl of confusion and fear.

But with the smell of pizza in the room, I can think of nothing else.

We eat crispy pizza on paper plates and talk about the party. "How did it go? Did they auction everything off?"

"Absolutely. My mother doesn't let anything ruffle her. She made sure the auction still happened and they earned five point two million for the children's hospital."

I whistle. "Wow, that's amazing. The Romanov Philanthropists it is, then."

He winks at me and takes the crust I tossed into the pizza box. He eats it in one bite. "Exactly."

"And did Volkov pull any more asshole tricks?"

"Of course, but nothing my brothers couldn't handle."

I take another slice of pizza. "I don't know if I've ever hated anyone, but he's definitely on the list."

"He's a man worthy of your hate, Aria."

"Do you think he'll leave us alone now that you've threatened him?"

He shakes his head. "No. You're in the worst danger of all now."

CHAPTER TWENTY-THREE

Mikhail

I HOLD her until she falls asleep. Aria is in greater danger than she's ever been. Not only have we outed her to our enemies just by showing up at the gala last night, but she's pregnant. And unlike our original plan of finding out about her pregnancy in private, I took her to a hospital.

Volkov will have his revenge.

When she brings our child into this world, Volkov's world is effectively over.

I lie beside her. Part of me wants to get out of bed and go to my piano. Being alone in my sanctuary, creating music under my hands, is sometimes the only way to soothe my nerves. Sometimes, it's the only way to feel emotion.

At least, until Aria.

But I will not leave her side. She will be glued to me whether she likes it or not for the next nine months. Yes, I'll have a security team on her. I'll have several. Yes, I'll have safety protocols put in place. But I told her that I would be her armor, and I meant that.

I mutter to myself for trying to remember what she said about crushing candy on an app. Turns out there are lots of apps where you can crush candy. It's not as relaxing to me as playing the piano, but I play the game until my eyelids grow heavy.

I'm dragged out of a sound sleep the next morning with the sound of my phone ringing.

I have it on "Do Not Disturb" when sleeping, but three phone calls in succession removes that. My brothers know to do that only in an emergency situation.

Aria is still sleeping beside me. I move as quietly as I can, take my phone, and go to the bathroom, where I can take the call in private without waking her.

"What is it?"

"We intercepted an attack on our family home last night," Nikko says.

"Who did? Tell me everything."

"Viktor and I did. We were with Mother, cleaning up. Staff was dismissed, security still in place. Polina was with you at the hospital. Everything seemed fine, but Viktor had a suspicion something was wrong."

Volkov. He will stop at nothing.

"What happened?"

"We swept the entire house. We found nothing, but Viktor didn't trust it. So he slept in the room adjacent to Mom's. We heard a scream and were in her room instantly. They were trying to abduct her, Mikhail."

"Who?"

"We haven't gotten them to tell us their identity yet." I'm already pulling on a pair of jeans. No. *Fuck.* I can't leave Aria's side, I won't.

"Where are you?"

"We have them in The Chamber."

"Any identifying marks?"

"Of course. They're marked Bratva."

When I threatened Volkov, he decided another insidious assault against my family was in order. If only I had the manpower, I would murder the man with my bare hands. He has too many allies and too many on his force. My brotherhood wouldn't stand the blowback. They would annihilate us.

But that doesn't mean we put up with this.

"I would come to you myself," I say, while peeking through the doorway at my sleeping wife. "But I will not leave Aria's side."

Loyalty to my wife and our future child means I may have tough choices to make.

"Tell me what's next?"

"We will interrogate. Permission to execute?"

"Only if you can't get answers out of them first. Send me footage. No, scratch that. I want a live feed. I want to feel like I'm there with you."

I will call the shots. Every blow. I want to account for every drop of blood and broken bone.

"Are you ready now? We're ready."

Nikko and Viktor haven't even slept, but that's how they are. Absolutely ruthless, dependable as fuck, as loyal as humanly possible.

"Who told you that she's pregnant?"

"You went to the emergency room, brother. Everyone knows."

Fuck.

Aria stirs in the other room, so I lower my voice.

"Show me."

"Stand by."

The camera pans to a wide-angle view of a room we call The Chamber. I can almost feel the chilly air and cold stone. The Chamber is a place for interrogation and execution, our take on a modern-day dungeon. Concrete is easier to clean than wood and doesn't get easily stained with blood.

The light is dim, reminiscent of an ancient dungeon with flickering torches. This is intentional. We want people who come here to be terrified. Terror is an excellent asset when you want answers.

There's a long, heavy table with high-backed chairs in the middle of the room. At the end of the room is a tiny, barred window that allows a sliver of sunlight but is impossible to exit.

All weapons are on clear display for Nikko. Lev is more likely to use psychological manipulation or deprivation, while Viktor chooses fists. Aleks is skilled at interrogation methods favored by Russian authorities. Unlike other methods of violence and intimidation, using observation and statements to elicit information gets him a long way, but he's far from above physical intimidation.

The Chamber is particularly structured to house a prisoner for a very long time.

The camera moves back to Aleks, sitting placidly at a table with his hands folded in front of him. He's dressed as if he's about to conduct a business meeting, wearing his signature black shirt and tie and slacks. But I recognize that cold, fierce determination in his eyes. Next, I see our prisoners – two men on the younger side, late twenties. They've already been beaten, now chained to the wall in front of us, their faces against the wall with their backs to the camera. Their bare backs and arms show markings of the Bratva.

"Gentlemen, it has come to our attention that you tried to kidnap my mother last night." Aleks's voice is ice-cold. "As you can imagine, I don't take too kindly to that, nor does my brother. You have forfeited your lives for an attempt of violence against my mother. But before we kill you, you'll give us what we ask for."

They are strategically placed in a stress position, arms just above comfortable so both are standing on their toes. Quietly, Viktor and Nikko enter the room.

Out of the corner of their eyes, with their peripheral vision, the prisoners can see my two brothers. One of them begins to tremble, the other stares stoically at the wall in front of him.

"We already know you work for Volkov," Aleks continues sternly. "We want you to tell us what you planned next."

They remain silent. A muscle twitches in Aleks's jaw.

"Nikko." It's then that I notice the small club-like bat in Nikko's fist. He takes a step toward each of them. I turn the volume down on my phone so Aria doesn't hear the sickening swish and thud of his weapon. The cries of pain of his victims. The sound of breaking bones and bruised flesh.

Nikko steps aside and casually wipes blood out of his eyes.

Aleks continues. "Anybody? Anyone want to offer information?"

They stare straight ahead. Aleks opens a slim silver laptop in front of him. "I've identified them both. Ilya on the left is a new recruit to Volkov, obviously, because he would've been more successful had he been more experienced. He has a wife and two small children."

Our prisoner stiffens in fear. "I'm confident you don't want to see your wife or children hurt, do you?"

Next, Aleks nods to Viktor. It's then that I notice the small device in Viktor's hand. He walks to the first man and presses it to his temple. He screams in pain from the electric shock. Aleks's voice is cold and confident.

"Tell us what the next move is."

I watch as neither one of the men move. The next is placed under the same electric shock treatment, but doesn't cave. Finally, one of them curses out in Russian, saying that he will never reveal anything even at the point of death.

Meanwhile, Nikko is sharpening a knife. He places it on the table in their peripheral vision.

Viktor speaks up, his deep voice booming in the enclosed area. "Allow me to explain what happens to people who cross the Romanovs. We will come after anyone and everyone you care about. They may die quietly, or they may be subject to a violent death. But make no mistake, they will die. We will find out where you live, and we will destroy it. We will find out everything that matters to you, from the smallest little puppy dog to the biggest truck that you drive, and we will destroy all of them. Nothing of who you are will remain."

"Viktor."

Aleks nods toward them.

I've had enough. I tap the button on my phone. This is child's play.

"Viktor, Nikko. They tried to take our mother. Uncuff them. Show them who you are." My voice is merciless. It is only out of love for my wife that I am not there exacting revenge with my own bare hands.

I steel myself against the sound of their pleas for mercy.

Viktor takes one and holds him up by the neck. "You had your hands on my mother. What happens in Volkov's family if someone touches one of his loved ones?" When he doesn't answer, Viktor drops him unceremoniously to the floor and kicks his ribs. "Tell me."

"He loses a hand," the man says. Viktor nods and takes the knife from Aleks. The man howls as they stretch his arm on the table in front of them.

"Mikhail?"

I silence my phone and place it face down on the vanity. I turn to her. "How did you sleep, my love?"

I have to trust that my brothers know what they're doing. What I would give to be there right now.

"I heard something disturbing. Someone screaming. What happened, Mikhail?"

She's standing by the side of the bed, looking pale.

"Someone tried to hurt my mother. They tried to take her last night. My brothers are finding out more information now."

Her expression turns pained. "Oh."

I don't give any more details, but I won't lie to her either. This is our life now.

"Are they hurting them?"

I take a step toward her and cup her face in the palm of my hand. "What would I do to someone that hurt you, Aria?"

Her voice is a whisper, but she doesn't look away. "I don't want to even think about that. But they would hurt. And likely not..." she swallows hard. "You know, like...make it."

I nod. "Come, sweet girl. Back into bed with you. Allow me to bring you breakfast. Don't think of those things, they don't matter right now."

I go back to my phone and see my text messages.

> **Aleks:** One caved. He's on the verge. Bleeding out on the floor now. Volkov knows about Aria's pregnancy. She and your home are the greatest risk right now.

Of course I assumed this would be true, but I'm grateful for the confirmation.

I send him a text back.

> As of today, I dismiss all of our staff. They will be under my payroll. I want no one but family at my house.

> That will be difficult, brother, but it must be done. Polina and mother?

> Everyone,

> They won't come easily,

I grit my teeth.

> Let me handle that. I'm getting a call from Kolya. Let me know what you get from the prisoners.

Within the hour, both of them will be dead. We will extract whatever we can from them before that happens.

I take the call from Kolya, walk to the bed, and run my hand along Aria's hair. I breathe more deeply. Her eyes close as I continue to brush through her hair with my fingertips.

"Hello?"

"Mikhail. A minute?"

"Hold please." I mute the phone and turn to my bride. "How are you feeling? Are you nauseous?"

She nods. "Yes, not as bad as yesterday. I was afraid that pizza wouldn't sit too well, but apparently our baby likes pizza. Do we have any left? For breakfast?"

I feel my brows pull together as I give her a curious look. "You want pizza for breakfast?"

She makes a face. "Only if it's cold. Not hot pizza. Can you do that?"

Cold pizza. "Yes. Anything you want, Aria. Just a moment." I send a text to my staff. I'll get the pizza delivered before I dismiss everyone. None of them will come back.

I sit on the bed next to Aria and rub her back. She gestures that she needs to use the bathroom, so I walk with her.

"I'm back."

"Mikhail," she whispers. "You can't come with me to the bathroom. I need to pee."

I clench my jaw and gesture for her to leave the door partially open.

She gives me a strange look but does what I say, as I take the call from Kolya.

"I had coffee with Volkov himself this morning."

"Did you? Playing good cop, bad cop again?" I cross my arms over my chest and watch for Aria as she washes her hands and begins brushing her teeth. She gags, and I throw the door open as Kolya continues.

"I'm fine," she whispers. "Might need cinnamon toothpaste..."

Kolya says, "There was a rumor that your mother was attacked last night. He's starting to crack, Mikhail. He's not in the right frame of mind. Nothing like he used to be."

Aria sticks her head out. "You alright?" I ask her in a gentle voice, covering the phone with my hand.

She shakes her head. "The toothpaste is disgusting. God."

Note to self: Get a different flavor toothpaste.

"How do you know? What do you mean?" I ask Kolya.

I help Aria back to bed.

"He began repeating words, over and over again, and some of the sentences he formed made no sense. He was completely incoherent at one point, and I had a difficult time following him. He repeated things that he already told me. He cannot recall some recent events or conversations that we had. I could even tell by the way he dressed himself, he has significant impairment of his cognitive and physical abilities."

Interesting. "This would explain why he's made advances on my family despite the fact that I'm married now."

"Precisely. We cannot assume that Volkov will obey our rules. You know that if we had passed the moratorium without you getting married, we would have been at risk.

But I'm telling you, we are at risk now. And if it's true he ordered an attack on your mother—"

"It is true. We just interrogated the intruders. It was his men that attacked."

Kolya is quiet for a minute. "You and Aria are in grave danger."

I quickly consider my options. With a snap of my fingers, I could command Nikko to assassinate Volkov. We could even make it look as if it were an accident, but right on the heels of the attack from his men, I don't trust the blowback to not be severe and annihilate us.

We could threaten him, but the same potential threat remains.

"He was confused, Mikhail. He called me Ilya several times. He was disoriented. And he made strange accusations. He's always been irritable, but this time it's much worse."

"I see."

"My suggestion is that we try to impair him in ways that are not as obvious. Psychological manipulation. A threat to his assets and safety."

"Aleks and Aria will be thrilled."

CHAPTER TWENTY-FOUR

Aria

I LIE AGAINST THE PILLOWS, my belly temporarily happy after breakfast. Mikhail brought me breakfast in bed this morning after promising to massage my feet with his strong, capable hands.

He does it every day.

"Why the feet? I asked him the other morning.

"I've heard that it is one of the best ways for someone to pamper a pregnant woman. Your feet get tired carrying the extra burden of a baby within you."

I moaned. He is excellent at this with those thick, strong fingers of his as he massages the achiness out of my feet.

"Mikhail, I'm not *that* far along."

I mean, aside from maybe a few extra pounds from the late-night pizza and fries I've been craving.

"Does that matter?" he said. I wondered why his accent was suddenly thicker. It's usually only this way when he feels emotional. I noticed a little furrow between his brows.

"Mikhail?"

"What?"

"Something's troubling you."

We've both been a little out of sorts with everything happening. While he's been very good to me for the past couple of weeks, taking care of all of my needs, spending every waking moment with me, he's also been hard at work with his brothers. I do catch wind of what they're talking about. There's some sort of rumor that Volkov has lost his mind, and his next attack on us could be unprecedented. There's even talk about Mikhail assassinating him, or having him assassinated.

I respect my husband's wishes and stay out of their online communications. Even though I *could* look into them if I wanted to.

Things have changed, though. The staff is no longer here, save one person his mother insisted on bringing from her own home, a woman who has stayed with them since their infancy. Mikhail says Yelena is like a second mother to them.

I like having Polina here, and his mother, of course. His brothers...that depends on which ones. Some are a little... friendlier than others.

But other things have changed, too.

For one, Mikhail has barely touched me. I shouldn't say that. He massages my feet and my back, but we haven't had sex in over a week, which is unheard of for us. The last time we had sex, I bled a little bit. According to my doctor, that's common for women in the first trimester. Their bodies are swollen in places they didn't even expect, and an ultrasound and some testing later showed that the baby is totally fine. But Mikhail hasn't really wanted to do anything since.

He's definitely not put me over his lap. He told me that he wouldn't hesitate to punish me, but now, I am not so sure.

I love being dominated by my husband. Whoever thought I would miss it?

I miss our intimacy.

"This is lovely," I say now, as the scent of lavender fills the air. He pours some lotion in the palm of his hand, rubs it between his palms to warm it, then applies it to the heels of my feet. "Mikhail, you need to stop treating me as if I'm going to shatter if you're too rough with me."

A beat passes before he responds. "I don't know what you're talking about."

"You know exactly what I'm talking about. Don't lie about it." I intentionally try to be a little rude, to ruffle him a little bit. He looks up at me from beneath lowered brows, stern. My heart does a little flip in my chest.

I lick my lips and swallow. Draw in a breath. "We need to have some fucking *sex*."

Yeah, I just said that. Even dropped the F bomb, which under normal circumstances would get my butt spanked. But now he only grumbles at me, the little rumble in his chest making my heart squeeze. And when he doesn't say anything else, I swallow the lump in my throat.

Why does it feel like rejection? It's strange.

"Don't try me, Aria. I'm doing my best here."

"Obviously you are. But we still are us, Mikhail. You've done everything, and I'm so grateful. Daily foot and back massages? Those love notes you leave me on my pillow when you walk across the room? Breakfast in bed? I mean, you had a tailor come out and help me pick out the most luxurious maternity wardrobe a mother can ask for. I know you're going above and beyond."

I play with the ring on my finger. "And I don't know what you're doing in the other room. But I suspect that also has something to do with me, and I'm excited about that. But I miss...us. That raw, primal thing we had going." A lump rises in my throat, and I try to clear it with no success. "I miss the tiger."

Every night I go to sleep, I can see the tattoo on the broad expanse of his back when he's lying on his belly, his hands tucked under his pillow. The tiger's eyes mock me now. I felt the bite of its claws so often, I long for it. And now...who would've thought I'd feel rejected because he's being too damn nice?

I kind of feel like a spoiled brat. I have a custom-made wardrobe behind those closet doors. A credit card with a ridiculous limit. I mean, does it even have a limit? Everything I could ask for, including the attention of the man that I love. Because yes, I know that I love him.

And while I'm not totally at peace with carrying his child? I'm telling myself I still have a good bit of time ahead of me. That's plenty of time to get used to the idea.

When I'm uncomfortable, he makes me comfortable. He has a team of doctors to take care of me and to monitor all of my symptoms. I have medication and Russian remedies for the nausea. He helps me sleep and holds me when I'm restless. Massages my back, and massages my feet.

But I crave more. I want *him*. I want a chance to reciprocate. I want the emotional connection.

I think what might be the most disconcerting part of all of this is knowing he's holding back from who he is. A tiger velveting his paws. I want to feel the bite of those paws again.

He gives me a curious look while concentrating on my feet.

"I don't want to hurt you. I don't want to hurt our son."

I guffaw out loud. "Oh no you don't. Who told you I'm having a son? Did you see some type of study or test that I haven't seen yet? Because as far as I know, this could be a girl. Maybe even two. "

I glare at him which only seems to amuse him. "You have many traditions in Russia."

"Traditions or superstitions? They're not the same."

Ignoring me, he continues. "Russian tradition says a man who has a firstborn son will be wealthy, and his son will rule with authority and integrity."

"But guess what, buddy. We aren't in Russia anymore. And while I may probably have some Russian DNA in me now that I'm actually bearing a Russian child, we're still American here. And here in America, both girls and boys are given equal opportunity."

It's our goal, anyway.

I try to cross my arms over my chest to make my point, but my breasts hurt today. That's when I see the twinkle in his eyes that goes with the twitching of his lips.

He is *so* giving me shit. I yank my feet away from him.

"You are so trying to fucking rile me up!"

His muscles clench; he really does hate when I swear.

"Are you really pushing the limits with me?"

"Of course I'm not," I lie. I'm not going to admit out loud that I actually want to go over his lap. Why would I do such a stupid thing?

He tips his head to the side, his tone dark and seductive when he insists, "You like it when I spank you."

I turn my head away. "Like punishment? You spank hard. Of course I don't like it."

I won't meet his eyes though.

He starts sliding his hands all over my body.

"You miss my dick."

"Is there some Russian superstition for that, too?"

He snorts. "Of course there is."

"Oh?" I say, as he bends his mouth to my neck and kisses me in that sweet, sweet spot, right between my chin and collarbone. I stifle a moan, because I don't want to give him the satisfaction.

"When I take you, superstition says that if you hear music, it's a good omen for our marriage. If rain begins when you climax, we will live long, fulfilling lives together. And the reason why I know you're giving birth to a son? We conceived on the full moon."

"Are you...mocking me right now?" The chuckle against my neck makes me shiver. He is so teasing me right now.

"Mikhail, you almost had me there."

While he holds me, the sun peeks from behind the clouds out the window, the direct opposite of a superstitious good luck rain. I don't believe in superstitions, but I can't help but wonder.

A knock sounds at the door.

"Who is it?" he barks.

"Polina. Don't try to bite my head off from behind the door. Jesus, Mikhail."

"What do you want?" he says in a voice that I know is trying to be a little gentler, but still sounds as if he's biting her head off.

"Mom wants you guys to come out here and come down to dinner. She says it's bad luck to spend so much time in a bedroom."

Mikhail smirks at me, as if underscoring the point that he's not the only one holding Russian superstitions in high regard.

"We'll be there! Don't listen to your brother."

He flashes his eyes at me. "Behave yourself."

"Yay!" Polina says on the other side of the door. "We have so much to talk about. God, let her out of there already." She pads away and we're left alone in the room.

"Aria," he says warningly.

"What?" I get out of bed and walk to the bathroom. "I need a shower."

"We have rules here."

"Oh, do we?" I turn on the shower. "Want to enlighten me?"

He follows me into the bathroom. "You know exactly what those rules are. You disrespect me in front of my family, I'll have to discipline you."

I turn around and look at him. "Ooh, big scary Russian guy's gonna punish me." I roll my eyes. "Do you really think I'm afraid of that by now?"

Oh, my God, what am I, *ten*?

He pulls up his phone to make a phone call. "You stay right there."

"Yes?" It's the doctor from the ER. I can see the contact on his phone, and he's got it on speaker.

"Is it or is it not dangerous for a husband to spank a disobedient wife?" My jaw drops. Oh my God. He did not just say that out loud. I am so embarrassed my cheeks flame.

"Mikhail," I say. My voice is shaky, with a little tremor. "Don't!"

"It's very dangerous," the doctor says, and for a second Mikhail's face falls. "If he wants his dick intact. Do you want her to kill you in your sleep? You might be bigger than her, but she could still smother you." I laugh out loud. God, I love this woman.

"I mean for her."

She laughs. "I know exactly what you mean, and the answer is no, with caution of course you can engage in all sorts of deviant sexual behavior."

Deviant sexual behavior. Oh my God. I'm so changing my name and moving out of state.

"Yes, Mr. Romanov. Kinky sex is fine. Once in a while, other things are fine as well. I'll send you an article that I wrote on this subject."

An article she wrote. Kill me now.

"Thank you."

"Anytime." He disconnects the call.

"You couldn't say something like...I don't know...can we have a little rough sex? You had to pull up that whole disobedient wife thing? Oh, my God." He's swiping through something on his phone, rapidly reading. One of the sexy things about him is that he's a speed reader, no matter the language.

"I don't think I'd be pushing that button right now, if I were you," he says. Dear God. Why did I have to do this? I jump into the shower, as if somehow a barrier of water is going to save me from his punishing palm.

And just as I suspected, just when I get to the conditioning part of my hair treatment, he's right in the shower with me.

"Mikhail!" I protest when he takes the bottle of conditioner out of my hand and throws it right out of the tub.

"Hands on that wall," he says in a low drawl in my ear.

I shiver. Yes. I've missed this so much. I brace myself against the wall and swallow hard. "Yes, sir," I tell him. Trying to remember what it's like to submit. Little push, little pull. Let him lead. Don't fight it.

"I finished that article. It was quite enlightening. It seems as long as I don't prohibit you from breathing properly, a good spanking can actually enhance your hormones, and make you feel better about things."

"Huh. Imagine that," I say, wryly. But I don't move.

"About that disobedience..."

"When exactly did I disobey you?"

"When I told you that you always speak respectfully to me in front of my family, and my men. Both hands on that wall. Now."

The first slap of his hand against my ass feels so hard I almost lose it. I come up on my toes right in the shower. I forgot that water can amplify the effects of a smack. I hiss in a breath, but I don't protest, because I know I need this. I need to take my medicine.

He spanks me again, and again, working his way all around my butt, my upper thighs, pausing between smacks, stroking between my legs. I'm already on the edge. They say some women hate sex when they're pregnant and some love it. Thankfully for me, I'm in camp two.

"I seem to remember a couple of curse words from your mouth as well, my love," he says, with feigned calmness.

He reaches across me and takes something off a hook. What the – no. Polina. For Christ's sake, why did you have to buy the bamboo bath brush?

"Stay right there," he commands in a harsh tone. I stay in position, cringing for the first smack.

I am not disappointed. The brush whistles through the air before it lands with a thud. I yell out loud, because it hurts.

He traces the welt on my ass. "I fucking miss seeing my stripes on you. Jesus Christ, you're gorgeous." By now I'm on the edge, practically ready to cry, but I don't want to. Not yet.

He leans one arm against the tiled wall, hot water cascading down his back and mine. His forehead to mine, he whispers, "You know that I love you. Do you know that, Aria?" There's a rare sincerity in his eyes, a vulnerability that makes me want to cry all over again. I nod and swallow. "I do," I whisper. "And I love you. Do you know that?"

"I do now." He bends down, and oh, thank heaven, wraps his fingers around the back of my neck, holding me in place just before his mouth crashes to mine. I taste the salt of my tears and the heat of the shower, his lips, and the memory of orange juice at breakfast.

I'm transported into another time and place where I do nothing but revel in bliss. I've surrendered myself to him, but even more? He's surrendered to me. The two of us have become one. We truly have. And right here between us –

Mikhail next to me, and the tiniest little heartbeat of a baby within me, we've formed our new family.

His rough hand cups my ass, massaging out the pain from the spanking that I craved.

"I love you, and I'm sorry I didn't give you what you needed."

"Mikhail, it feels so greedy for me to complain about anything when you give me everything I could want. All those clothes, the massages, and the breakfast in bed. The bubble baths and everything that I wanted. The computers and the monitors and everything, it's just...It's too much."

One sharp shake of his head. "It isn't too much. It would be too much if you didn't deserve it, Aria. But you are my queen."

That's it. Now I really am crying. Damn these pregnancy hormones.

He bends to take my mouth again, and after a long, lingering kiss, he spins me around and rinses my hair. I relish the feel of his thick fingers on my scalp. Hot water across my aching ass...

When the loud blast of an alarm tears us out of our reverie.

CHAPTER TWENTY-FIVE

Mikhail

I'M out of the shower in seconds, my phone to my ear.

"Someone's broken through the perimeter." It's Viktor. "Lev got a notification that one of our security systems has been disabled. All-hands-on-deck, Mikhail. Keep her safe." There's a shout behind them, the sound of shattering glass, and his phone goes dead.

Fuck.

I turn to see Aria standing in the doorway, stricken. Water streams down her body and pools on the floor while she stands wrapped clumsily in a towel.

"Get dressed. We're taking you to the safe room."

My entire house is a fucking safe room. I designed it this way, and when my family retreated here, we were ready. It's reinforced with bulletproof glass, extra surveillance systems, and my brothers have upped their weapons to auto-

matic guns, stationed at various points throughout the
house. Even the doors are reinforced steel. But we designed
a room just for Aria.

"What's going on? If someone breached security, Mikhail, I
can help – "

"No. We need to get you to safety, now."

"At least let me bring my laptop!" I know she hates feeling
helpless, but I don't care about her helping right now. I want
her safe.

"Leave the fucking laptop," I snap. I take her by the hand
and yank her over to the dresser. "Put some clothes on.
Now!"

She purses her lips, but doesn't respond, just reaches in her
dresser and grabs fistfuls of clothing. She yanks them on. I
open the door of my bedroom, armed.

"I have a secure room on this floor, designed for this
purpose."

"What purpose? I have no idea what you're talking about."

"To keep you safe if the home is under attack."

This room is strategically located off the main hallway, in a
discreet area of the house difficult for outsiders to locate.
While the bedrooms are on the perimeter of the house, this
room is in the dead center.

It was a large closet that I once used as an office, but I
quickly had it converted. The walls, ceiling, and floor are
constructed with thick bulletproof material that will not
cave under gunfire or an explosion. The entrance is a heavy
reinforced door, but the outside looks like it's a large

tapestry. Inside there are multiple locks and deadbolts. I pull up my phone, tap the app that Aleks and I designed, and when I slide my hand against the panel of the door, it opens.

"Wow," Aria says, obviously awed. "That is impressive."

Inside the room I have a secure internet connection, and more safety measures. There are closed-circuit television cameras with a live feed around the surrounding area, supplies such as food, water, basic amenities, and medical supplies. One bed, a television, a few comfortable chairs. And while it's well ventilated, there's no window in this room.

"I knew that you took security to the next level, Mikhail. But the security infrastructure here is really something else." I half push her in and shut the door behind us.

According to Kolya, Volkov has lost his mind. This is no longer about a moratorium, or honoring the rules of our brotherhood. This is revenge, pure and simple. And while I will not hide for any length of time, and I will not cower under his threat, we need a minute to gather our resources.

She sits on the bed, lifts the remote control, and does a quick surveillance of the equipment I have in here.

"Really, this is incredible, but are you sure you're not overre-acting? What happened?"

"I'm not sure yet."

I tap a button on my phone and call my brothers.

The conference call quickly picks up with Aleks, Viktor and Nikko, swiftly followed by Lev and Ollie.

"Jesus," Viktor says, scowling at the camera with his arms crossed on his chest. "The fucking balls of these guys. "

"Tell me."

I'm pacing the small room while she looks over everything I have on the computer.

"We've detained one attacker," Viktor says. "Kolya wouldn't let me kill him."

"Of course you can't fucking kill him," I tell him. "We need him to talk. Did you get any information out of him?"

Aria cringes on the bed and shakes her head. Maybe this is all a bit too much for her, but I don't care. Her safety is more important than anything right now.

"Yes. He broke more easily than I thought he would. He says there are no further attacks, that Volkov wanted to warn us. He said that he's gone mad, and even his own men don't trust him anymore."

That corroborates with what Kolya told us. "I see."

"You don't have to keep her in the safe room, Mikhail. We have everything stabilized out here."

"Do you know how they breached security?"

"Not yet."

Still, I don't want to risk anything happening to her. But we can't stay in this room forever. This is a temporary hold, and if it was a false alarm, she should be able to go see the rest of my family.

And even though she and our baby are the most important people to me right now, I have other responsibilities as well.

Jesus.

"Mikhail? I suspect based on what I'm looking at here that this is nothing new. They've been staging an attack on your home for a while. Since before I was here."

I turned to look at her. "How do you know that?"

"I've located several drones that may have been placed to gather intelligence on your home security measures, your routines, where you and I are...Looking for potential weak points."

Of course. Volkov knew that I would be getting married, and if he couldn't prevent my marriage, he could definitely threaten the safety of my family.

"Looks like Nikko has shot down two drones. But there may be a third in place. With this particular strategy, it's common to use three drones. The tripod, we call it."

"Are you telling me that Aleks fucked up again?"

She shakes her head. "No, not at all. It looks as if all of this was very covert and off the record, until Volkov just didn't fucking care anymore."

For once, I let her language slide. We have bigger things to deal with, like locating the one remaining drone and disabling it.

"They found someone, you said?"

I nod.

"Find out what you can from them, that's the best strategy. It would also be best if I could deal with Aleks, the two of us, one on one, so we could put a more secure system in place."

She bites her lip for a moment, looking contemplative. "Mikhail," she says. "How long though? How long will your family hide here? You are not people that hide from danger, so I know you can't be planning on doing so for very long."

"You're right. We're putting together a plan of offense in place of defense. We just need some time. "

I get a call, and my brother tells me that the coast is clear. I blow out a breath, reluctant to remove her from the safe room now that she's here.

"We can't stay here forever," I tell her with a nod. "I know you're right. Let's go eat with my family."

She looks down at herself in rumpled sweats, her hair still damp from the shower.

"Can I at least freshen up first?"

"Fine."

We go back to our room and I'm preoccupied. She quickly puts on a pair of jeans and a sweater and does some kind of messy knot thing in her hair that looks adorable.

While she freshens up with a little bit of makeup, I lean toward her, catching her gaze in the mirror, and wrap my hand around the messy knot of a bun at the nape of her neck.

"Do you remember when we first met, and you walked in my office with your hair up? Do you remember what I told you?"

She snorts. "Remember? Of course I do. It was the first time in my life I had ever encountered someone that made me think they were a total asshole while also making me want to be pressed against the wall and kissed by them at the same time. I was so mad at you for making me all kinds of attracted to you."

I grin against her hair and give her a kiss on the back of her head. I love her.

"Are you hungry?"

"Starving, as usual, but you know how it goes. My appetite is a little weird right now."

"We'll find you something you like."

Polina claps her hands together in glee when we make it to the dining room. My mother sits in the background, tapping on an iPad.

"Mikhail. Aria! It's so good to see you. I wondered if you'd ever let her come down."

They seem remarkably calm.

They haven't been told of the attack. Why would they be? My brothers had it covered. Aria gives me a questioning look, and when I shake my head, she shrugs and sits next to my mother.

"How are you feeling?" my mother asks, reaching for Aria's hand and giving it a gentle squeeze.

"Much better. Still kind of yucky, like I have weird aversions, and cravings, and nausea comes and goes all the time. I can't stop crying over everything."

"Understandable. I got you something."

"Did you? "Aria says, her shining eyes looking at me in surprise. I knew she'd love my mother. I knew my mother would love her. But right now, I have more important things to worry about.

I call all my brothers down to the dining room so we can go over what just happened and fill my sister and mother in as well.

"Oh my goodness, I love these." Aria unwraps a set of Matryoshka dolls, traditionally known as Russian nesting dolls here in America.

"You know each doll contains a smaller one, and I thought it would symbolize the stages of pregnancy, as you get further along."

"Thank you!"

She pulls out a package of herbal teas designed for pregnant mothers, a little tin of pastilles you melt under the tongue for nausea, and a soft, thick woolen shawl.

"In Russian tradition, it's exceptionally important for pregnant women to stay warm. While your body uses up all your resources to grow that child, you have to take care of yourself. Here, I made this myself." She arranges the shawl over Aria's shoulders. I'm alarmed to see Aria wiping at her eyes.

"Thank you," she whispers, leaning in to give my mother a kiss on her cheek.

Aleks storms into the dining room, his eyes on Aria. ""Good. You're here. We need to put our heads together. Goddamn drones."

"Oh my God, tell me about it." Aria rolls her eyes at me. "Drones are one of the hardest devices to track. It has to do with short range communication, the way they are so rapidly mobile, and how everything is encrypted."

"Right. The ones Volkov's using have anti-jamming techniques. It means they're built to resist any attempt to stop them from communicating."

"He's been at this for some time, Aleks."

I can't blame Aleks for this. I've never made my private home part of his responsibility. And while he recently came in to help with surveillance and security, it's still new to him.

Viktor storms into the room next, formidable and intimidating. He's been working out in the home gym with Nikko, because when Nikko comes in, I notice they're both wearing thin workout tanks and shorts, sweat still glistening on their skin.

Viktor takes a look at the large platter of bread on the table. "Are we eating lunch?"

"Of course we're eating lunch, sweetheart," my mother says as she rises to her feet. "I'm glad you're hungry."

When Viktor came to us, he was severely malnourished and underfed. My mother took great delight in making his favorite meals and feeding him thoroughly until he put on weight. In high school, he started lifting and honing his body to where it is now.

Nikko sits at the table, bottle of water in his hand. "I interrogated him myself," he says, obviously not caring that our mother is within earshot, Polina is somewhere nearby, and my wife is sitting right next to me. "He knows almost nothing. I don't blame our questioning techniques. It seems like

Volkov doesn't have much of a plan. He's flying by the seat of his pants, and from what information I've gathered, his own brothers don't trust him anymore."

"It makes sense," Aleks says. "His reckless disregard for the rules we all agreed on. Dangerous risks, like drones and sending new inductees here to fulfill whatever it is he demands." He shakes his head.

"And Kolya says Volkov is losing his mind. We can no longer reason with him."

I lean back in my chair, thinking.

"If he's unpredictable, we won't sit waiting anymore. We'll work as usual because he will strike when he thinks we'd least expect it. Tomorrow, we're back to work and we stay vigilant and in constant communication."

He reaches for my hand. "That includes you, little hacker."

CHAPTER TWENTY-SIX

Aria

"CANCEL ALL NOTIFICATIONS, meetings, and anything else on my calendar until further notice," Mikhail snaps at Chantelle.

We are back in the office where I first met him, and I suspect his administrative assistant doesn't really like me. She pretends that she does, because of course she's a professional, but as soon as I stepped foot in there, she narrowed her eyes at me, and I didn't miss the way her jaw tightened. She speaks to Mikhail but never to me. Who could blame her? I fucked things up for her when I first met them.

Now here I am, living in the lap of luxury and little does she know I'm carrying the mob boss's baby. I guess she'll know soon enough. And is it really a tragedy for me? I'm safe. As safe as I can be, anyway.

Ollie was right. No one has attacked. Mikhail is back to work because, as Ollie suggested, we all need to pretend that we are not afraid. We all need to pretend that things are normal, that we're not expecting blowback from Volkov. That we're not expecting anything. We know, though. We know he hasn't given up on us, and that we can expect an attack. We just won't wait in hiding anymore.

When Mikhail has me alone in his office, he lifts me and puts me on his desk. "This is the sexiest fucking thing I've ever seen," he says, in a deep growl of a voice.

"What? What are you talking about?"

"My pregnant wife with her legs spread wide on my desk," he bites back, as if surging through his own emotions. "I imagined you here. And now I want to remember you here."

I swallow and bite my lip. "How might we do that?"

Standing, he removes his belt. I watch greedily, my body heating at the look he gives me. Wordlessly, he lifts my hands above my head and secures them with the belt.

"Legs open," he drawls, his accent thickening. "And remember how I punished you for coming without permission."

Oh God, do I.

"So what are you going to do, Aria?"

Inhaling deeply, he stifles a groan as he drags a finger down my damp panties.

"Ask for permission," I breathe, as my hips jerk. "May I come?"

I swear the sound of his deep chuckle vibrates through me. My body clenches with need. Wordlessly, he lifts my legs and drapes them over his shoulders before he presses his tongue to the heat between my legs. I whimper and bite my lip, my head falling to the side.

"You may come when I tell you. Not a second earlier."

I want to stab my fingers through his hair, but my wrists are secured tight, of course. Damn that doctor. I could've played the pregnancy card before, but now I'm toast.

"Okay, yes, alright." I nod maybe a bit too eagerly as his thick fingers deftly remove my panties. He arranges me back over his shoulders and without warning, gives me a long, lazy stroke of his tongue.

I cry out, it feels so damn good. "Oh, God, *yes*." When I realize how loud I am, my cheeks heat. What if someone hears?

I lose myself to sensation, the warm feel of his mouth on me, the way his hands grip my ass possessively. I close my eyes as waves of ecstasy begin to course through me until I'm on the edge.

"Mikhail," I whisper. "Please?"

"Not yet," he says against my thigh, taking a moment to scrape his stubbled chin along the sensitive skin.

I whimper and moan, holding myself back with everything I've got. Oh God, he *will* punish me if I come now, but it's gonna kill me –

"I said not yet," he rasps, then in Russian, *"Ty krasiva, no upryama. Mne nravitsya, kogda ty podchinyaesh'sya mne."*

Oh boy.

You are beautiful but willful. It pleases me when you submit yourself to me.

Why is it so damn sexy when he talks to me like that?

I bite my lip and start mentally reciting the Russian alphabet, so I don't lose it, when he finally stops, kisses my thigh, and whispers, "Come, my love."

I let myself totally succumb and fall head over heels into ecstasy. My muscles contract, my breathing hitches, my skin flushes, and I scream out loud in pleasure. When I'm on the cusp of another climax, he rises and spreads my legs further, his eyes blazing into mine as he unfastens his pants. In seconds, he plunges into me. The walls of my pussy convulse, clenching around him. Having just crested my first orgasm, the second hits hard as he fucks me.

Slowly, he drags his cock out, his thumb pressed to my clit as he watches me come. I whimper and beg for his cock. When he's nearly fully out, he takes his time thrusting deep within me all over again. "That's it, my sweet girl. Take my cock. I want to fill you. Your pussy belongs to me."

Gripping my hips with a punishing hold, he thrusts into me so hard a tremor reaches all the way to the base of my neck. I cry out in pleasure as a third orgasm overtakes the first two. "Come with me," he grates in my ear. "Come with me, my filthy, beautiful little slut."

Another thrust, another, I'm half-crying in pleasure as nerves tingle up and down my spine. Oh, God, I love him. *I love him.*

He rocks his hips in time with me, his own release on the heels of mine. He holds his breath, his body stills, and with the next thrust, he throws his head back in ecstasy. I writhe with my own orgasm, enhanced by his, until he leans into me and holds me against him.

"I love you," he whispers in my ear. "I love you, Aria."

Still panting, I cherish the feel of his lips brushing against my cheek. "And I love you."

Footsteps sound outside the office, voices rise and fall. I stifle a giggle and press my hand to my mouth.

"So what if they hear," he says, his hair a little mussy and his clothes disheveled. "If I want to fuck my wife on my desk, I'm gonna fuck my wife on my desk."

I love that about him, too.

With trembling hands, I arrange my clothes, fix my makeup, and try to smooth my hair, but it's a little bit of a disaster after what just happened.

Oh no. I turn my head to look in my compact's mirror and see pink finger marks on my neck.

Jesus, Mikhail. Why couldn't you grab my waist or some-place that I could hide under clothing? It has to be my neck. Still, I'm pleased though. Every married woman wants to be loved by her husband. I am sexy, and he makes me feel that way. My husband loves my body.

Even as I'm growing a child in me. Even as the angles of my body soften, and my belly rounds.

A knock at the door. Mikhail scowls at it. Sometimes I think if his scowl or the laser of his glance could cause heat, he'd incinerate everyone and anything in his path.

"What?" he snaps.

"Your lunch has arrived, sir."

Mikhail looks at me sharply while he cleans us up. "I didn't order lunch."

I reach out a hand to his arm. "Easy there, killer," I say. "I ordered lunch. I'm craving one of those turkey burgers, okay?"

"Aria," he warns. He doesn't like to order without making sure that one of his men personally watches the food be assembled so no one can, I don't know, slip arsenic in it, or something.

"Test it for poison, I don't care what you do. All I want is one of those avocado turkey burgers on a grilled bun, okay?" And maybe their sweet potato fries.

He grunts. "I happen to know that Lev is down at the milk-shake factory today. He's got something going on, I don't know what, but if you want a milkshake –"

I grin. Of course I want a milkshake.

"Do you want one?"

"I'm all set but I think...I think the baby might." He grins and winks at me. My heart flips.

He's busily arranging the food on his desk, inspecting it and sniffing at it. "Mint chocolate chip." I smile and go to open the DoorDash app but realize it's not on my home screen. Nothing's on my home screen.

Wait a minute, that's because I grabbed *his* phone by accident.

I go to put it back on the desk when I see a text come in.

> Tatiana: Received the last payment.
> Thank you.

The last...payment? Is this another Tatiana? How common of a name is that?

I shouldn't be looking at his phone. I glance up at him and then back at the phone, confused.

"Oh," I say with a forced laugh. "I took your phone by accident. Sorry."

I put his back down and lift mine up, but I've forgotten what I wanted it for.

He doesn't even look at me.

Milkshakes. I want Lev to pick me up milkshakes.

Why is Tatiana's name on his phone? Under normal circumstances, I know the right thing to do is to flat out ask him. But I happen to have a world of hacking experience at my fingertips, and I don't want to put him in a difficult position...

"Have you heard from Ollie today?" I ask. I'm nervous about his job right now.

"I have," he says but offers no other information. "The fewer questions you ask, the less I tell you, the better it is."

I watch him inspect my turkey burger and suddenly think he's being ridiculous.

"Feeling alright?" he asks. He peers over at me and brushes hair out of my eyes. "Sweet girl," he says with a smile. "Tell me. What's on your mind? You look preoccupied."

Why is the woman who told me to come to you texting you? Is it a different Tatiana? Do you know her?

"I'm just nervous about everything," I tell him, which is not a lie. Who wouldn't be nervous when you're told, "pretend everything's fine, let them think that you've become complacent. That's when they'll strike."

What will happen when they "strike?"

Does anyone really know?

"I want you to talk to me, little hacker."

He doesn't always call me that anymore. It's always something sweet or my name. My throat tightens.

Could there be another Tatiana? There must be. There's no way...well.

Maybe there is.

Mikhail's leaning over the Styrofoam trays. First, he checks all the food over carefully, moving things around with a plastic fork before he leans in and smells everything. Finally, he takes the smallest bite of each item on the tray.

"Alright," Mikhail says, bringing me the tray with my food. "This is fine. No more ordering without going through me first, Aria."

I feel practically smothered beneath his over-the-top protection, and today is definitely a day where I need some space.

"Thanks. I'm going to take this into the conference room if that's alright. I need a little privacy."

"A little privacy?" he asks curiously. "No, not now. Stay here with me."

"Mikhail..."

"Aria." The tone of his voice leaves no room for debate. "You know what's at risk."

Yes, I do. I know an attack is imminent and maybe I have gotten a little complacent from weeks of peace.

I need to know if that's the same Tatiana. I know I could ask him, but — what if he lies to me?

I nibble my food, my appetite gone. I'm completely obsessed with the need to find out more information. Thankfully, Mikhail is occupied himself. I wait until he gets a call from one of his brothers, the only ones that get through when he silences notifications. I pull out my laptop and quickly open an incognito browser.

I was going to show Aleks how easily one could access our texts, so I have everything right at my fingertips.

My stomach flips with nerves when Mikhail's voice grows harsh.

"What do you mean you can't find him?" he growls into the phone. "Find him *now*. Stop everything else. Pause all operations. This is of paramount importance, do you understand me?"

He slams his phone down and curses. With a shaking hand, I hide my browser.

"Everything alright?"

He stews but doesn't answer at first. Finally, he shakes his head. "Ollie's gone radio silent."

Oh no.

I knew this was a risk they took but the actual knowledge that someone might've made a move makes apprehension rise in the pit of my stomach. Where is he? How far have they all gone just to keep me safe? Or more accurately, the baby I carry, the heir to the Romanov throne, safe.

I swallow hard and feel like a jerk that I'm totally going to take advantage of this situation to get answers.

"I'm sorry, Mikhail," I say. "Do you want me to help?"

I would and maybe could, but he shakes his head.

"Not yet, but thank you. Aleks has some ideas and I want him to follow those first."

"Got it." I pretend to be preoccupied while he makes another call. When he rises, his back to me, I swiftly pull up what I found. Right here in front of me, I have a transcription of every text conversation these men have had in the past six months.

With dread, I start searching. I don't need six months.

It takes me two terrifying minutes of rapid work while Mikhail is preoccupied to find the woman's name again.

Tatiana.

I stare at the date and feel my eyes water. I feel sick.

This one came the day before I met him.

> Do you? Perfect. Tell me details.

> Woman named Aria Cunningham. Super smart, really pretty but a bit nerdy. On the run from several major organizations because she found out information she shouldn't. I'm going to send her to you to offer her skills and you can see if she suits you.

> Will send the first payment as we discussed. The second if I decide I'll take her.

I jump at the feel of Mikhail's grip on the back of my neck. He's found me out. He sees what I'm doing.

I look up to him but only see a look of concern on his face.

I exhale a trembling breath.

He always grips the back of my neck. It's his signature move, his hand on the nape of my neck. Normally, I love it. It's possessive and intimate and I love knowing that I'm his. Right now, though...

"Are you alright, baby?" he asks gently.

I shut my laptop but it's too late. I feel as if I'm going to be sick.

I begin to tremble, facing him. I need time to process this before I accuse him of anything.

No. No, I'm not okay.

I can't lie to him.

Why not? He lied to me.

He bought me. Paid a finder's fee to Tatiana.

I was set up from the beginning. I think I'm going to be sick.

"Stay here, my love. Don't move. I know when you look like this, you may be easily made nauseous."

He knows because he's been by my side for the past few weeks. He's taken the very best care of me I could've asked for. He knows when I get sick and what helps, how to soothe my morning sickness. He massages my feet and draws warm baths. He's been the picture of a doting husband, everything a woman could ask for.

Only...only it isn't real. I was bought to fill a role.

Hell, I'm filling it now. I'm carrying his baby for him because he needs an heir to the throne.

Do I even mean anything to him?

He bends and kisses my temple. "You work too hard, sweetheart. Take your milkshake and have a little break. You can nap if you'd like."

Because of *course* he's so perfect he even has an area in his office he's set up for me to comfortably nap when I need it. I look over at what I call "the nap zone," a cozy nook with a full-sized chaise lounge, adorned with fluffy pillows and a blanket in warm, neutral tones that's so soft I swear it's made of cashmere. It's even got a shade I can pull for privacy. He keeps bottled water in a mini fridge and an electric kettle on a low table with herbal teas.

He really is perfect, except for that *minor* detail that he's a criminal and ex-con who doesn't seem to have a moral compass and he just may very well have *bought me.*

There's a knock at the door. Mikhail frowns. He was explicit in his instruction that we shouldn't be interrupted.

"Maybe the milkshake?" I suggest, my voice wavering while I wonder if it could be Aleks. If he comes in here and tattles on me...

I run through possible lies.

I accidentally stumbled on this when trying to do research. No idea how those popped up on the screen but they mean nothing to me.

I was trying to remember a conversation I had about something he researched for baby gear and accidentally scrolled way, way back.

But it's Chantelle on the other side of the door, her pale face and wide eyes a clue that she knows he'll be pissed, and she isn't wrong.

"I told you not to interrupt me unless it was an emergency."

She swallows. "I'm so sorry, sir. This is an emergency."

"What is it?" Mikhail's tone softens the merest fraction.

"Anton's called and said he's trying to get in touch with you. He said to check your messages immediately and to call him if you still have time."

If he still has time?

Mikhail whips his phone out of his pocket and curses.

"Mikhail, what is it?"

"Chantelle, you're dismissed." She fairly runs from the

thunderous voice and the look in his eyes, though I know it isn't directed at her.

"Anton's our informant on the police force, out of Manhattan. They oversee The Cove."

He shows me his phone. Either he doesn't remember he has a text on there from Tatiana, or he thinks I won't understand why it's there.

> Hide. Now. They're putting you under arrest. I'm on it.

"They're arresting you? Where can you go?"

But it's too late. He opens his mouth to tell me when the blaring sound of sirens fills the air.

The building's surrounded.

CHAPTER TWENTY-SEVEN

Mikhail

THERE'S no time for me to take Aria to a safe room or house. My office building's surrounded in seconds by a goddamned SWAT team.

Aria looks stunned when the door to my office is shoved open and masked and uniformed men and women swarm into the room. I grit my teeth and don't resist. I know this routine.

Either someone trumped up a charge to neutralize me or I'm under arrest for something I did, but we pay Anton well for a reason. He'll get me out on bail and all charges dismissed, but it'll take some time.

One luxury I don't have.

My guess is that someone wants to take me out of the picture so they'll have better access to Aria.

"This isn't happening," I say when they enter my office. "You can put your guns away."

"No, sir. You're under arrest for violation of human trafficking laws in New York. We have evidence to support your involvement."

Aria's eyes widen.

Trumped-up charges. Of course I never did anything involving human trafficking. Volkov may have, though. And whoever's behind this is the enemy of my wife.

"I don't know what you're talking about and don't see anyone showing a warrant."

They don't need a warrant, but I'm buying time until my brothers are here and ready to take over surveillance with Aria.

"We don't need a warrant, sir, not when we have reasonable cause."

"Please!" Aria says. I swear she's curving her back and pushing her belly out. She's hardly showing more than a little, but she'll play that pregnancy card. "I'm pregnant and at high risk. If anything happens to me, it's on you."

They remain unyielding. "Step aside, Mrs. Romanov," one of the women says. Her jet-black hair's slicked back into a bun at the nape of her neck. "We don't want you to get hurt should there be any altercation."

Aria steps back, her eyes wide. I'm not sure what to tell her. Normally, I'd go with them until we could sort this shit out, but I can't leave her.

Footsteps sound outside my door. My brothers responding to the call.

Viktor enters first. He has quite the reputation with local law enforcement. It helps that he's huge and intimidating.

"What's the meaning of this?" he asks in a dangerous voice. They repeat their rigamarole.

"So you obviously must know that's a lie," Viktor says as he crosses his arms on his chest and glares at them. The female officer with the slicked-back hair stares, her jaw agape. He's terrifying when he pulls himself to his full height.

"It doesn't matter, sir," one of the officers says. "And I'm beginning to lose my patience. It's imperative Mr. Romanov come with us so we can continue our investigation."

Viktor nods to me, stalling so my other brothers have time to get here. If this is an attempt to get Aria isolated, we won't let it happen.

"I want to see that warrant."

"We don't have time for this," one of the other officers snaps, but when Viktor glares in his direction, he quickly folds himself behind the others.

Pussy.

"At least let me say good-bye to my wife." Another delay tactic. I want more of my brothers here to protect her in my absence.

Aria walks to me and stares. I reach for her neck, but she pulls away. "Human trafficking, Mikhail?" she whispers. "How could you?"

"It's a lie, Aria. Jesus, that's not what I did."

"Didn't you, though?" She brushes at tears on her cheeks, her voice wobbly.

What the hell is going on?

"Jesus, you have to believe me. Come here," I say to her, just before they put the cuffs on. I lean in and kiss her, but she doesn't kiss me back.

The door to the office opens and Lev, still wearing workout gear, his tight frame slicked in sweat, and Nikko, as terrifying as ever, enter. Thank fuck. Aria will be safe.

"Problem here, officers?" Nikko asks.

"They're arresting me for human trafficking," I say with an eye roll. But then I see Aria. She's staring at me as if she's never seen me before.

Wait. Does she think I'm actually guilty?

"I didn't do it, baby," I say, even as they pull my arms behind my back and slap handcuffs on. "We don't do that shit."

We do a lot of things that *could* get us arrested, but that's beside the point.

Anton instructed me to get my brothers in here and once they were here, to allow them to take me away.

He'll work on the rest.

It takes everything in me not to resist. The sooner they take me, the sooner I'm freed. I have to trust Anton's doing everything he can.

"You keep her safe," I snap at Viktor, who stands like a brick building beside Aria. Aria stands behind him, almost cowering. She doesn't look at me.

"I'll be back, Aria. Be careful, baby."

I turn to my brothers. "You watch her while I'm gone or I'll personally beat the shit out of each one of you before I—" I turn to the officers. Probably not smart to issue a death threat while being arrested. "Keep her safe."

"She'll be safe with us," Lev says, his brooding eyes holding a promise.

I let them lead me away. I have to get out and get back to her as swiftly as possible. If it takes longer than it needs to, heads will fucking roll.

I will find who orchestrated this and I will end them.

I look straight ahead as they shove me into the back of a cruiser. The officer driving exhales, as if she's been holding her breath, waiting for me to retaliate.

I'll retaliate, but it won't be the officers that have to worry.

Someone is behind this. Someone wants me taken away from my wife so she's at risk, I'd bet money on it.

Someone will pay.

Why didn't Aria look at me when I left?

CHAPTER TWENTY-EIGHT

Mikhail

I PACE the cell over and over again, waiting for a call from Anton. This must run deep. Under normal circumstances, I never would've seen the walls of this cold, dark cell, but here I am.

My fists are clenched with barely suppressed frustration. My worst fear in the world is being helpless, and knowing the people that I love are at risk. If I didn't think it would break my fist, I'd slam it against this wall to help release the fury that's cascading through me like an erupting volcano. But that won't solve anything. When I was younger, though...

"Mikhail Romanov? Is that you?" I look into a corner of the cell. It turns out I'm not alone.

"Who is it?" I don't recognize him from where I sit. He stands, uncoiling himself like a snake.

"Has it been that fucking long?"

"Jesus Christ." I cross the cell and embrace my former military brother, Saul Bianchi. We were rivals for a short time but laid that to rest. Sometimes it helps to have friends, and sometimes it's more helpful to have allies that hate your enemies alongside you.

"There was a time when I would've wanted to kick your ass for coming in here," Bianchi says, and when he grins, I see he's missing a tooth. Newly? Who knows. "But I heard how you stood up to Volkov. Fucking brilliant. You know we all want Volkov dead."

Of course they do. He runs all of New York with an iron fist, mercilessly and selfishly. He annihilates anyone in his path, after building a group so large no one has a chance to withstand him.

"He's why I'm in here."

Bianchi swears. "Of course he is." His voice drops. "You need to get out, don't you?"

I nod. Of course I fucking do. I tell him about Aria and the baby. His eyes shine with conviction. "We'll bust you out of here." He lowers his voice even more and brings his mouth to my ear. "Do you see that guard over there?"

I nod.

"He's on my payroll. I'm here voluntarily. I have connections, and I needed face-to-face interaction with a couple of the detainees. I get out tomorrow, if all goes as planned."

"Yeah?"

"You have an informant, yeah?"

I nod.

"And you're willing to pay?"

I laugh out loud. "What do you fucking think?"

Bianchi grins at me. He reaches a fist out, and slams his knuckles to mine, a universal code of loyalty. We may have rival clans, we may be in different groups, but loyalty runs deep when it comes to the law.

"Romanov."

The guard comes to the bars, looks at Bianchi. Bianchi nods, and the guard gestures for me. "You have a call. Let's go."

CHAPTER TWENTY-NINE

Aria

IT TURNS out Ekaterina's home is closer to the office than ours. Or...Mikhail's. Whoever's.

I can't think of it as my home anymore. Not now.

If only I had somewhere to go. A part of me feels as if it would be not only a betrayal, but an act of great cowardice. Yes, my husband used me. Yes, I've been betrayed. But I didn't make this commitment to him out of love. That only happened as a result of drawing close to him.

A lump rises in my throat, and I put a hand to my forehead. I don't want to cry. Not now. Not when I have so much to do.

A knock sounds at the guest room door. "Who's there?"

"It's me, Polina."

I open the door and let my sister-in-law in. She takes one look at me and gathers me into a huge hug. "I know, I know.

But don't worry, you have to believe me, they get arrested all the time. It's fine, I promise. We have ways out. It's not what you think it is."

It's kinda sweet that she thinks I'm upset because Mikhail was arrested, although...I'm not immune to that either. The vision of my husband being taken away in handcuffs is something that I won't easily erase from my memory.

"You'll see, he knows how to get out. You just have to give him time. It's probably fucking killing him, knowing that you're here and he's there. He's been glued to your side ever since you had those two lines on the test."

I nod, turn away from her, and pace the room. "I understand. I know where you're coming from. How's your mother?"

Even in my own distress, I feel badly for her. It must not be easy seeing her sons go through something like this.

"Oh, Mom's *fine*. She takes it all like a champ," Polina says. "And I think if she didn't already have completely silver hair, she'd get more gray. But you have to keep in mind, this stuff's been going on for a really long time. She's steeled herself against them. I mean, when Viktor was in grade school, he made the owners of this lemonade stand on the corner pay him protection money, and he'd guard their money. It's kind of hilarious, when you think back on it. And Nikko? Nikko was bad news. He's always been excellent at what he does."

She pauses. "Not that you know what he does. Uhm, not that I'm supposed to know, either. But let's just say his skill with a weapon started *long* since before he was old enough to actually carry one. And Lev got in trouble for some petty theft, but by the time he was old enough to get into real trouble – namely, drug dealing? My father was traveling in Europe, and the older guys were all in charge. And they put a very quick end to *that*. Not that they have any trouble with drugs, like don't get me wrong. They're not exactly good guys? But they didn't want him to get involved with the wrong people."

Polina continues her efforts to distract me. "Viktor was always, and I mean always, *always* getting into street fights. He always won, but my parents kept having to pay all these bills for like you know, medical bills and broken property and things like that." She shakes her head. "It's not easy raising a gang of mobsters. So my mom, she's learned a lot along the way."

Turns out, so has Polina.

"What did Mikhail do to get in trouble when he was younger?"

Why am I asking this? Why do I need to know?

She knits her brows together. "His escapades were more like...protecting people he cared about. Like if someone disrespected Mom or double-crossed Dad or something. He has always been so loyal and protective, to a fault."

I swallow. "What do you mean?"

Why do I want to know?

"He always put other people's needs above his own, to the point of neglecting sleep or food. And when he lost all those men in one night..."

I blink. "All those men in one night?"

"In the military? When his entire squad was killed? He'd been sleeping in a bunker after an all-night mission, and he came out to find they'd been bombed. He lost all of his brothers, every damn one of them, including the very last one he found still unconscious. He carried him on his back four miles to the nearest medic, only to have him die, too."

Oh. Oh, God. That's awful.

"Ever since then he's sort of just taken on this role of like... protector. Sometimes I wish he'd take better care of his own needs." Leaning forward, she gives me a hug. "That's why I'm so glad he has *you*. Finally, after all these years, he isn't alone."

Well that makes me feel like absolute shit. *God.*

She lets me go and gives my arms a little squeeze.

"Why don't you join us for dinner."

I hesitate. "Who's here?"

"Yeah, so...um, everyone. Mikhail made everybody take care of you when he got taken away. Since he couldn't actually protect you himself, he did the next best thing. As we speak, right outside this door, we have *all* of my brothers. It's kind of ridiculous. I'm sure there are other things I'd like to do, but if they leave your side, when Mikhail gets out of jail, he would kill them. Literally kill them."

I draw in a breath and let it out.

Interesting. I have work to do, and I'm not very hungry. I'm not feeling social right now. Thankfully I have a pregnancy card I can use.

"Okay. Wow. So...it's been a long day, I'm tired." I just don't feel like it.

There's a gentle knock on the door. When it opens, Ekaterina steps in and shuts it behind her. I've never seen her wearing jeans and a sweater, but she looks younger in them somehow. Her hair is still swept up in an elegant updo, but she doesn't have any makeup on, and she's wearing house slippers.

"How are you, Aria?"

I'm not good.

I don't know how I'd actually leave him, but I am no longer giving myself to him. I will carry his baby, only because I'm being forced to. It doesn't make sense for me to leave, because no matter where I go, he'll find me. I'll have his *child*.

But I need to find a way.

He called me an hour ago.

I let it go to voicemail.

"We'll make you anything you want," Ekaterina says. "The boys want to make sure you're alright. Mikhail can be a little...overbearing."

You don't say.

"Are you hungry?" I am. My stomach growls as if to answer her.

"A little." I have to play it casual. Even as I make my plans, though, my heart feels as if it's been torn to pieces.

I thought he loved me, not just the idea of me.

I thought he cared for me, but it turns out I was wrong all along. He wanted a wife to fill a role and have his baby, and I was the most expedient choice.

I feel so *used.*

What will he do with me when I no longer suit his purpose?

When we open the door, I'm faced with a wall of stern, intimidating men that are all very familiar.

"Why hello, boys," I say, barely tempering an eye roll. I can barely breathe for the phalanx of men standing in my way. "We're going to get some lunch. *Lunch,* as in that meal between breakfast and dinner. You really don't need to follow me."

"We absolutely do," Lev says, his arms crossed on his chest. "Rules."

Right.

"First," Ekaterina says, reaching for my arm and walking down the carpeted corridor with me, pretending like I'm not surrounded by a human forcefield. "We have to get some food in you and take care of that baby, don't we?" She winks. I feel nauseous. Am I only a baby mama to all of them? "Then I have something to show you."

Interesting.

As I step down the hall, I'm flanked on both sides by the guys. They walk as one, their steps synced. I notice Lev carries a weapon and his mother doesn't even say anything. How strange. This is just normal for her, then.

There's a small commotion outside the window. I'm reminded of our wedding day.

Our wedding day.

A pang hits my heart. *He didn't mean it.*

As I walk, his brothers are an impenetrable wall. Even though they're here to supposedly protect me there's no way *I'll* be able to find a way out. But if I could get onto one of their computers, I could maybe bypass security...I'd need to do it in a way that Aleks doesn't realize.

I barely pay attention to what we're eating. The food is tasteless, even though Ekaterina has done her best to get me everything I like. I'm thankful and tell her as much but my appetite is gone. Thankfully most people understand this about a pregnant woman.

"Got a call from Mikhail," Lev says. Everyone looks his way. I try to pretend my heart isn't hammering out of my chest.

"He's got some connections, it seems." He looks at me. "He'll be home soon."

"Thank you. I knew he would."

I did, to be honest. Because whether I want to admit it or not, Mikhail isn't exactly one to let his hands be tied – no, *he's* the one that does any tying.

Lev speaks to Nikko in a low voice. They speak in Russian, but surprise, boys – I understand a bit of Russian now.

They're talking about *me.*

I put down the remains of my sandwich and gingerly wipe my fingers on a paper towel. It's hard to participate in one conversation while listening in on another, but I manage to do it. It helps that Polina is currently more concerned with telling me about the cute doctor with dimples on rotation who likes to wink at the nurses, while I'm listening to Lev talk to Kolya.

"Teper', kogda on zhenat, on neprikasaemyy."

Now that he's married, he's untouchable.

Kolya nods.

"No rebenok prinosit bolshe bezopasnosti."

But the baby brings more security.

They only solidify my greatest fear – I'm an object to be used, and my baby will be their prized possession.

"Aria?" I look up to Ekaterina's hand on me. "Let's go. It's time I show you something."

CHAPTER THIRTY

Aria

SOMETHING TELLS me what Ekaterina needs to show me will be monumental.

A part of me wants to run. *Don't pull me in any more, please don't give me a reason to stay.*

And then of course, as soon as I rise from the table, almost every single one of Mikhail's damn brothers rises with me. *Seriously.*

"She's fine, boys," Ekaterina says, her silvery eyes kind but firm. "She's coming with me."

"We're under strict orders to not allow Aria out of our sight," Nikko says, taking a step toward us.

"Nikko, can't a woman have a conversation in private? Honestly, boys. Your insistence on protecting Aria is admirable, but we need to chat in private. It's not like I'm even taking her out of the house."

Nikko shakes his head. "I'm sorry."

Viktor unfolds himself from the table, all six foot whatever of solid muscle and testosterone. I'm a little intimidated by him if I'm honest, but Ekaterina raised these men.

"Fine," she finally agrees, steel lacing her voice. "You may come with us but you'll stay outside the door so we can have some privacy."

Stern Nikko and Implacable Viktor look at each other and I can tell already they're immovable, but Polina pleads her case with Lev. Seems the younger ones in the family unite from time to time.

"Lev, can you talk some sense into these boneheads? Seriously. We have a few things to discuss."

Lev is thoughtful as he folds his arms across his chest. Ollie sits at the table, silent as usual, whittling something in his hands. He finally looks up.

"You can go to the room. We'll stand guard outside. No one leaves the room or goes near a window without one of us nearby."

I finally can't take it anymore. "You guys are treating us as if we're royalty under attack from an enemy. This is ridiculous. It's been weeks of nothing happening. Are you just going to continue to smother us for the rest of our lives?"

Polina snickers.

"If we need to? Yes," Ollie says, looking back at the little wooden figure in the palm of his hand. He takes the sharp knife with his right hand and holds the figure with his left, then scrapes the tiniest detail with the tip of the knife.

"This is exactly what Volkov wants you to think, Aria. What's the fun if you're anticipating an attack? No. He'll wait until you've let your guard down." When he looks up at me, my heart rate spikes. His green eyes sparkle with intensity. *"That's* when he'll strike." He stands, easily as tall as Viktor but not quite as bulky. "You may go, but we come with you."

I roll my eyes to Polina, but Ekaterina only smiles warmly and takes my arm. "Let's go."

Once again, with every footfall, the heavy step of my guard falls in unison, like a marching band. Ekaterina leads me down a hallway to an open door. "In here," she says, escorting me into one of her guest rooms. The second Polina and I are over the threshold, she peeks her face in the doorway. "Thanks so much for the escort, gentleman. We'll be right back."

Then she effectively slams the door in their faces.

"It's fine, they can stay out there," she says with a wave of her hand. "These windows are reinforced with steel bars and bullet proof glass. If anyone gets past that kind of protection, I'd like to know how. Now," she says, walking to a corner of the room where she has a desk. "Have a seat, Aria."

I look from her to the desk again, then to Polina, who looks about as baffled as I feel. The white wooden desk is L-shaped and takes up a good deal of space in this corner of the room, but there's only a slim gray laptop on its surface. There isn't so much as a paperclip in sight.

I pull out the seat in front of the laptop and look up at

Ekaterina. She folds her hands placidly and speaks in a low whisper of a voice so the guys don't hear.

"If I told them what I had in here, they'd be all over it," she says in the tiniest of whispers. "And I won't have that. I trust you, Aria, because Mikhail said you're a genius with these things."

I still have no idea what she's talking about.

"I'll be quick," she says, continuing in the barest hint of sound. "I've had Fyodor Volkov here weekly for months now. My sons didn't like it because they don't trust him. What they don't understand is that I don't trust him, either."

Her eyes gleam. The hairs on the back of my neck stand up. Ekaterina's been playing Volkov?

"I got him to trust me. As Kolya may have explained, Fyodor's growing senile in his old age. He repeats stories over and over again, confuses dates and times, and some-times doesn't even remember my name." She shrugs. "So it was an easy matter to get him to bring me his toys then conveniently 'lose' them. Open the drawers, Aria."

I look down at the desk drawers in front of me. My heart is beating too fast. My mouth is dry. Every instinct in my body tells me something's about to happen.

I open the drawers and find two more laptops and four cell phones.

"Those aren't just his, some belong to his friends as well."

"And he just...*handed* these to you?"

She smiles. "Not exactly. I can be very persuasive when I need to be. But you don't have to worry about that. All I need *you* to do is to find information on these devices that will destroy him." She leans in closer, her voice still a whisper. I jump at the sound of a fist on the door.

"Everything alright in there?"

"Yes, fine!" I yell. "And unless you want to learn more about the dilation of a woman's cervix during labor or the tenderness of my breasts, I'd suggest you stop now."

Polina snorts. "I adore you, you know."

My heart melts a little bit. I don't want to give her up. I don't want to give Ekaterina up. But how can I stay knowing I mean nothing to Mikhail?

"Fyodor hurt my sons. He may have been the one who orchestrated my husband's death." Ekaterina's voice hardens. I look up at her. "Destroy him, Aria."

My hands fly over the keyboard of the computer on the desktop in front of me. Unlocking it is child's play. I feel my eyes widen and my jaw unhinge as I systematically unlock everything. I go as quickly as I can, which is pretty quick since I have the tools to do it. I know how to bypass the security measures Volkov has in place, and within three minutes, it's all here. *All of it.*

Communications and criminal records. Financial transactions. Detailed ledgers and personal information as well. Pictures and family information, and enough digital evidence of crimes to send him to jail for ten life sentences. But as I read, I feel nausea curling in my belly.

"He isn't working alone," I whisper, as I recognize names and places. Panic sweeps through me. "He isn't the one we need to fear."

I leap to my feet. I have to sound the alarm, I have to —

The sound of a deafening roar shatters my world.

CHAPTER THIRTY-ONE

Mikhail

"PULL OVER."

Before I was made *pakhan* he might've given me shit for making him pull over, but now he only does what I say with a tight-lipped look.

He's driving too fucking slow for me.

"Listen," he growls as he reluctantly gets into the passenger seat. "Driving so fast you get pulled over won't get you there any faster."

"You sound like Mom. Shut up and let me drive."

Aleks only sits up straighter and crosses his arms on his chest.

"I've got a lot to tell you, Mikhail," he says with a note I can't quite identify in his voice.

"How convenient. I have a lot I have to tell you, too."
Namely, how he's directly impacted by the deal I made to
get out of jail. There's no "get out of jail free" card in real
life, ever.

"I'll let you go first. Oldest brother and all that."

I know it's his curiosity, though.

"Bianchi got me out. I owed him a favor, but a small one, so
we made a deal."

"I suspected Bianchi had something to do with it. Mario
Rossi texted me and told me you'd probably cross his path."

"I did." The fact that we were in the same cell wasn't lost on
me either. "And we struck a deal."

"Oh?" Now I have Aleks's attention.

"He has a younger sister who's causing him some trouble.
She's tried to leave on numerous occasions, and he's done
with it. Says it's time to marry her off and he'd rather
marry her into a group he trusts than take his uncle's
advice."

I don't blame Bianchi. His uncle's a greedy son of a bitch
who'd auction his niece off to the highest bidder, character
and integrity be damned.

Aleks laughs out loud. "So enter the Romanovs, because
we're so reputable and trustworthy?" He flattens a palm
against his chest. "I'm fucking honored."

"His uncle was talking with Volkov."

Aleks's eyes darken. The last woman who entered an
arranged marriage to Volkov ended up marrying a man

thirty years her senior who locked her in a cage in his bedroom and shared her liberally with his peers.

There's a reason Polina isn't allowed contact with that side of the family.

"You thinking what I'm thinking?" he says, his dark eyes glittering.

"That you and I both tying the knot within six months gives us a decided advantage? Fuck yes."

He sits up straighter. "Wait, *me*? Jesus, Mikhail."

"I have my reasons."

I noted the tension between Aleks and Aria and while I was ready to step in if necessary, it would be far easier for all of them if I didn't have to.

I also happen to know, thanks to Bianchi, that while his sister's a handful, she's much more Aleks's type than Viktor's.

"Well, then. Happy birthday to me," he mutters, looking out the window. "Not only do I get a wife, but I also get the unique privilege of taming her. You got a pic?"

"I do."

I pull out the picture of tall, elegant Harper Bianchi. Honey-brown eyes and sun-kissed skin complement her long, blonde beach waves. Her smile is a bit impish, if staged – the byproduct of hundreds of selfies she's liberally posted.

"She's been spoiled," Aleks says, his eyes fairly gleaming. "Hasn't she?"

"Without a doubt."

"I can't decide if I should thank you or deck you."

"So soon you forget the punishment for striking your *pakhan?*"

"Dammit, that's right," he says with a laugh, then quickly sobers. "Alright, we can talk about this with everyone else later. I have a more urgent matter we need to address."

I hit the gas and watch the needle hit eighty-five. I need to get to Aria. She hasn't answered my calls or texts, and it would concern me if I hadn't left her under the total wall of protection that's the entire Romanov brotherhood. I know she needs to nap often and is sometimes so busy with her work that she doesn't notice notifications.

We're ten minutes out.

"What did you need to talk to me about?"

Aleks sobers, which isn't a good sign. When he clears his throat, I feel my hands tighten on the steering wheel.

"Aria's been poking around. I'm almost certain she intercepted some texts, and when I looked through yours, they were potentially damning."

Texts? She intercepted texts?

"What kinds of texts were damning? What are you talking about?"

"You got a text from Tatiana, brother."

Ahh. Shit. "She knew we didn't exactly meet in a traditional way..."

"No, but she might not be too crazy about the fact that you arranged for her to be sent to you and the woman you paid a finder's fee to was posing as her friend."

It's how we do things here. I fucking kidnapped her, for Christ's sake. It's not like we met in a traditional way by any means. Hell, I didn't even give her a choice about vows or a baby.

"Is this why she isn't answering my texts?"

"Could be, but I also don't want to – *shit*."

"What?" I say through gritted teeth.

"I get an alert when there's been any tampering with security measures. It looks as if she's been unsuccessful, but Aria's been attempting to circumvent security."

She is in so much fucking trouble. I clench my teeth together and push the gas pedal even harder. "How?"

"I need to catalog these alerts before I..."

All of a sudden, he goes still.

"Aleks." What the fuck?

"*Fuck.* Mikhail, there's something more urgent we need to respond to, *now*. An alert's come in that says there's been a security breach at the primary residence – Mom's home. The fire alarms have been triggered and window alarms as well."

I will myself to stay calm but even the road in front of me goes a little hazy.

Jesus. Fuck. Volkov and his goddamn sons of bitches –

I hit the steering wheel. "Call Viktor."

The phone rings and rings.

I systematically go through every one of my brothers and get no response. I turn the corner so hard we're on two fucking wheels. My mother's estate looms in front of me, smoke billowing into the sky. My heart hammers in my chest, adrenaline nearly choking me.

"Multiple unauthorized entries at the main gate. Detection of explosives. Fire safety alerted."

Fuck.

"Check real time family status." My voice sounds as if it's coming from inside a tunnel, hollow and echoing. I need to stay focused.

"Jesus," Aleks says in a choked voice, running a hand through his hair. He blows out a breath. "Polina's in Mom's guest room. Heartbeat accelerated. Mom's detected in the same room with her, but her heartbeat's well below the normal range. Viktor's nearby, heart rate accelerated. Nikko as well. There's..." He's having trouble continuing. "No reading on Lev or Ollie."

"And Aria?"

"She's off our radar."

CHAPTER THIRTY-TWO

Aria

I'M UNDER A BODY. Someone's heavy, steely body. And it's not the body I *like* being under.

Liked.

LIKED.

I think whoever's on top of me is unconscious. I blink, trying to piece together what happened, when a wave of panic shoots through me.

The baby. Is the baby okay? *Oh my God.*

The windows shattered, glass shards flying through the air like a deadly snowstorm. The noise was deafening, triggering alarms in the echo of the bomb's explosion. The air is ripe with the acrid scent of gunpowder.

"Get *off.*" I try to push but it's about as effective as trying to lift a small elephant. I look up to see Viktor's scarred face.

He's still conscious, but there's a large gash on his forehead dripping blood into his eyes.

He grunts and rolls over but grabs a weapon. I've never seen him grab a weapon before. If the fact that a *bomb* detonated isn't enough of a clue that something's terribly wrong, him grabbing a weapon absolutely is.

He grimaces with the effort of moving off of me. I don't even remember how he got here. There must've been something that triggered an alarm and he only had seconds to shield me with his body before the detonation took full effect.

"Where is everyone? Is everyone okay?"

"Stay down," he growls, pushing himself up. He's wobbly on his feet. "Do you know how to use a gun?"

"Of course I do."

He shoves one into my hand. "That bomb was a distraction and a way in. You're in grave danger. Don't pull any of your shit, Aria, you stay fucking *there*."

I glare at him but hold the weapon anyway and give it a quick glance. You pull the trigger, right? My mind churns with questions and fears.

If I never hear the words "you're in grave danger" again for the rest of my life, I'll be a happy camper.

"Polina?" he calls out.

"I'm fine, Viktor. It's Mom I'm worried about." I look up to see Polina kneeling over her mother, a look of concern on her face. They're handling this with such calm, it's a little unnerving.

Ekaterina's unconscious, her forehead streaked with blood.

Oh no.

I push up and feel a painful stab in my abdomen. Stricken, I put my hand to my belly. Polina looks about as terrified as I feel. "You fell," she says, even as she holds her mother's wrist between her fingers. "Did you hit your head? Are you in pain?"

Gunshots ring out. Viktor's on his feet. I look up to see the entire wall between us and the hallway's been demolished. Even though there's still a ceiling over us, there are gaping holes in the roof overhead.

I can't even figure out who's where because of the debris and smoke in the air.

Smoke?

"I have a pulse," Polina says, blowing out a breath. "Thank God."

Gunshots ring out again, and again. My hand trembles on my weapon. Will I be able to use it if I need to?

"They're here for you," Viktor says in a harsh whisper. "We need to hide you."

He looks around the room, his keen eyes taking everything in. With one quick movement, he yanks down the desk, shoves everything onto the floor, and pulls it so the top forms a barrier between me and the doorway. It's fruitless, though, because there's no safety at my back. Still, it's something. "Get *down*," he orders, grabbing me and pulling me down.

Another gunshot rings out. Another.

"Viktor!" Polina screams, as an armed man in all black, wearing a face covering, walks into the room holding a huge gun. Viktor's faster than he is, though, and he pulls his trigger, just as a second assailant comes in through the broken wall. I scream and pull the trigger of my own gun, unprepared for the way it bucks against my shoulder. I miss by a mile.

"You said you could fucking shoot."

"God, I lied, alright?"

"Don't shoot again, you're likely to kill someone and not the ones we want."

He isn't wrong.

But we're outnumbered and we can't hold them off for long.

I hear the sound of screeching tires. The boom of a car door. Multiple weapons — machine guns? — being fired.

Someone screams something in Russian, and Polina and Viktor's heads whip to the open gash in the wall. They share a look as our assailants retreat. They look...they look like they're running for their lives.

Viktor won't leave my side. He has me shoved behind this broken desk, wielding his gun in one hand, when something hits me on the back of the head. I scream, and on instinct swing the gun I'm still carrying. It connects with the head of another man dressed in black just as I hear a roar behind me.

Mikhail launches himself at my assailant. I cringe at the animalistic shriek of sheer terror my assailant releases

seconds before Mikhail's got him in his grip. He lifts him
bodily with both hands and throws him against the wall.
The man's body crumples against it and slumps to the
ground, but unfortunately for him, he's still conscious.

Mikhail grabs the broken drawer from the desk and slams it
over his knee, takes the wooden plank, and whacks my
assailant with it. Over and over he hits him while the man
cries for mercy. I cringe when he kicks his ribcage but can't
look away. The human body when under attack is so much
more fragile than one might think.

He beats him until the man begs for death. He holds his
head between his hands when Viktor shouts out, "Don't kill
him. Not yet. We need answers."

Mikhail chokes the man out until he slumps to the ground.

He's covered in the blood of another man, drenched in
sweat from the effort of the beating he administered, but
there's nothing but concern in his eyes when he reaches for
me. He kneels on one knee and gently grabs my chin,
forcing my gaze to his.

"Are you hurt, my love?"

No, you can't, I want to tell him. *Please don't call me that,
not now.*

"I don't know. I was unconscious. I – I felt a pain in my
belly, Mikhail." My voice quavers. I reach my hand to his.
He strokes his thumb against my chin, and I'm confident
he's smearing blood on me, but I don't care.

Someone screams in the background amidst the sound of
more gunshots, and I hear a phrase in Russian that
chills me.

Sibirskiy tigr.

I hate that I want nothing but to go to him. I try to remind myself why I'm angry, why only a short while ago I began the process of getting past their security system so I could make my escape. But now that he's here? Now that I'm afraid that our baby could be harmed? There's no one else I want but my husband.

I didn't know a human could hold such conflicting emotions at the same time. I can't even begin to sort through the feelings of repulsion at the utter, unapologetic violence I just witnessed, relief at his tender concern for me, and a whole bunch of other emotions I haven't begun to sort through yet.

"We'll get you to the hospital." It makes me nauseous to see blood streaked across his white tee and know it isn't his. He beat a man to the point of almost death...for me. I should be more troubled by that than I am.

Viktor watches, standing guard against any other attacks.

"Polina?" he says.

"Mom's pulse is faint. She's alright. We need to get both of them to a hospital immediately."

Mikhail holds me to him and stands with me held tightly against his chest. He leans in and kisses me. I almost turn away, but at the last second...I let him.

"We have a lot to talk about," he whispers in my ear. "But know that you are mine and that I love you."

The rest of what I wanted to say fades. I can't even remember why I'm upset with him anymore.

You are mine and I love you.

It might be the only thing that can sustain me through what I have to go through next.

CHAPTER THIRTY-THREE

Aria

"THERE," the doctor says, pointing to the screen in front of her. I squint my eyes to see what she's pointing at, but only see blurry, indistinct images. It's a bit unnerving to me that I'm able to see patterns on a screen in ways other people never can, but I can't make heads nor tails of the ultrasound screen in front of me.

"Where?" Mikhail snaps.

I squint harder, but it doesn't help.

I'm lying on my back and Mikhail is scowling at the doctor and the screen.

"There's a heartbeat," she says. "You likely pulled a muscle when you fell, but thankfully the female body is remarkably resilient and built to protect and nourish growing life. You're fine, Aria, and so is your baby."

Tears prick my eyes. I'm not fine, not at all, but I'm glad I don't have to face the reality of a lost pregnancy. I close my eyes to stop myself from crying, but I can't. Sometimes you don't know how much something means to you until you almost lose it. I'm not super good at stopping myself crying when I'm overcome with emotion, and the feel of Mikhail's strong arms around me only makes matters worse.

I want to sob it all out to him.

I couldn't bear the thought of losing our baby.

I hate that you bought me.

I hate myself for going behind your back and not addressing it head-on.

Is your mom okay?

Did your brothers all survive?

I was the one that brought this on all of you.

Instead, I swipe at my eyes and swallow the lump in my throat for the umpteenth time.

The doctor turns and pats Mikhail's shoulder before she hands me a white towel to clean the goopy mess up with. Who knew that ultrasounds are a messy business?

"Looks like you two can resume business as usual. Now if you'll excuse me, I have a date to return to," she says with a wink before she leaves. My cheeks burn when I suddenly remember the conversation she had with Mikhail.

"Mikhail, you pulled her away from a date!" I say as the door shuts behind her.

"And?"

"There are plenty of other people who could've met us at the ER."

"Or I could give her fifty thousand dollars to drop what she's doing because she's the only doctor I trust."

I balk. "You gave her *fifty thousand dollars?*"

He's still scowling, even as he gently helps me off the table. "I did, and I'd do it again. She works for me, Aria."

And I know by now that Mikhail Romanov is very good to those who belong to him in any capacity at all.

Like...me.

Unless, of course...they betray him. My heart sinks.

We hear a knock at the door.

"What?" Mikhail snaps. He's stressed as hell since half his family's been brought here tonight. I don't blame him. This whole ordeal has pulled the edges of my nerves so taut I feel ready to snap at any second.

Polina enters, a bandage across her forehead, looking even paler than usual. She looks wordlessly from me to Mikhail. I hand her the little printout the doctor gave me and point to the tiny bean. "The baby's fine," I say in a whisper since I don't trust my voice tonight after everything that's gone down. "I'm fine."

To my surprise, Polina bursts into tears. In seconds, she's gone from pale and holding her shit together to full-on sobbing. I sit up and reach for her but before I can get to her, Mikhail takes one step toward her, wraps his enormous arms around her, and holds her. Tears prick the corners of my eyes again. She lays her head on his chest and sobs.

"I was so afraid I failed to protect Aria and the baby," she weeps. "And Mom, when she was passed out, I thought she was gone. I was so worried, Mikhail, and I was so afraid we'd fall apart."

Her wracking sobs shake her thin shoulders, and I find my own cheeks damp with sympathy tears. Or maybe I'm crying because I'm seeing a side of Mikhail I've never seen before. My scary monster of a husband is a giant teddy bear when he comforts his sister. He strokes her back as he soothes her.

"Shh, *milaya devushka*. Shh. You did so well. I am so proud. You've made us all proud, Polina. Aria is safe."

Milaya devushka.

Sweet girl.

After a few minutes, her sobs quiet and she nods. "Okay," she says, still teary, her voice wobbling. She gives a loud sniff. "If you say so."

"I do," he says, a hint of a smile on his lips. "I say so, and you know that what I says goes."

"How are the others?" I ask.

"Lev and Ollie are stable. They sustained head trauma on impact and Ollie has a cast on his right hand. Lev's pissed because he can't lift for a few days, and he's mad as a hornet he didn't get to beat any of Volkov's men."

I feel sick. They don't know yet.

"Mikhail," I say in a whisper. At first he doesn't hear me as Polina updates him on their mother – stable, needed some oxygen and pain meds for a headache, but she only sustained scratches. Her house *was* built like a damn fortress. Viktor was the only one who sustained a gunshot wound, when he used his body like a human shield to protect me.

"Mikhail," I repeat after another minute. My voice is shaking. "We need to talk."

The burning heat of his gaze over Polina's shoulder makes me freeze. He lets her go. She squares her shoulders and blows out a breath. "I'm going to check on Mom then work with them on releasing her so we can keep a close eye on her."

I nod. "Okay." She reaches over and gives my hand a squeeze before she leaves the room.

I was taken into Mikhail's custody to begin with because I hacked into his family's confidential information, and now I've done that and so much worse.

"We absolutely need to talk, little hacker."

I swipe again at the tears on my cheeks. "Damn pregnancy hormones," I say in a whisper, but I know it's so much more than that.

"We all need to reconvene in a private location after everyone's been sent home," he says. Under normal circumstances, the injuries some of them have sustained would likely mean a hospital stay, but he'll want them all safe, where he can keep a close eye on everyone and everything. His mother's home is no longer safe and needs major renovation after what's gone down today.

"We do." When my stomach growls with hunger, he slides a hand to the small of my back.

"Are you hungry?"

I nod. "Starving. Something between the aftereffects of adrenaline wearing off and being too stressed to eat..."

"Right. You need to eat." For some reason, his reaction now reminds me of how things were when we first met. That very first time he admitted he actually used a private detective and nearly scolded me for subsisting on cereal bars.

"I do, but we need to talk more than anything."

"Okay, Mom's resting and I've started the process rolling to have her released." Polina's back, her normally pale cheeks flushed from crying but her eyes bright. "Pro tip? They have a cafeteria here. You use your pull to get privacy and food for you both, and then you can ensure everyone else under your care is taken care of." She grins triumphantly. Mikhail mulls this over with his characteristic frown, then finally nods.

"Yes, I would *love* a slice of cake," Polina says with a wink.

"What kind?" I ask her.

"The kind with sugar and frosting," she retorts. "I mean, chocolate is a bonus, but beggars can't be choosers."

We leave Polina with Viktor and Aleks. Aleks has given me some not-so-friendly looks in the past, but this time he looks damn near murderous.

The fact that Mikhail allows it is even more concerning.

Right now, though, my biggest concern is getting some food in me. When I go too long without food, the nausea returns with a vengeance.

"Send me a detailed update the second you have it," Mikhail snaps at Aleks.

Aleks is looking at me when he responds. "Oh, I promise you, I will."

Gah-reat.

I have no idea what strings Mikhail pulled, but he made some kind of phone call before we came down on the elevator. Once we're in the cafeteria, every one of the staff members stands at attention like they're his personal staff at home.

"What can we get you, sir?" A young man with an earnest expression on his face and a scant beard stands in front of a grill, his hands folded behind his back.

"Anything she wants," Mikhail responds, taking a step back.

"And you, too. I mean I have no idea what they feed anyone in an NYC jail, but I can imagine you weren't eating borscht or blini."

Someone stifles a gasp. Oops. Guess I shouldn't have said that.

"Vodka. I want vodka. But I doubt they have that here and I need to stay alert, so I'll get something hot and be fine with it. What do you want, Aria?"

I look at the menu and mull it over. I'm starving, but nothing here appeals to me. I barely know what I'm pointing at when I ask for something hot, but the tray of macaroni and cheese with a side of grilled chicken and roasted broccoli looks mildly appetizing.

"I'll take the same."

We're completely alone in the center of the large cafeteria with our food and drinks. Mikhail grabbed four different types of cakes and a pile of cookies at the checkout.

"Polina will be happy."

"Perhaps the baby will, too. Polina won't eat all this."

Why is he being all sweet?

Does he know what I do?

Does he know what I've done?

I open my mouth to ask him when he gives me a stern shake of his head. He's so hot even sitting in a flimsy plastic chair under the glare of fluorescent overhead lights. Even with his hand bandaged and his clothes rumpled. I love him so much my heart aches.

"Eat first, Aria. Put some food in you, then we will talk."

It's only been a short time since we've been together, but I'd made the decision to leave. When I don't eat right away and he gives me that one-brow-lifted look, though, I realize that I would miss this so much. Even his hard-ass, grumpy temperament. I've never had anyone in my life to take care of me the way he does, to watch over my most basic needs. There's a lump in my throat when I think about the little nap nook he built in his office for me. The way he carried me in his own two arms, swearing off paramedics, and insisted I get medical attention.

I nod and eat, because it's the sensible thing to do as he checks his phone for updates on his family. While it's nowhere near the best food I've ever had, I remember what my mother used to say when she served hot ramen. "Hunger makes everything taste delicious."

It does indeed.

"Are you feeling better?" he asks, pushing his completely empty tray to the side. He eats with brutal efficiency, likely a throwback to his military days.

"From hunger? Yeah."

I twist the plastic lid on my iced tea to still my trembling hands.

"Your mother managed to obtain so many of Volkov's devices, I was able to hack into them and discover what's really been at play here."

The lift of his brows shows mild surprise. "Did she? And she came to you?"

"Yes. She trusts me. Probably was afraid that you'd nuclear bomb Volkov or something."

He doesn't deny it but seems to be thinking this over. "I see. Go on."

I lick my lips and swallow. I have to address everything with Tatiana, but I need to tell him all of this first. "When I came to you, I'd unearthed a scandal unlike any in American history. The Epstein scandal, you remember that? What I stumbled upon was so much worse. Multiply that a hundredfold. You told me at the time I didn't know your enemies, but the truth is, I did. I do. I might not know all of them and I hope I never will. The World Independent Leadership Consortium – WILCo -- funded this crime ring, Mikhail."

He nods. "I know. Aleks took the lead after you came to me and found every detail he could."

I blink. Aleks?

"I looked through Volkov's data, and his attack on us? It wasn't him at all. WILCo was tipped off by Volkov, but the dates on communications I've witnessed show me he basically gave us over to them after our wedding. Yes, he's senile, there's no denying that, and he has a vendetta against you. But my going to jail and the attack on the house?"

"WILCo."

"You weren't to blame, Aria. Aleks released intel intentionally as a power move during the strengthening of our Bratva. We made it very clear you were part of this family now."

I feel my shoulders sag in relief. "I didn't bring them to all of you? Oh, God, Mikhail. I thought it was me. I thought they were trying to get to *me*."

He reaches for my hand across the table and gives it a squeeze. "No. It wasn't your fault. Where everything went to hell was when I was sent away. I knew that no matter the protection my brothers would give you, our enemies wouldn't hesitate to initiate an attack like they would if I were there."

Ahhh. I nod in relief. "I understand. Good God, what a complicated mess, isn't it?"

Mikhail reaches for one of the cookies he bought and breaks it in two, handing half to me.

I take a bite. "Mm." I sigh, relieved that I've gotten that off my chest, when he leans across the table.

"We have more to talk about, though, don't we?"

I swallow and nod. "We absolutely do."

His phone buzzes with a text. "Everyone is ready for discharge. We will not be going home, though, after all."

I give him a curious look. I'm exhausted and ready to discuss everything else I've been holding onto.

We need to.

"Where are we going?" I can't imagine a single place that's safer than his own home nestled right in the heart of The Cove.

His eyes shine as he stands and reaches for my hand. "I'm taking you to Russia."

CHAPTER THIRTY-FOUR

Mikhail

ABOARD THE PLANE, I make sure my bride is comfortable before I look in on everyone else. Our private planes allow us to travel in luxury. The plush furniture converts from chairs to roomy beds, each nestled in the confines of private suites. The bathrooms are well equipped and climate controlled, and we have a well-trained and attentive crew with us.

Aria lies in bed in our private suite, but she isn't asleep. She watches me attentively, her eyes never leaving me.

I'd arranged every detail of business before we traveled. My staff will take time off except the few that will come with me to Russia. The press release was pretty innocuous: Upon my release from jail, my mother's home was under attack by a nameless assailant. Nameless assailant spent time in the ICU before he passed away.

The others have similar histories and fates.

Volkov's been arrested on charges of human trafficking. While my charges were fabricated, his were absolutely true. The pace of what's happening makes my head spin, and I can hazard a guess Aria's no different.

I finally strip down to my boxers and join her in bed. It will take us about ten hours to fly to Moscow which gives us time to sleep.

But first, we have to talk.

When I join her in bed, she does this thing that I love. She snuggles up closer to me, nuzzles under my arm, buries her head on my chest, then crooks her knee up so her whole body is flush against mine. "It was a waste buying that body pillow, you know," she says. "You're my body pillow."

I run my hand through her hair, and she sighs.

"I want all of this behind us, Aria. This whole ordeal."

"Me, too," she whispers. "Which is why you need to know that I looked at your texts and I know that Tatiana sent me to you."

I nod. "I told her I needed a wife. She told me she was on it."

Aria swallows. "How much did you pay her?"

"Does it matter?"

She pauses before she finally nods. "It does, Mikhail."

"I paid her two point five million."

Her jaw drops. "*Two point five million?* I'm not worth that much. Are you crazy?"

"You aren't worth that much." I kiss her forehead. "We cannot even put a price on your worth, my love."

She sighs and doesn't speak for long minutes.

"I...I need to let this go. I know I do. I thought...I felt so betrayed, I wanted to leave, Mikhail."

"I know. Aleks told me you'd intercepted the texts, bypassed our security measures, then took yourself off our tracking system so he couldn't get a heartbeat on you after the attacks." I run my fingers through her hair. "You know what would happen if I had you alone right now, don't you?" I lean in and kiss her cheek. "You'd be over my knee for being so reckless, Aria. For taking your life in your hands like that. For making a decision that put yourself at risk without coming to me, first."

Even though she pouts, I know a part of her likes when I take her in hand.

"But don't worry, love. We'll have plenty of privacy in Russia."

She squirms adorably before continuing. "Mikhail, I felt so betrayed. All this time you told me that I was your prisoner because of what I did, when I hacked into your computers."

"You were."

"But you'd orchestrated my coming to you!"

"I did."

She pulls away and frowns at me. "Explain that to me, then."

I easily frame her face in my hands, holding her gaze to mine. "I told Tatiana I needed a wife. Tatiana told me you needed protection. It fell into place as if you were sent to me. *Kak s neba svalilsya,* we say in Russia. As if fallen from the sky. Sent from above."

I shake my head. "I kidnapped you, Aria. You were my little hacker. I took you, drugged, to my home and forced you to marry me. Are you offended or hurt that I didn't go about this by conventional means? Your reasoning makes no sense to me."

When she swallows and tries to look away, my grip tightens. "No, Aria. You look me in the eye and tell me why you're upset."

She blinks, fat tears rolling down her cheeks. "I thought I was just...a vessel to you. Someone to be used for gain. You needed a wife and child...then I came along. I could've been anyone. *Anyone.*" Now she cries freely. I release her long enough to pull her body completely on top of me. I sit up and arrange her so she straddles my lap.

"My love. *Aria.* Have I failed to demonstrate how much you mean to me?"

"You bought me," she whispers. "You bought me like I'm a rare trinket you wanted for your collection to keep under lock and key."

"I paid a price for Tatiana's services, Aria," I say gently. "Not for *you*." I lay my hands on either side of her, my fingers laced at the small of her back. "There is no price for perfection."

She sniffs, and I pull her to my chest. I hold her to me while she cries freely.

"Aria, don't you know? If I'd only known you, I would've chased your shadow from the very first time I ever saw you. I would have reinvented myself, become the man you needed me to be just for the merest glimpse of your smile or a moment of your attention. I would have fought full armies for your favor and destroyed anyone or anything that pulled us apart. I would have razed the earth to clear a path to you and make you mine."

"Oh my God, Mikhail," she sniffs. "*Stop.*"

"Stop what?" I ask, bemused.

"Being so damn perfect," she sobs. "I was totally convinced I was only your trophy and someone you'd used to get your way. And then you go and say all these perfect things..."

"Oh I have *every* intention of using you."

EPILOGUE

Aria

THE CRACKLING fire warms the interior of the living room where I sit – no, *lounge* on a chaise built for a king. It seems Ekaterina furnished the Russian home with furniture strong enough to withstand the weight and heft of the Neanderthals she raised. Not that I'm complaining. I quite like that Mikhail and I can snuggle here comfortably. Or, more accurately for the moment, *I* can snuggle under blankets and enjoy the fire while he massages my feet, which he's back to doing and I am *not* complaining.

"I researched all the latest equipment," he's telling me, his eyes on me so earnest he looks almost boyish. "The safest bassinet, the safest car seat, the best baby monitors and strollers." He pauses, his capable hands holding my foot. "Do you know the benefits of breastfeeding?"

I almost laugh out loud. It's amusing as hell to see the way my monster of a husband has turned into a pile of mush.

"I have, Polina and I were researching the different feeding options." I look down at my ample breasts. "I mean, mine are big enough..."

He shakes his head. "The volume of breastmilk a lactating mother can produce has nothing to do with the size of your breasts." He looks momentarily amused. "Though, I have to admit, yours *are* perfect."

I smile. "Why, thank you."

"Oh, God, will you two get a room already?" Polina walks in the room carrying a tray with a large pitcher of water and a plate of something that looks delicious. She's grinning, though. "And don't worry about the baby gear. Auntie Polina's on it."

Mikhail scowls. "Run anything by me, first. Some of those things are marketing ploys with no actual focus on safety or endurance."

Polina nestles the tray beside me and *pats his head.* "You're so *cute* when you get all baby growly," she says. "It's quite unlike you."

His scowl deepens. "What did I say about calling me cute?"

She winks at me. "We don't do baby showers here in Russia," she explains. "I know they're common in America, but we consider them to be bad luck."

I nod. "Ah. Imagine. A Russian superstition!"

She snickers. "Not like Mikhail will let anyone else buy anything for the baby, anyway. But you can't stop me from buying all the little outfits." She points to the tray. "Try these.

They're Russian tea cookies and they are *so* good with tea. I'll make you *pryaniki* when you get close to labor. They're spicy little cookies and supposedly help with the onset of labor."

Mikhail, predictably, looks concerned. "We have a ways to go."

"Oh, I know," she says. "I love how liberally you men use plural pronouns to discuss pregnancy. *We're* pregnant. *We* have a ways to go. You, my friend, do not have any ways to go."

He dismisses her with a grunt and reaches for my right foot. I lean back and take a cookie. It's delicious – rich and buttery and a little crumbly. "Yummy," I say around a mouthful of crumbs. "She's gorgeous, brilliant, *and* bakes. You can't ever marry her off, Mikhail."

I'm joking, of course, but I don't miss the look that flashes across Polina's face.

She quickly recovers. "Fortunately, we don't have to worry about that anytime soon. We do need to talk about going back to America, though."

Mikhail nods. "We do."

Now that things have settled back in America, Mikhail's been itching to get back home. I love it here in Russia, though. After the controversy and struggles we faced in New York, the comfort and warmth of his family home set deep in the heart of Moscow, built like a fortress to withstand the bitter cold, feels *amazing*.

It isn't just the home, though, of course. Mikhail and I have our own *floor* here. The rest insisted. I was amazed at the sheer size of this place and half expected that anyone who grew up in a home like this would be absolutely spoiled, but that's not how they did things here with the Romanov family. I don't completely understand why they ever left Russia to begin with, but know it has something to do with his father burning bridges.

We don't have a commute while we're here and thankfully my nausea's a distant memory, so we get to spend more time with each other. We revel in each other. Mikhail's also different here in Russia, in his homeland. Maybe it's because the threat against us has been put to rest and he can finally breathe a little more freely. Or maybe it's because we're in his homeland and he finds a bit of himself here. But Mikhail seems to be easing into his position as *pakhan,* as leader of the family. It's a role he was born to fill.

I'm not on the run anymore. Mikhail and his brothers put a decided end to that, and thanks to Aleks's prowess, Volkov and everyone he was working with are either dead or in jail. Aleks orchestrated a high-profile exposé, outing the names and crimes committed that both he and I found.

For the first time in a long time, I feel like I can *breathe.*

Mikhail has promoted me and while he hasn't demoted Aleks, he's given him another job as well. So now I feel like I'm not Aria Cunningham, Professor by Day and Hacker by Night anymore.

No.

I'm Aria Romanov, head cybersecurity expert, a pivotal member of the Romanov family business. Aria Romanov, wife to Mikhail, mama to our unborn child, sister to Polina and the Romanov brothers.

"Mikhail? Polina? Aria?" Ekaterina's voice rings out.

"In here!" Polina responds around a mouthful of cookie.

Mikhail gently lays my foot down and stands, stretching. Here in Russia he doesn't often wear the formal clothes he does in America. While I love the look of him all dressed up, I could get used to the tees and jeans. There's something so damn sexy-casual about it. Who am I kidding? I love Mikhail in *anything*.

Ekaterina opens the two large doors to the living room, an uncharacteristic look of concern on her face. "Where is everyone?"

Mikhail looks up. "The short answer is, everyone's working except Viktor and Nikko, who were lifting last I heard." He sobers at the look on her face. "Everything alright?"

Ekaterina nods, but she's rarely fazed by anything, so this isn't super reassuring. "Call them, please."

Mikhail snaps to attention. I pull out my phone and tap the security feed at the same time Polina stands tall and squares her shoulders. "What is it?"

"We have visitors. The guards at the front gate told me there are two of Volkov's men asking for permission to enter."

A muscle twitches in Mikhail's jaw. He lifts his phone to call Viktor and Nikko. "Aria, what do you see?"

I pull up the names and profiles based on a quick facial recognition check. "Dmitri Petrov. Pavel Kuznetsov. Confirmed affiliation with Fyodor Volkov."

Ekaterina watches us thoughtfully when the sound of heavy footsteps comes from the hallway. Viktor looms in the doorway, barring any light from coming in, Nikko close at his heels.

"Volkov's men are at the gate. Bring them to me." Mikhail nods to his mother. "You and Polina, leave us, please."

"Mikhail..."

He looks up at his mother. "Yes?"

She cringes. "No blood on the carpet, son."

The two of them leave. Mikhail curses.

"They're nice carpets," I say, more because I feel the need to back her up than because I know anything about the quality of carpet. He grunts in response.

Polina follows her mom and gives my hand a little squeeze on the way out, leaning in and whispering in my ear, "Tell me if either one of them are cute."

My eyes widen in shock that she'd dare to go there, but it only makes her laugh out loud as she leaves.

"They can't be here to attack. If they were, they wouldn't have entered by the front *gate*, Mikhail."

"Mm. I make it a rule not to assume until I have all the data. Get behind me."

Heavy footsteps return but there's no sound of a scuffle or bodies being dragged down the hallway.

"We come bearing gifts," Viktor says with a sardonic smile.

"I can fetch a silver platter..." Nikko says, his eyes twinkling.

Mikhail stands in front of me, his large, muscled back rippling under the thin fabric of his tee when he places his hands on his hips. "On your knees," he snaps, in that voice that makes a shiver go from the base of my neck down the length of my spine. *"Now."*

Viktor and Nikko shove the men to their knees. I quietly peek to the left to catch a glimpse. Okay, cute is not a word I'd use to describe either of them, but I can report back to my sister-in-law that one of them *is* hot.

Even while pushed to their knees, they're just a few inches shorter than I am. The first is blond with ice-blue eyes that chill me, an athletic build with taut muscles under simple street clothes. The other is older and stockier, with dark hair and midnight eyes.

"Tell me why you dare defile my family home with your presence," Mikhail snaps. Okay so maybe he *isn't* more relaxed in Russia. I'm pulling stats and info as quickly as possible. "You'll speak in English so my wife can understand every word you say."

Um. About that...

How sweet is he, though?

"Aria. Report, please."

God, I love when he gets all bossy on me, and I can show off.

"Dmitri Petrov. Thirty-two. Born in Siberia. Father former KGB operative. First came on the scene in the arms trade. Oversees international arms smuggling." I look up. "Likes eighties rock music and matcha lattes."

Mikhail's lips twitch. I like to throw a little personal touch in just to show that I can. I have his financial records, medical history, record of online communications and the names of every woman he's fucked in the last three years, but I don't want to bog my husband down with unnecessary details.

Mikhail jerks his chin at the second.

"Pavel Kuznetsov. Forty-two. Raised in Moscow where his family makes their home. Father died when he was young, forcing his hand to learn to earn money. Overseas high-end prostitution in the Red Square. D'awww. Has a penchant for owning long-haired cats."

"Do you confirm or deny your identities?"

"Confirm," the men say in unison.

"You have thirty seconds to tell me why you defiled my family home with your presence."

Thirty seconds or what? I look around the room and cringe when I notice a large open floor space with no carpet. He can do a lot of damage and still maintain clean carpets...

The older one speaks first. "You will soon hear news of the death of Fyodor Volkov, our former *pakhan*. He died by his own hand two hours ago in America. Volkov intentionally kept his men at odds with one another with no strong leadership. In the wake of his death, our group is unstable."

The second continues. "Your brotherhood is built on loyalty and a hierarchy of power. We come to you of our own accord and submit ourselves to your authority. You are a man worthy of respect, Mr. Romanov, and we humbly ask you to consider us as future men of the brotherhood."

Mikhail scowls at them. "The only reason I'm still allowing you to live is because I'm curious what you have to offer." These men knew they could be facing a death sentence with Mikhail. And yet they're here. He nods to Nikko. "Keep them in holding until further notice."

The men are brought to their feet and led out. They hang their heads in silence, their fates undetermined and resting in the palm of my husband's hand.

Yikes.

Mikhail reaches for my hand. "Would you like to go out to dinner?"

So we won't talk about the fact that he has two men "in holding," which means that this gorgeous home has a *dungeon* somewhere or something. He won't talk about what just went down at all.

Double yikes.

"Sure," I say. "That sounds perfect."

We walk hand in hand out of the room. "Am I wobbling?"

"Of course not."

"I'll eventually wobble, though."

"And if you wobble, you wobble. You'll still be gorgeous and adorable, and *mine*." I love the feel of his heavy hand on the small of my back.

It's kind of cute hearing him say "wobble" in his accent.

"I can't tell you how pleased I am to have you here in Russia, my love. My homeland. Bearing my child. It seems at times to be more than I deserve."

"Oh, it's definitely more than you deserve," I tease. We're in a vacant hallway with a large window that overlooks the garden nestled behind this house.

"Is that right?" he asks. I squeal when he presses me against the window and slaps my butt, hard.

A rush of heat suffuses my cheeks. I turn to him, my tone demure. "I was only teasing, of course. You deserve so much more."

"Do I?" He turns me to face him. The sun from the window glints on his handsome features. Shadows dance along the walls. He stands in front of me, his warm eyes reflecting a storm of feelings.

I love the feel of his warm hand on the back of my neck. He brushes a stray lock of hair from my face. I shiver. He rests his other hand on the small of my back. Heat curls in my stomach.

When his lips meet mine, it's so much more than just physical – a joining of two hearts and minds.

I wrap my arms around him and lose myself in the passion of the moment. When we finally pull apart, we're both gasping for air. He frames my face in his capable hands. "I love you."

I lay my hands atop his. "And I love you. I feared this would happen, you know."

"What would?"

"That I'd fall in love with my captor."

He looks boyish and vulnerable when he looks up at me. "And?"

Does he really not know?

I grin. "It totally happened."

I've made peace with a lot of things. My place in his family. Being a mom.

Being married to a tiger.

He reaches for me. "Aria, you opened the door to a world riddled with darkness and let the light in. You've given me a reason to hope. I love you for who you are and who I am with you." He brushes his lips to mine. "I've lived many lives. But this one? This one is my favorite."

When he holds me to him, I close my eyes and feel like we got a bonus wedding scene. The vows I took to him were under duress. But these? These words came freely and of his own accord.

Mikhail is sovereign over all, but most of all? He is king to my heart.

BONUS EPILOGUE

Can't get enough of Mikhail & Aria? Scan the QR Code below to get a FREE bonus epilogue to "Sovereign: A Dark Brava Forced Marriage Romance"!

CHAPTER ONE

Aleksandr

"I'LL DO WHATEVER IT TAKES. Whatever our family fucking needs." When I close my eyes I can still see my brother Lev, his face beaten to a bloody pulp. Unrecognizable. It was a threat, a thinly-veiled warning meant to send a message to my brothers: we're watching.

Jumped after a late-night gym session, it was five against one. Lev is a formidable opponent but his pair of fists didn't stand a chance against the pack of five masked men wielding broken bottles, a length pipe, and a goddamn baseball bat.

We'll find who did this and when we do, they'll wish they were never fucking born. But until then, we have to plan our next move strategically.

My older brother Mikhail paces in his dimly-lit office, his hands shoved into his pockets. The blue light from our computer monitors cast shadows on the floor.

We've been at this all night damn night. Empty pizza boxes sit haphazardly in the corner of the room, the emergency stash of vodka long gone. The entire atmosphere of the room is charged, the weight of our decision impacting all of us.

We haven't been able to find out who beat him. Not yet. But we got the message. The death of our enemy Fyodor Volkov was only the beginning.

I pinch the bridge of my nose, my eyes stinging from staring at the computer screen for way too long.

Mikhail blows out a breath. "I know. That's the problem, Aleks. I'm not sure if marrying the Bianchis is the next best move."

I push away from the desk and stretch, my muscles aching from lifting earlier and sitting too damn long. On instinct, I glance at my phone to check the security details of our family. I'm always on hyper alert, but ever since Lev took a beating I'm damn near glued to the screen.

I glance through the list. My mother and Polina are both at home, Viktor and Nikko in their homes, our younger brother Ollie in Moscow. Lev is still in the hospital. I can fit my entire world in the palm of my hand.

The security cameras show nothing out of place, including the two men we have in holding we've transported back here to America.

I sit back down while Mikhail continues to pace.

"Mikhail, it's probably not best for us to make decisions when we've been up all night." Kolya leans back in his chair and strokes his beard threaded with silver. The group mastermind, my dead father's war buddy, Kolya's taken on father figure of the group even though he's only a few years older than us. While Mikhail and I have stripped to tees and jeans, Kolya's still fully clothed in a dress shirt and neatly-pressed trousers.

He's well-meaning but ought to know by now you don't talk me or Mikhail into letting anything go when it means the security of our family's at stake.

Still, Kolya tries. "Go to bed. Go home to Aria."

"Home to Aria?" The door beside Mikhail's office opens and Mikhail's wife Aria stands in the doorway, wearing Mikhail's tee and sweats, the only clothes that apparently fit her when she's stuck in the office nine months pregnant. Her hair's in a messy bun, her glasses perched on the edge of her nose. She has a laptop in one hand and a large plastic cup with a straw with something vibrantly pink in it in the other. "You need to sharpen your senses, Kolya. I've been here working in between naps the whole time, I just didn't want anything to do with the vodka shots for obvious reasons."

Before Aria came, I was the group cyber security expert...at least ostensibly. We all knew the real job I got paid the big bucks for doing was hacking — until Aria showed me she was better. I've gotten over it, though, mostly because she isn't just better than *I* am. She's better than anyone in the goddamn world.

Aria isn't well versed in Bratva business, though, which is why she sticks to some jobs and I do others.

"C'mere." Mikhail sits in his office chair and gestures for her to come to him. She sidles onto his lap and plunks her computer on the desk. The real reason she's here is because Mikhail doesn't let her out of his sight. Not that I blame him. If I cared for anyone half as much as he does, I wouldn't let her out of my sight either.

"I've been listening to everything you said, I just needed to do so in a comfortable position." She nestles in against my brother. "Though if I knew you were *this* comfortable..."

He kisses her temple and wraps his arms around her, whispering something I can't hear in her ear.

I look back at my computer, a headache forming behind my eyes.

"Aria, what's your take?" I ask. If there's anything I love about my sister-in-law, it's that she is absolutely Mensa-level brilliant, likely the smartest person I've ever met in my life. Just for fun, she learned *Russian* on her downtime in a few short months. She can outcode anyone in the goddamn world. In the digital age, having the world's best hacker team puts us at a decided advantage.

But even Aria hasn't been able to identify the perpetrators.

"Alright, I'll fill you boys in on what I'm thinking here." Her fingers fly over the keyboard like she's performing a magic trick. "We have two informants that we can trust, and I think—"

"*Maybe* trust," I interrupt. "I'm not convinced. You know we haven't released them yet, right?"

Mikhail's eyes narrow on me. He doesn't like that I interrupted his wife, but we can throw down about that later if he wants to be a dick about it.

"You still don't trust them?" she asks, her eyebrows rising above her eyebrows. "Seriously?"

"Of course not."

"What will it take?" she asks, giving me a curious look.

"A decided show of loyalty. Some skin in the game. Talk is cheap." I shrug. "They need to fucking bleed for us before I'll trust them."

"I agree," Mikhail says soberly.

"As do I," Kolya says with a nod.

"Alright, alright," Aria says, shaking her head. "Simmer down. All I was going to say was that they might be able to point you in the right direction."

I shake my head and Mikhail and I respond in unison. "No."

Aria sighs. "This is driving me batshit crazy."

"You and me both," I mutter. "The masks mean we can't use facial recognition."

She nods. "And the quality of the video looks like an iPhone at a rave. I just think your prisoners might have some useful info is all."

Dmitri Petrov and Pavel Kuznetsov turned tail on their former mob after the death of their *pakhan,* Fyodor Volkov. Volkov's life mission, before he hung himself in in prison, was to decimate my family. He kept his men at odds and kept them in control with intimidation tactics. There were no leaders, barely a hierarchy, and in the wake of his death, they've begun to fall apart.

Petrov and Kuznetsov turned themselves into Mikhail following Volkov's suicide. We've had them in holding now for several months. They haven't had any contact with former associates. I would know, because they're under my charge.

"Maybe if you sent *me* in."

Mikhail curses and grips her more tightly. "Are you out of your mind? *Khristos,* Aria. You're not going anywhere near them."

"But if I could ask the right—"

"*Enough.*" Mikhail rarely raises his voice to her but what she's suggesting is unthinkable. For all we know, they could be moles. Patient moles, but moles nonetheless.

With a sigh, Aria leans back thoughtfully against Mikhail. "Do you guys know about the sequoia tree?"

Jesus. I clench my jaw to keep from snapping. I'm fucking tired and I don't want some fucking science quiz—

"Aleks." My gaze snaps to Mikhail. He doesn't say another word. My name is only a warning. It's uncanny how he can read my mind.

I blow out a breath and shut my laptop. My eyes need a break anyway. "Yes. The sequoia tree is one of the largest in the world. They can grow up to something like three hundred feet in height and they're so big in circumference, some of them have actual tunnels large enough for cars to drive through them. What about them?"

Aria gives me that smug look she sometimes gives me when she beats me in a hacking race. She's lucky I love her like a sister.

"And what can you tell me about their roots, Aleksandr?" she asks in a tone a teacher might ask a student to recite the alphabet.

I would so flip her the bird, but I still value my life and Mikhail's watching me.

"Don't know anything about the roots," I admit through gritted teeth.

Aria's eyes grow triumphant. She loves one-upping me.

"One might *think* they have massive roots, right? But no, they don't. Their roots are quite shallow. It isn't the *depth* of their roots that make them so sturdy but how far they spread."

Kolya's eyes twinkle at her. He slowly nods, and Mikhail gives her a little squeeze.

"You guys are *sequoias*. Kings of the jungle. Volkov *who?* Good riddance. He *thought* he was going to overtake you guys, but no way. And lucky for you, he was so full of himself he practically self-destructed on his way out."

She fires up her laptop. "So yeah, you're right. This isn't looking good. While you're strong *financially*, our group is comparatively small. While you're strong *physically*, you're still lacking reliable manpower to fortify. And while we're doing our best to grow," she says, patting her ample belly, "It will take time that we really don't have. Mikhail was right when he suggested marrying with the Bianchi family, Aleks. We need to consider further unions as well for the other men."

"Yes. We've suffered three physical attacks and two cyber attacks since Volkov's death. We aren't the only ones who want to capitalize on his demise," Kolya says. "We need to solidify our alliances sooner than later. We can't underestimate the potential for ruin if we don't."

My mind whirs. "Right. What does Bianchi bring to the table?"

"A dowry and connections," Mikhail says. "I agree with Kolya. We need to secure an alliance that fortifies our defenses. We need a lifeline."

Aria nods. "Right. Also, you guys, we've looked at accounting, and while you are all still richer than God, some of your investments have gone belly-up. While you've been all hard at work establishing yourselves as the premier Bratva group here in The Cove, others have been trying to do the same."

The Cove, nestled in the heart of New York smack dab between Coney Island and Manhattan, is our stomping ground, the place we own.

A chilling clarity cuts through the fuzzy haze of exhaustion. The burden of what happens rests squarely on my shoulders. I draw in a ragged breath. We don't have the luxury of time any more. Every second that passes could mean my family's demise.

"There's no more time. My marriage to Harper Bianchi has to happen *now*."

I hold Mikhail's gaze and hide my clenched fists. I can't put into words why the thought of a loveless marriage makes me want to hurl my laptop against the wall of his office. I thought by now I'd have gotten used to the idea. It isn't the first time we discussed it, but I thought I still had a few more months to warm up to the idea.

It's only a wedding.

For life. To a woman I don't love and haven't even met.

But I owe this to my family.

I swallow the anger that boils inside me at the thought of what I have to do.

Mikhail's still holding my gaze.

"Your loyalty to the brotherhood is admirable, Aleksandr," he says softly.

I despise what I have to do to prove it.

I loved once, and once is enough for a lifetime. I already know I'll never love again. The least I can do is bring peace to my family.

I owe this to my brothers. To my family. If someone ever got to my sister Polina, or my mother, or God forbid, Mikhail and Aria's innocent baby... I'd never forgive myself.

I won't make the same mistake twice.

My phone buzzes with a text. Mikhail nods, silent permission to take the call.

I stare at the screen. "Speak of the fucking devil."

Order your copy of 'Sanctum: A Dark Bratva Arranged Marriage Marriage Romance" by scanning the QR code below:

Fueled by dark chocolate and even darker coffee, USA Today bestselling author Jane Henry writes what she loves to read – character-driven, unputdownable romance featuring dominant alpha males and the powerful heroines who bring them to their knees. She's believed in the power of love and romance since Belle won over the beast, and finally decided to write love stories of her own.

Scan the QR Code below to receive Jane's Newsletter & be notified of upcoming new releases & special offers!

Be sure to visit me at www.janehenryromance.com, too!